THE BERWYN RIVER KILLINGS

A DI Ruth Hunter Crime Thriller Book #5

SIMON MCCLEAVE

STAMFORD

THE BERWYN RIVER KILLINGS

By Simon McCleave

A DI Ruth Hunter Crime Thriller
Book 5

First published by Stamford Publishing Ltd in 2020

✿ Created with Vellum

Your FREE book is waiting for you now

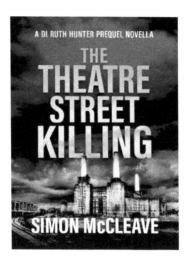

Get your FREE copy of the prequel to
the DI Ruth Hunter Series NOW
at www.simonmccleave.com
and join my VIP Email Club

For Sian, Cass and Ben

Prologue

T he Berwyn River ran for eighteen miles along the eastern edges of Snowdonia in North Wales. From the southern slopes of Moel Fferna in the Berwyn Mountains, the river's source started at an altitude of around 1,800 feet before flowing west through the Ceiriog Valley. From there it passed by Chirk Castle and then to the small town of Chirk, where an aqueduct carried the Llangollen Canal high above the river.

The early-morning sunlight dappled the water as Damian and Kelly Fielding paddled their dark green Canadian canoe up the river. The overhanging branches formed thick awnings that plunged pockets of the water and banks into darkness.

Damian had only had the canoe for a few months – it had been a thirtieth-birthday present to himself – and ever since, Sunday mornings were often spent with his younger sister, Kelly, down by the river. They both loved the peace and tranquillity as they glided effortlessly along with the gentle flow of the water. The only sound was that of the water lapping against the boat and the swish of their paddles. It was the perfect antidote to their busy lives.

Damian remembered their *taid* – Welsh for 'grandfather' – had told them that the Berwyn Mountains were the gateway to King Arthur's ancient lands and the kingdom of the Celtic Otherworld. Taid Thomas used to take him and Kelly, when they were teenagers, up the craggy south face of the mountains and then east along the undulating ridge as far as possible to a place he called *Bwrrd Arthur*, King Arthur's Table. Here, Damian would imagine himself to be Arthur, king of the Britons, standing with pride as he viewed his lands stretching from the mountaintop to the sea. Snowdonia was the land of giants, monsters, magicians and all the creatures of enchantment.

Cutting his oar into the water, Damian skilfully guided the canoe from the back of the boat as they navigated a long bend in the river. Over to the right, he could see deep peat blanket bogs characterised by plants dependent on wet soil conditions. Peat forming mosses, known as sphagnum, and heathers and cotton grass were interspersed with such species as sundew, bog asphodel, and the famous cloudberry.

To the left of them, the edges of thick woodland were ablaze with the colours of early autumn. The trees were densely packed and Damian could only see for a few yards before the eerie darkness came.

'You okay?' Damian called to his sister as he let his paddle dangle in the icy river. He was working up quite a sweat under his waterproof jacket.

'Yeah, fine. I might just get a drink,' she replied, placing her paddle down and turning to reach into her rucksack.

She smiled at him and, as the light caught the freckles of her face, he saw the little girl that she had once been.

'Pub lunch on the way home?' Damian asked as he dragged his hand into the chilly water and then smoothed it onto the heat at the back of his neck. It was cool and refreshing. Red and orange leaves floated and twirled together on the river's surface like dancers.

'My shout, isn't it?' Kelly said as she put away her drink.

'Makes a change,' Damian teased her with a smirk.

'Hey!' She flicked him with water.

A sharp snap from the undergrowth grabbed their attention. It had come from the shadowy woodland and sounded like someone was walking in there. Then a rustle from further away.

Damian knew it could have easily been an animal. A fox or a squirrel maybe? But it had spooked him. They had never seen anyone on this stretch of the river before.

'Come on, we've still got an hour to go before we get to Chirk,' Damian said brightly.

'Slave driver,' Kelly chortled as she dug her paddle into the water to get the canoe moving again.

Glancing up, Damian caught sight of something up ahead beside the water. It was a person sitting against an enormous tree, their feet dangling into the water, looking out at the beautiful view. Given the temperature of the water, Damian was more than surprised. It was bloody freezing.

As they got closer, the man didn't seem to respond to their presence.

Odd, thought Damian.

'Morning!' Damian called over. The man didn't move.

'Do you think he's drunk?' Kelly asked in an almost-whisper as they slowed so that they were now parallel to the man.

'Bit early,' Damian said under his breath.

With a mop of greying black hair, the man was gazing out into space, completely oblivious to them. He was wearing a black denim jacket, black T-shirt and jeans, which were rolled up to avoid them getting wet.

'Hello!' Kelly shouted over at him. 'Are you okay?'

'Hi there!' Damian yelled, now concerned. Still nothing. Damian looked at Kelly and then shrugged.

There was a moment of eerie silence and stillness.

It was then that Damian realised that the man's eyes weren't blinking or moving at all. His face and his body were frozen still. Damian's stomach lurched as he gazed, waiting, hoping, for some kind of movement.

The man's face was grey.

'Oh, God. I think he's dead,' Damian said, as the sickening realisation dawned on him.

'What! No ...' Kelly glanced anxiously back at him, her own face losing its colour in shock. 'Are you sure?'

'No. I don't know,' Damian said before waving over at the man again. 'Hi there ...'

Nothing.

'Oh God, Damian,' Kelly said, sounding upset.

'It's all right ... I'll call for help. Don't worry,' Damian said, trying to reassure his sister.

Grabbing his mobile, Damian looked to see if he had signal. As he tapped 999 into his phone, he could see that where the man's hands rested casually on his thighs, there was dark blood.

Chapter 1

Pulling up slowly by the wooden fence, Detective Inspector Ruth Hunter stopped the car and turned off the radio. It was a Sunday morning. The village of Dinas Padog was dark and quiet. She was picking up Detective Sergeant Nick Evans on the way to Llancastell. Calculating that she was ten minutes early, Ruth pulled out a cigarette, wound down the window and lit it. Drawing on it deeply, her body instantly relaxed. She blew a plume of smoke out into the chilly morning air.

That's better, she thought. *That's so much bloody better.* Now all she needed was a strong coffee and her morning would be complete. She and Nick would grab one from a roadside buttie van once they got going.

The wind picked up and brushed a stray lock of hair away from her face. It was grey. One of the numerous ones that had been making an appearance of late, it seemed, now that she had turned fifty. *Bloody hell, how did that happen?* It only seemed like yesterday that she and her friends were screaming at George Michael and Andrew Ridgeley as they danced around in Fila tennis shorts at the Hammersmith Odeon in 1984. Wham!'s Club Fantastic Tour. That was thirty-five years ago! How? Poor old George.

The pungent smell of a nearby farm broke Ruth's train of thought. She should have got used to it by now. It had been nearly two and a half years since she transferred to the North Wales Police from the London Met and she would take the fresh air and occasional farm yards smells over the London smog any day. Gazing across the valley, Ruth saw that the fields and trees were filled with autumnal colours. It was a beautiful part of the world to live and work in and a vast improvement on the crack-infested estates of Peckham.

Opening the car door, Ruth twisted the sole of her foot to put out her ciggie old-school style and went to the front door. She rapped on the door before realising that Nick had now fitted a doorbell. Since Amanda had moved in, Nick's cottage had a few more modern, feminine touches. A couple of hanging baskets with bright purple petunias rocked in the wind either side of the door, which was painted a tasteful Farrow & Ball green. The garden path was weeded, level and tidy. There was even a comedy gnome wearing a police helmet sitting watching from the porch. That was probably a touch too far in her book.

Ruth glanced down at the recycling box. A few empty bottles of water and two cans of Coke Zero. It's what she expected. Amanda was heavily pregnant and due to give birth in about two weeks' time. Nick had been sober for a while. When she had first arrived in Wales, Nick had still been suffering from chronic alcoholism, and it wasn't pretty. Even though he was a functioning alcoholic, Nick had been thin, grey and constantly stank of booze. The change in him had been miraculous; he put it down to going to AA.

A metallic sound of the door being unlocked. Nick

smiled when he saw her. He was putting on his coat and already had a dapper black-and-grey scarf wrapped around his neck. It might have only been early September, but it was bloody cold in Snowdonia.

'Oh, it's you, boss,' Nick said in mock disappointment.

'Charming … Who were you expecting at seven thirty in the morning, Nicholas?' Ruth asked with a smile.

'I dunno. Scarlett Johansson looking to get her knickers back?' Nick quipped.

'Jesus. Your girlfriend is upstairs about to give birth and you're acting like a randy eighteen-year-old,' Ruth said, rolling her eyes. Over the past two years, she had grown used to Nick's laddishness. It was all an act, usually to get a rise out of her. Her offence was part of the fun.

'Randy?' Nick asked with a grin.

'Yeah, or for people of your generation I mean "horny".'

'That's right, I forgot you're in your fifties now, boss,' Nick said as he pulled the front door closed quietly.

'I'll let that go … No early signs of Evans Junior yet?' Ruth asked.

'Nope. We've been told to try nettle tea, hot curry and sex when we reach the due date.'

'Not in that order, I hope,' Ruth quipped as they got to the car and tossed Nick the car keys.

'I know. I drive, you smoke,' Nick said sardonically as he got into the driver's side. It was their little saying.

The roads were virtually empty as they left Dinas Padog and got onto the major road that traversed Snowdonia Park. It was no longer tourist season, so the endless stream of visitors and caravans had slowed to a trickle.

Ruth had been playing the latest Lewis Capaldi album on a loop in recent weeks.

Nick pulled a face. 'Are we still listening to this?'

'What's wrong with it?' Ruth asked, feeling defensive.

'Lewis Capaldi is like Coldplay. It's music for people who don't really like music. It used to be Dire Straits,' Nick said, teasing her.

'God, you're such a snob when it comes to music,' Ruth said, shaking her head. He was winding her up.

The car's Tetra radio crackled into life, 'Three-six from Control, over.'

'Three-six, receiving,' Ruth replied as she reached over to turn on the car's heating. It was bloody freezing.

'We have a suspected suicide on the northern bank of the Berwyn River. Uniform patrol at the scene. Exact location to be confirmed.'

'Three-six, received. We're en route,' Ruth said.

Looking down at the map on her phone, Ruth frowned.

'Where the hell is the Berwyn River?' Ruth asked.

'Why don't you look at the car's satnav, boss?' Nick asked.

'I don't understand it. I prefer Google Maps,' Ruth explained. 'Fifty minutes at an average of fifty miles an hour is …?'

'Twenty minutes, give or take,' Nick said with a smile.

'What?' Ruth asked. *What was so bloody funny?*

'I just know that maths isn't your thing, that's all,' Nick shrugged.

'All right, smartarse,' Ruth said – he wasn't wrong, of course.

Going through the gears, Nick took the Astra up to sixty in a few seconds.

'I'm gunning the engine,' Nick said to her as he floored the accelerator.

'What?' Ruth didn't know what he was talking about.

'I've been reading a Rebus book.'

'Didn't know you could read.'

'Funny … In it, Rebus "guns" the engine when chasing these two toerags through Glasgow,' Nick explained.

'Edinburgh,' she corrected him.

'Wherever. Scotland.'

'I didn't know "gunned" was a word,' Ruth said as they hurtled around a long bend in the road and climbed a steep incline. 'Gunning or not, your driving continues to terrify me, Nick.'

TWENTY MINUTES LATER, NICK AND RUTH PULLED INTO A car park close to a wooded area in Ceiriog Valley. Nick had been lost in thought and the car had become noticeably silent. The idea of becoming a father was weighing heavily on him. His own father had been a cold, nasty and sometimes a violent drunk. The possibility that Nick might turn out to be just like him was terrifying. The anxiety and uncertainty of the future had churned around his mind in recent weeks. *What if I relapse and start drinking? What if something is wrong with the baby?* Even though he was putting on a brave face for Amanda, who wasn't coping too well with the last few weeks of her pregnancy, he was finding it exhausting.

Turning the car around on the noisy gravel, Nick parked up close to a uniform patrol car with its blue and yellow markings and *HEDDLU – POLICE* written clearly on the side. Although uniform thought it was suicide, CID needed to have a look before anyone moved the body or trampled on the scene.

As Nick turned off the ignition, he sensed Ruth looking over at him. He glanced at her. 'What? Have I got a bogey hanging off my nose or something, boss?' he quipped with a smile.

'No … I'm just seeing if you're all right?' Ruth asked.

'Fine,' Nick said.

'Really?' Ruth asked, raising an eyebrow.

'Just waiting for that bacon buttie and coffee to kick in, you know?' Nick said. He wasn't sure if he was in the mood to talk about the thoughts doing laps around his brain, even though Ruth was an incredibly supportive boss. They had been through a lot in the two and a half years since she arrived from the Met.

'Come on. You've been a bit off for a couple of days now. Weeks, actually,' Ruth said.

'I'm fine,' Nick said.

'You're not fine,' Ruth said sternly.

Nick took the keys out of the ignition and then shifted in the driver's seat to look at her. He sighed; he needed to get this off his chest. 'I've got a baby arriving in two weeks. We see people's lives destroyed every day. We spend all our time with people at their worst, whether that's victims or criminals. And this morning, I've got to look at the dead body of someone who thought the world was such a terrible place, they've topped themselves,' Nick explained.

'And your job is to make the world a better place for everyone, including your child, isn't it?' Ruth asked.

'Doesn't feel like that this morning,' Nick explained as he opened the car door.

'Everyone gets nervous before the birth of their first kid. Don't worry. Most of us have been there,' Ruth said with a kind smile as she patted his arm reassuringly.

She meant well, but Ruth's words hadn't helped much.

A young, male, uniformed officer, blond and muscular, approached as Nick and Ruth got out their warrant cards.

'DI Hunter and DS Evans. Llancastell CID. What have we got, Constable?' Ruth asked.

'Body on the riverbank, ma'am. Two canoeists spotted it this morning and called it in,' the officer said and then gestured to a narrow pathway that led from the small car park down into the woods. 'It's down here.' He began to lead the way.

'Any ID?' Ruth asked.

'Nothing obvious, ma'am. The man's wrists are slashed. It looks like he bled to death sitting at the bottom of a tree by the river,' the constable explained.

Sounded like suicide to Nick. Most people hanged themselves in garages or the woods – it was the UK's most common method of suicide. People believed it was a relatively painless, certain and 'clean' method of killing themselves. No technical knowledge was needed and the body would be left intact for identification and for members of the family to see if they wished. But Nick had attended suicides where wrists had been slashed too. They required a stronger stomach.

As Nick heard the faint swish of the Berwyn River, the pathway turned and he could see the water and the dark, wooded bank that ran alongside it. His Uncle Mike had taken him fishing just along here when he was a boy.

'He's just there, ma'am,' the officer pointed, and Nick could see the man's body slumped at the foot of the tree.

Taking out their purple forensic gloves, Nick and Ruth approached.

'Thank you, Constable. Could you tape off this path and make sure no one comes down here?' Nick said.

'Sir,' the officer said as he turned to go.

Snapping on his gloves, Nick trod carefully towards the dead man. There was something unnatural about the way the man was sitting. His back was at an angle to the thick tree trunk, with his knees and thighs pointing the other way.

The man's eyes, now opaque like stone, were wide open as though still gazing out across the river. He had a growth of stubble and a mop of greying black hair. Around his neck and wrist were chunky silver chains. He looked like one of those 'cool' art teachers that seemed different from every other teacher in the school. Nick remembered Mr Tudor, or 'Ken' as the sixth-form students at Ysgol Dinas Padog used to call him. He smelt of tobacco and beer. Fleetwood Mac or Pink Floyd seemed to be perpetually on his old cassette deck. In those days it was unheard of to have music playing during lessons, and that made Mr Tudor totally 'cool'.

Hearing Ruth approach from behind, Nick looked at her and then down at the man's wrists that had been cut deep and were now matted with dark, sticky blood. The tops of his jeans were also stained dark.

'Looks like he slashed his wrists and just bled out here,' Ruth said.

'First time I've seen double denim since Shakin' Stevens,' Nick quipped.

'Suicide?' Ruth asked.

'Looks like it,' Nick said and then gestured to an empty litre-bottle of vodka that lay propped against one of the tree's roots. 'Maybe he's an alky, although I haven't seen him around the rooms. Never a surprise when one of our lot tops themselves though,' Nick said, a hint of pain in his voice.

Statistics showed that a third of all suicides were committed by people with a drink problem. Nick had certainly contemplated it himself in his darkest moments.

Nick felt a drop of rain on the back of his hand and then another. He looked up at the grey cloud that seemed to have loomed into view over them. A fleck of water landed in his eye and he blinked it away.

'Great, that's just what we need,' Nick said, gesturing to the cloud. 'We'd better get on with it.'

Taking out a pen, Nick began to move the denim jacket carefully and look for ID – wallet, phone, keys. He pushed the skin on the man's neck with the pen – it was firm.

'Signs of rigor mortis,' Nick said to Ruth.

Crouching on her haunches, Ruth looked at the man's face. 'Some signs of purple lividity.'

'So, he's been dead for quite a few hours now, but the pathologist will confirm,' Nick said as he reached with his gloved hand inside the man's denim jacket and pulled out a wallet and handed it to Ruth. 'Bingo'

Ruth opened it. There was fifty pounds in cash and some bank cards, which she took out.

'Mark Fisher,' Ruth read aloud. 'Three credit cards, two bank.'

'Shouldn't be hard to find, fingers crossed,' Nick said as he stood up.

'Doesn't look like he was homeless or anything like that,' Ruth observed.

'I doubt it. That's a Diesel denim jacket and jeans. That's about three hundred pounds' worth of clothing,' Nick said.

A fairly routine suicide, Nick thought, relieved that they'd soon be able to pass it on.

The rain had started to fall steadily and was making a pattering sound on the leaves and trees around them.

As they turned to go, Nick stopped and looked back.

'What's wrong?' Ruth asked.

'I don't know. Something doesn't feel right,' Nick said as he looked back at Mark Fisher's body propped up at the base of the tree. It just wasn't a natural way to sit. The spine was twisted and the back wasn't straight. In fact, it looked painfully uncomfortable.

It was rare that something at a crime scene unnerved

Nick, but his instinct told him there was something more here.

'What do you mean?' she asked.

'No one sits like that. And it's very painful and cold when you bleed out like that. And it's freezing out here already. But he sits under a tree and dangles his feet in the water like it's a beautiful summer's day? However drunk he is, no one is going to do that.' Nick pointed to the body. 'Look, his back is twisted.'

'You mean it feels staged?' Ruth asked.

'Possibly. Maybe I'm just tired and overthinking it,' Nick said with a shrug.

'Let's see what the preliminary PM throws up,' Ruth said and looked up to the grey sky. 'We need to get the body moved asap.'

A sudden snap of a twig or stick breaking caught Nick's attention. It seemed to come from about a hundred yards further into the forest.

'What was that?' Nick asked. He peered into the darkness of the tightly packed trees.

The rain was now lashing down. It battered rhythmically on the trees and ground around them. Pulling up the collar on his coat, Nick glanced at Ruth.

'Did you hear that?' Nick asked.

'I don't hear anything apart from the rain. Let's go before we get soaked,' Ruth said.

'There!' Nick said, pointing to a dark figure further into the woods. About seventy yards away, wearing an army-style camouflage coat.

'Where?' Ruth said, trying to follow his gaze.

The figure began hurrying away into the shadows of the forest.

'Oi! Police, stay there!' Nick bellowed.

'Come on,' Ruth said. They both broke into a jog.

Nick led the way, weaving in and out of the trees on the muddy path.

Up ahead, the figure had started to run.

'Police! Stay where you are!' Ruth shouted.

Breaking into a run, they gave chase. Rainwater filled the shallow dips in the pathway. Nick could feel his feet slipping in his shoes. They weren't designed for chasing a suspect. The sole of his foot landed heavily on a tree root. It hurt like hell.

For fuck's sake! It's too early to be doing this.

Nick looked through the trees. The figure was escaping. Their large hooded camouflage coat made them difficult to follow and from this distance it was impossible to tell height or build. At first Nick had instinctively thought it was a man. Now he wasn't sure.

Nick was now running flat out. Breathing hard. Behind him, Ruth was also in full stride. The hooded figure disappeared out of sight.

Nick splashed through the deepening puddles. Water soaked his socks and shoes, creating an unsettling squelching sensation with every stride.

Nick sucked in breath. His lungs were burning. He wiped the raindrops from his eyes with his coat sleeve and blinked.

That's better. I can see again.

They stopped. There was no movement from within the forest.

'Where've they gone?' Ruth gasped, getting her breath back.

'No idea. You okay, boss?' Nick said, panting. His heart and pulse were banging.

'Brilliant!' Ruth said sardonically.

'You're doing well for—' Nick said.

'If you mention my age, I will kick you in the shins,' Ruth growled.

Nick's eyes scanned around. He looked for the smallest movement. The incessant rain wasn't helping.

Then a twig cracked. The figure emerged further up the incline on the left-hand side.

'Come on! I thought you were fit?' Ruth beckoned to Nick as they broke into a run again.

'I'm giving you a head start,' Nick joked. He then slipped, losing his footing on the muddy bank. 'Bollocks!'

They sprinted through the dark passages created by the tightly-knit rows of towering pines and birch. Trunks that reached over a hundred feet above their heads. A canopy of trees that shielded them from the rain.

The forest was now quiet. An eerie stillness replaced the lashing rain.

Where the bloody hell have they gone?

Suddenly, there was movement. The figure was in the undergrowth about two hundred yards straight ahead. Nick's chest felt tight. Running uphill was bloody hard work.

Spotting a clear, wide pathway, they both sprinted at full pelt. They were gaining on the figure. A hundred yards. Maybe less.

'Oi! Police! Stop where you are!' Nick shouted through gasps.

Up ahead, Nick could see light where the edge of the forest thinned out into a clearing. He had lost sight of the figure again. His eyes zipped right and left across the greenery.

Where the hell are they?

More branches cracked a hundred yards away, bringing Nick's attention hard left. He could see undergrowth moving.

'This way,' Nick said to Ruth.

Zigzagging quickly through branches and brambles, Nick found a pathway and picked up speed. His shoes were rubbing painfully. He could feel the sweat running down his back.

Nick reached the large clearing and glanced around. Nothing but trees in every direction. The rain fell heavily without the protection of the trees.

Ruth frowned as they spun around, looking intently.

'Where the hell have they gone?' Nick mumbled, trying to get his breath.

'No idea,' Ruth said, bent double.

They waited quietly for a minute to see if they could hear movement.

Nothing.

The figure had vanished.

Chapter 2

I t was early afternoon by the time Ruth and Nick walked into the mortuary. Chief Pathologist Tony Amis was just starting his preliminary post-mortem on Mark Fisher.

Ruth had cleaned herself up and recovered since their morning chase through the forest. She and Nick still weren't certain whether the figure they had been running after had anything to do with Mark Fisher's suicide, but the person was so intent on not being caught that it made Ruth uneasy. Why had they made such an effort to get away?

Looking around the mortuary, Ruth was already feeling unnerved as they made their way over to Fisher's pale cadaver. Her shoe slipped on the smooth, white-tiled floor below them. Her shoes and the bottom of her trousers were stained a little with mud, despite Ruth's best attempt at cleaning them in the women's toilet at Llancastell nick.

Nick gestured around the morgue with a raised eyebrow as he addressed Ruth. 'Your favourite place, isn't it, boss?'

Mortuaries freaked Ruth out. A normal reaction for

most of the general population, but Ruth was an experienced murder detective who had seen dozens of dead bodies. She had attended more post-mortems than she cared to remember, and yet each time it felt like her first.

'Think I prefer a trip to the gynaecologist than coming here,' Ruth quipped.

'Which is probably too much information,' Nick said, pulling a face.

'You'd better get used to it. You're going to be at the birth of your first child soon,' Ruth said.

'Don't remind me,' Nick said.

'That's not the attitude. It's a beautiful thing, bringing a child into the world.'

'Is it?' Nick said with a suspicious frown.

'Well, apart from the grunting, screaming, blood and placenta …' Ruth joked.

'Don't! My mate told me to stay by Amanda's head. He said if you go down the business end, it's like watching your favourite pub burn down. You know it's going to be rebuilt, but it will never be quite the same again.'

'Jesus, Nick. What a delightful metaphor,' Ruth said, with a mock-disgusted face. She had heard it all before – and far worse.

They stopped talking as they arrived at the metal gurney, which gleamed in the stark, cold lighting.

Ruth shivered as though someone had just walked over her grave. Mortuaries were just too quiet, too sterile and too lifeless for her liking. A dead body lying on the street or in a home didn't bother her one bit. But a bluish corpse laid out clinically in front of her like a shop mannequin gave her a dark sense of unease. Maybe it was the thought that in death, that was all we were. A long, four-limbed creature with strange patches of hair.

She looked up and down Mark Fisher's skinny body.

The essence of life, of personality, was gone. She didn't know if she believed in any type of god or a 'life after death'. She had seen enough pain and death to question any formal religious belief. But certainly, in this world, all that was left was flesh and bone.

The underlying buzz of fans and the air conditioning added to the unnatural atmosphere. Smells of sterile clinical disinfectants and other cleaning fluids masked the odour of the gases and beginnings of rot and decay. She'd rather be anywhere but here. Right now, all she wanted was a glass of wine and a cuddle with Sian on the sofa in front of a good film.

'Good afternoon, detectives,' Amis said brightly. Ruth often questioned how happy Amis seemed in his work. She supposed that he treated it in the same way as a mechanic looking under the bonnet of a car. 'How are we doing this afternoon?'

'Fine. I wouldn't want to be anywhere else, Tony,' Ruth said sardonically.

'You say that, but I actually wouldn't want to be anywhere else,' Amis said with a smile.

'You might want to keep things like that to yourself,' quipped Nick.

Amis laughed as he walked around the body. 'Never a dull moment with you two, is there?'

'Do we have a time of death?' Ruth asked, cutting to the chase.

'Given the lividity, I would narrow it down to between midnight and two in the morning,' Amis said.

'Are we looking at suicide, Tony?' Ruth asked. She didn't want to spend any longer there than necessary. After chasing the unknown figure through the forest, she wondered if there could be an element of foul play in Mark Fisher's death. It seemed unlikely that the figure was unconnected to what had happened to Mark Fisher. In her twenty-five years as a copper, Ruth knew that wasn't how the world worked.

'I think so,' Amis said as he continued to inspect the wounds on Fisher's wrists. He seemed distracted and deep in thought.

Now they had been washed and cleaned, Ruth could see the incisions in the flesh clearly. They were dark but thicker in width than she expected.

'You think so?' Ruth asked with a frown. 'That's vague, even for you.'

Dressed in pastel-green surgical scrubs, Amis chortled and adjusted his black rubber apron and microphone. These days, post-mortems were recorded digitally.

'Okay. Well, the wounds on the right wrist aren't that severe. Not life-threatening. On the left wrist here, however, the man has a severed ulnar artery,' Amis explained, pointing to the deep cuts.

'And they're definitely self-inflicted?' Ruth asked.

'Possibly. Hard to say,' Amis said in a voice that lacked its usual confidence.

'What's the problem, Tony?' Ruth asked. She could see that he was unsure about what he had found, but 'possibly' wasn't going to help her.

Get to the point. Is this suicide or not?

'It's unusual to see the ulnar artery severed rather than the radial, which is how the cuts would "naturally" have been made – from left to right, with the right hand.'

Ruth had no idea what Amis had just said, but she sensed his implication.

'You think someone else made the cuts?' Ruth asked, trying to clarify the sub-text; he was vague at the best of times.

'Again, it's possible. I've seen many suicides from cutting wrists,' Amis said.

'And?' Ruth asked, prompting him.

'They just don't look like this,' Amis said, pointing to the wounds on Fisher's left wrist. 'I think the evidence is inconclusive as to whether or not this is suicide. I would even go as far as saying that the death is suspicious.'

Ruth exchanged a look with Nick – it confirmed their uneasy feeling at the scene.

It also meant that they might have a murder case on their hands.

Chapter 3

I t hadn't taken long for Llancastell CID to track down an address for Mark Fisher. He had been living with his elderly mother for the past few years. Detective Chief Inspector Drake, Ruth's boss, agreed with her that although the injuries to Fisher were still inconclusive, they should treat his death as suspicious. Therefore, Ruth and Nick were on their way to Tregarth, on the western edges of Snowdonia, to talk to Mrs Fisher. A uniformed patrol had been dispatched soon after the body was identified that morning to break the news of her son's death to her. Ruth was glad that she didn't have that job now she was a senior-ranking detective in CID; watching relatives dissolve into the utter pain of grief before your eyes was something no police officer ever got used to. Sometimes it was the quiet of complete disbelief and shock. And sometimes it was the ear-splitting wailing of unbearable sorrow and heartache.

The village of Tregarth had grown up around the local slate industry, with houses being built for the quarry workers and their families in the 1800s. Tregarth was infamous for Tanrhiw Road, which was built by Lord Penrhyn, proprietor of the Penrhyn Quarry. All the houses on that street were built to accommodate the workers that refused to strike during the Penrhyn Lockout Strike between 1900 and 1903. Tanrhiw Road was known locally as *Stryd y Gynffon*: Traitor's Row.

As they entered the village, Ruth looked up at the greying sky. The trees were resplendent in a plethora of autumnal colours and waved and swayed in the wind. She loved this time of year. In fact, for a long time, autumn was her favourite season. Making stews and casseroles while drinking heavy red wine. Long walks through leaf-strewn parks. It was the time to unpack cosy jumpers and scarves. Halloween and Bonfire Night were always great fun and a chance to get together with friends.

However, the autumn also saw the countdown to the 5 November – a date that had a painful, sombre significance in her life. On the 5 November 2013, Ruth's partner and love of her life, Sarah Goddard, had gone missing. She got onto the 8.05 commuter train from Crystal Palace station to Victoria but never arrived. She vanished off the face of the earth. No contact, no note, no idea where she had gone. As a copper, Ruth had made sure the CCTV footage from that day had been scoured and re-scoured at every station on that line. There had been television appeals and articles in the press. There had been sightings of Sarah everywhere from New Zealand to Newquay. Ruth had found herself stopping to follow women she thought looked like her. It had shaken her to her very core and the problem was that there was no end to it. No closure. Sarah had simply disappeared off the face of the earth and was nowhere to be found.

The Met had used CCTV at Victoria and eyewitness statements to identify a German banker, Jurgen Kessler, who was seen by various passengers talking to Sarah on that train. He was the last person to talk to her. The case took a darker turn when Berlin police linked Kessler to the murder of two young women in the city a couple of years ago. Kessler had vanished but had then been traced entering the UK on a false passport.

However, Ruth had decided in the summer to move on with her life. To try to put Sarah's disappearance behind her. She had promised her partner Sian that they would build a life together and that Ruth would stop living in the past. She had to get on with living in the present and so far, it had proved to be a positive, rewarding decision. Life was good and her relationship with Sian had never been better.

Sticking her hands into her pockets to keep them warm, Ruth looked over at Nick as they made their way up the garden path to Mrs Fisher's neat stone cottage. They knocked at the door and showed warrant cards to the uniformed officers, telling them they would take it from there.

Eileen Fisher was sitting in the living room with a cup of tea on a patterned saucer. She was thin, with dyed-brown hair, angular-framed glasses and must have been in her early seventies.

'Mrs Fisher. I'm Detective Inspector Ruth Hunter and this is my colleague, Detective Sergeant Nick Evans. We're from Llancastell CID … I'm so sorry for your loss,' Ruth said.

Eileen looked up, giving them a vacant stare, and gestured. 'Do you want to sit down?'

Ruth and Nick nodded and took a seat on the large deep-burgundy sofa. The living room was tidy but a little twee. Ruth could smell more than a hint of vanilla from an air freshener that plugged into the wall. They seemed to be the preserve of the over-sixty brigade.

'We're just here to ask you a couple of questions about Mark as part of our enquiries,' Ruth explained.

She noticed that a series of black-and-white photographs dotted around the room featuring musicians playing at various concerts had distracted Nick. They seemed out of keeping with the décor.

Had Mark Fisher been a photographer? Ruth wondered.

'No one will tell me what happened to him,' Eileen said, her voice trembling a little.

'That's because we're not sure what happened to him yet, Mrs Fisher,' Nick said gently.

Eileen blinked. Ruth could see her mind was going ten to the dozen, and it didn't help not knowing how her son had died. Ruth thought that Eileen reminded her of her own mother, Liz. It wasn't just the physical similarities. Eileen also had the same fragile, even brittle, quality.

'All we can tell you is that we're treating Mark's death as suspicious until we know more … It would be helpful if we could ask you about how Mark had been in recent days?' Ruth asked.

Eileen shifted back on the sofa. 'You know what … I've been waiting for that knock at my door for over twenty years,' she said grimly.

'What do you mean by that, Eileen?' Ruth asked. It was quite a statement.

'Mark's had trouble with drugs, alcohol and depression for a long time now. He would go missing for a couple of days, then he'd come back and stay clean for weeks, sometimes months before it happened again …' Eileen pushed her lips together as a tear rolled down her face. 'And I knew that one day he would disappear and not come back.'

If Mark Fisher had committed suicide, it sounded as if his mother wouldn't have been surprised.

Ruth's heart went out to her. Not only because Eileen reminded her of her own mother, but Ruth also imagined the pain and torment of sitting at home for years on end, never knowing when or if your son would come home. Ruth thought of her own daughter, Ella, who was in her early twenties. Although Ruth often worried about her daughter, as all mothers do, it would be torture to worry about her like that every day.

Grabbing a tissue from her coat pocket, Ruth handed it to Eileen with a kind smile. 'Here you go.'

'Sorry … Thank you.' Eileen wiped the tears as she sniffed.

'And he lived here with you?' Nick asked, holding his pen and notepad.

'Yeah. He's got a family over in Corwen, but she slung him out years ago. He didn't have anywhere else to go,' Eileen explained sadly. 'I didn't want him on the streets.'

'And did Mark seem any different in the last few days?' Ruth asked.

'Hard to tell. He could be happy and dancing around in the morning and then take to his bed depressed in the afternoon. I thought he had that bipolar, but he never got diagnosed with it,' Eileen explained.

'So, there was nothing about the last few days that was noticeably different?' Nick asked, writing in his notepad.

'Not really,' Eileen said with a shrug. She couldn't think of anything.

'Did Mark work?' Nick asked.

'Not really. Not anymore.'

'What did he do?' Ruth asked.

'He was a guitarist,' Eileen explained.

'Hence all the photos,' Nick said, gesturing to the wall.

'Yeah. Session stuff. But he toured a lot too. Mainly in the nineties and just after the Millennium … Not my sort of thing …' Eileen said and then stopped as the reality of Mark's death overwhelmed her again. 'Sorry.'

'Please don't apologise, Eileen,' Ruth said, giving her an empathetic smile.

'You said that Mark didn't work very much anymore?' Nick said, looking down at his notes.

'It was the drugs and the drink. I suppose it made him unreliable,' Eileen said, thinking aloud.

'Something else?' Ruth asked, probing for the second reason.

'He got RSI … You know, repetitive strain injury. And then that led to him getting arthritis in his hand. The drugs and drinking got a lot worse after that because he couldn't really play,' Eileen explained.

Ruth could see how that would make sense. And then she had a thought.

'Was Mark a right-handed guitarist?' Ruth asked, thinking aloud.

Eileen frowned, thinking this was a strange question.

Nick caught Ruth's eye – he was already on the same page as her. That's why they worked together so well. Copper telepathy.

'No, he was left-handed. He had to have all his guitars re-stringed.'

'So, it was the arthritis in his right hand that prevented him from playing?' Ruth asked, knowing that one hand strummed while the other did all the hard, complicated movements to create the chords.

'Yes.' Eileen was still confused.

'When you say Mark's right hand was arthritic, how bad was it?' Ruth asked.

'Oh, he had hardly any movement or strength in it. He couldn't lift a kettle, and I had to cut up his food for him. Sometimes he couldn't even hold a pen,' Eileen explained.

Ruth looked at Nick. Was that significant? It didn't sound like Mark Fisher had the strength or ability to slash his left wrist deeply with his right hand.

And if he hadn't slashed his own wrists, it meant that someone else had.

Wandering back through CID, Ruth spotted DC Sian Hockney walking towards her with a walking stick. Ruth and Sian had been living together as a couple for over nine months now. Their relationship within the department was common knowledge but never talked about. It wasn't very professional, but Ruth was a detective inspector and no one would challenge her on it. She also made sure that she treated Sian the same at work as everyone else. If anything, she overcompensated the other way.

'Getting the hang of it?' Ruth asked Sian, gesturing to the stick. Sian had been in an accident during the summer and at one point it had been touch and go whether she would walk again.

'I don't think there are any Paralympians in danger of losing their medals any time soon, but it'll have to do,' Sian said with a wry smile. She had only been back to work for a few days.

'Don't overdo it,' Ruth said, catching herself sounding motherly.

'I need to keep swapping or I'm going to get a whopping bicep and shoulder on my right-hand side and nothing on the other,' Sian joked as she sat at her computer.

Ruth put her hand on her shoulder and Sian reached up and touched it. There had been a few days when Ruth thought Sian would be in a wheelchair for the rest of her life. She was so grateful to see her back at work and mobile – even if she had to use a stick for the meantime.

Ruth's train of thought was broken as Nick came in with some printouts.

'Boss, Amis sent over more detailed findings from the preliminary post-mortem,' Nick said, raising an eyebrow.

'Something wrong?' Ruth asked, sensing something was off.

'There's heavy discolouration and lividity on the left-hand side of Mark Fisher's body,' Nick explained.

Ruth was experienced enough to know that meant that after death, Mark Fisher had been resting on his left-hand side. The stationary blood would have pooled and settled, causing purple discolouration. That meant that someone had moved Mark Fisher's body after he was dead and positioned him sitting under the tree where they had found him.

'Right. Someone moved the body?' Ruth said.

Nick nodded. 'And if that's the case, he didn't kill himself.'

'Our mystery person in the forest? And given Amis's reservations about the cuts on his left wrist, and from what his mother explained about his arthritis, this is looking more than just a little suspicious,' Ruth said, thinking out loud.

'What do you want me to do, boss?' Nick asked.

'Call another briefing for an hour in CID. Book the incident room. Can we get some scene boards going? And get everyone in. I'm now convinced we've got a murder case.'

She was going to need another coffee.

Chapter 4

'Afternoon, everyone,' Ruth said, looking up at the clock on the wall in Incident Room One. It was five o'clock. Now there was a murder case, the CID homicide team needed to regroup before the end of the day. She pointed to a makeshift photo of Mark Fisher playing the guitar that had been printed from Google. In the photo, his hair was black and wet from sweat, and a cigarette hung from his bottom lip Keith Richards's style. 'This is our victim, Mark Fisher. As some of you already know, Nick and I were called to a potential suicide on the banks of Berwyn River this morning. We spotted someone in the forest nearby. When we told them to stop, they ran, but we lost them. We have no idea if they're connected. Time of death is between midnight and two this morning. The pathologist's initial findings were inconclusive, but the wounds to Mark Fisher's left wrist didn't seem consistent with a self-inflicted suicide attempt. We spoke to Mark Fisher's mother. It seems due to a long career playing guitar, Mark Fisher had severe RSI and arthritis in his right hand. Eileen Fisher told us that Mark sometimes struggled to hold a pen or cut up his own food. This ties in with the patholo-gist's concerns that someone else inflicted the wounds on Mark's wrists.' Ruth looked over to Nick. 'Nick?'

Standing up from the table, Nick looked down at the pathology notes. 'Too early for a "Stairway To Heaven" joke?' he asked with a grin.

'Yes,' Ruth said, with a roll of her eyes.

'Okay … Full post-mortem revealed significant lividity on the left-hand side of Mark Fisher's body. So, after he died, Mark's body was on the ground on his left side.' Nick went over to a small photo that showed Mark's body as they had found it, resting upright at the bottom of the tree. 'This is how we found Mark when we arrived on the scene this morning.'

'Someone moved the body post-mortem,' Sian observed.

'Yes. We're waiting for Forensics to look at his clothes to see if there are signs that the body was dragged,' Nick explained.

'What about the toxicology report?' Ruth asked.

'We found an empty bottle of vodka beside Mark's body. But the report is gonna take a few days, boss. They're backed up,' Nick explained.

'Okay, see if you can lean on them. We need a house-to-house on the road opposite the turning to the woods' car park. ANPR on the approach roads for that morning. Let's start from ten o'clock last night,' Ruth said.

ANPR stood for Automatic Number Plate Recognition – a computer could spot and recognise certain number plates from traffic cameras. It could also register any vehi-cles within a specific time slot.

'We need to know where Mark Fisher was last night. Who was he with and what was he doing? Nick and I will go back and talk to Eileen Fisher. Let's look at bank records, social media, P45 and employment records. I want to know about everything that was going on in Mark Fisher's life. Anyone done a PNC check yet?'

PNC was the Police National Computer Database and had records of prior convictions or cautions. It was the first port of call in any investigation.

'Dan's on it,' Sian said, getting up from the table.

French approached. 'Boss, PNC check on Mark Fisher.'

'Anything interesting?' Ruth asked.

'Mark Fisher was interviewed in 2015 by officers from North Wales Police, but there are no notes. But more interestingly, Mark Fisher came out of prison just over three months ago,' French explained.

'What was he in for?' Nick asked as he came over.

'Causing death by dangerous driving while intoxicated,' French said, looking down at the PNC print out.

'Sentence?' Ruth asked, knowing that it carried a maximum sentence of fourteen years.

'Ten years. He served four and a half,' French explained.

'Eileen Fisher failed to mention that,' Ruth said, raising an eyebrow.

'Maybe we should jog her memory?' Nick suggested.

RUTH AND NICK SAT IN THE LIVING ROOM AT EILEEN Fisher's home. It was clutter-free except for the collection of small porcelain figurines that ran along the windowsill. Ruth knew that she shouldn't judge, but they were bloody horrible. 'Precious Moments' she thought they were called. The nearest of them featured a small girl with a basket full of puppies. Tat didn't begin to describe it, but each to their own.

Ruth's train of thought was broken as Nick shifted on the sofa and looked up at Eileen, who handed them both a mug of tea.

'Thank you,' Ruth said as she glanced at the tea, which looked like milky hot water that someone had dunked a tea bag in for all of five seconds. Ruth wasn't so thirsty after all.

Nick sipped his 'tea' and pulled a face – he was thinking the same thing.

'You said there had been some developments?' Eileen asked as she sat down.

'Yes, that's right. I'm very sorry to have to tell you this, Eileen. But we do now believe that Mark was murdered,' Ruth said gently.

Eileen looked at them both blankly. She hadn't quite taken in what Ruth had said.

'What? … Right …' Eileen took a breath and shook her head. 'My God … I don't understand. I thought he had killed himself?'

'There are various things that we think are suspicious about his death that we can't discuss with you at the moment, but we're certain that he didn't take his own life,' Nick said as he took out his notepad and pen.

Ruth watched as Eileen blinked as her eyes welled. She took off her glasses and reached for a tissue. She wiped her eyes and nose.

'I don't understand …' Eileen whispered.

'Eileen, is there anyone you can think of who would want to harm Mark?' Ruth asked.

'No, no. Mark wasn't like that. He didn't make enemies. He wouldn't hurt a fly,' Eileen said, looking totally bewildered.

'We understand that Mark had spent some time in prison recently?' Nick asked.

'Yes, that's right. Drink driving,' Eileen explained naively.

'A little bit more than drink driving, Eileen,' Ruth said. She could see that Eileen was one of those mothers who wouldn't hear a bad word said about her son.

'Yes. It was a terrible accident. Terrible,' Eileen said, as if thinking out loud.

'Can you tell us what happened?' Ruth said.

'Mark hit another car. He said that the car came out of nowhere … And his wife, Donna, was severely injured in the accident. She died three days later. It was so sad. She was so beautiful … and so young.' Eileen said getting emotional.

'Did Donna's family blame Mark for her death?' Ruth asked.

Eileen looked down. 'They didn't want to see it as an accident. They said that Mark had killed her…'

'Do you know if Mark has had any contact with Donna's family since he left prison?' Nick asked.

'No, I don't think so. He didn't say anything. And they wouldn't want anything to do with him,' Eileen explained.

'So, when I asked you if there was anyone that might want to harm Mark, it sounds to me as if Donna's family could hold some kind of grudge against him?' Ruth said. If Eileen had told them this earlier, it would have saved them a trip. Under other circumstances, this would have annoyed Ruth, but Eileen looked so vulnerable it was hard to feel anything but pity.

Eileen nodded. 'Yes … Now that you've said it, I suppose that is right.'

'But, as far as you know, there was no contact between

Mark and anyone from Donna's family in the last few months?' Nick asked.

Eileen shook her head. 'I really don't think so … You can't think that one of them killed him?'

'Was there anything else in the last few days or weeks that was out of the ordinary?' Nick asked.

Eileen wiped her nose again and then thought of something. 'Last week. A couple of times I heard a noise outside. Sounded like someone was out there. Mark went to take a look.'

'Did he see anyone?' Ruth asked.

Eileen shook her head. 'No. He said it was probably kids messing about.'

Nick caught Ruth's eye. *Is that something we need to look into?*

Shifting forwards on the sofa, Ruth looked over at Eileen. 'We're going to have a look in Mark's room, if that's okay, Eileen? In case there's anything that might help us find who did this to him.'

'Yes, of course … Straight over at the top of the stairs,' Eileen gestured – she was still lost in shock and grief. 'Do … Do I need to come with you?'

'No, no. You sit here and have your tea. We won't be long,' Nick said with a compassionate smile.

Snapping on their purple forensic gloves, Ruth and Nick made their way up the stairs. The carpet was dark red, patterned and thick. The walls had watercolour prints of various types of horses.

'What do you think?' Ruth asked, gesturing downstairs to Eileen.

'I don't think she would have mentioned prison, the accident or Donna's death if we hadn't brought it up. I think Mark was "Mummy's little soldier",' Nick said cynically.

'She's just a mother covering for her son. My mum used to do it for me. And you'll do it for your child,' Ruth said.

Nick nodded as if to say, 'Fair point.' They went into Mark's bedroom, which was cluttered with clothes, vinyl records, plates and an overflowing ashtray. Ruth looked around; it looked like a student's room rather than that of a middle-aged man. Under the small table about twenty empty bottles were stacked – mainly whisky and red wine. It smelt of cigarettes and deodorant.

Ruth spotted Nick looking at a large black-and-white photograph of a rock concert. It had writing underneath it: *World Tour – Irving Plaza, New York. 6 November 1997.* Nick pointed to a figure stage left playing a guitar – it was Mark Fisher.

In 1997, Ruth was still married to Dan and it was just after Ella had been born. Maybe it was her rose-tinted glasses, but to her, it seemed to be a far more positive time. New Labour had just been voted in, Britpop ruled the world and the country had called the royal family to task over the death of Diana.

'Must be hard to give up that lifestyle?' Nick said.

'Even harder if it's taken away from you because you can't play anymore,' Ruth said.

Wandering over to the wardrobe, Ruth opened it to see a few stylish shirts and jackets hanging up. In the stillness, she couldn't help but feel sad that Mark Fisher would never wear them again. Never open those wardrobe doors and pick out a shirt for the day.

Pushing the wardrobe doors closed, there seemed to be nothing in the room that gave any clue as to who might have killed Mark.

'Anything?' Ruth asked Nick as he shuffled through a box.

'Old photos mainly,' he replied as he walked over and showed her a large photograph. Mark had his arm around an attractive woman. It had been taken a long time ago, but they looked very rock'n'roll and glamorous.

'I'm guessing that's Donna?' Ruth said.

'Yeah. Pretty lady,' Nick said, going back to the box.

As she stood up, Ruth noticed a pale blue shoebox on the bedside table. It seemed out of place.

Wandering over, she opened the lid and saw there was an object inside wrapped in an old tea towel. And then she got the unmistakable waft of something. It smelt like petrol.

I recognise that smell. What the hell is it?

'I think I've got something,' Ruth said as she picked up the object. It was far heavier than she was expecting.

Nick came over and before he even looked inside, he also sniffed the air and frowned. 'Boss, I think you need to be very careful with that,' Nick said.

'Why?' Ruth asked, still holding the object.

'I can smell gun oil,' Nick said.

'That's what it is,' Ruth said, now realising why the smell was so familiar.

It was an odour that took her straight back to being in the Met.

'I'll do that,' Nick said as he unfolded the towel slowly, revealing a black handgun. It was a revolver with a cylindrical barrel that held six bullets.

'Bloody hell,' Ruth said, slightly shocked. 'What is it?' Ruth knew that Nick knew a lot more about firearms than she did.

Reaching down carefully, Nick turned the gun to look at the model number. 'Webley Service Revolver. Mark IV, I think. Probably made in the late seventies.'

Ruth rolled her eyes. 'You really are a gun nerd, Nick.'

'Your lot had them down in the Met for a while. It's what Jack Reagan used to carry in *The Sweeney*,' Nick said.

Ruth looked at the gun again and then exchanged a look with Nick.

'Mark Fisher kept a loaded firearm by his bed, which tells us he was a very scared man,' Ruth said.

'Yeah, and now he's dead.'

Chapter 5

Cutting across the eastern edges of Snowdonia Park, Ruth and Nick picked up the A452 and headed for Barford. Having talked to Eileen Fisher, Ruth knew that they needed to speak to Donna's family about the accident and her death.

Barford was a tiny hamlet that stood at the confluence of the Afon Angell and the Afon Dyfi. On the north side of Barford, the long ridge of Pen y Clipau swept down from the summit of Foel Dinas, which stood at 1,600 feet and was part of the Cadair Idris mountain range. The Afon Mynach joined the Afon Angell just west of Barford, with the rounded slopes of Moel y Ffridd beyond.

The discovery of the gun in Mark Fisher's house the previous day had surprised both Ruth and Nick. North Wales Police firearms officers had to be called to make the gun safe and Eileen Fisher had to vacate her house until that had happened. When it came to firearms, Ruth knew that you couldn't be safe enough.

Ruth had a flashback to a terrible case that she had worked on ten years earlier on the Lettsom Estate in Peckham. CID officers had been called to the flat of a well-known low-level crack dealer, Tremaine Thomas. Ruby and Ruben Thomas, Tremaine's six-year-old twins, had found a handgun, a Beretta 9000S, in Tremaine's bedroom and played with it. As Ruben and Ruby fought over whose turn it was, the gun went off. It took three of Ruby's fingers clean off her left hand and she nearly bled to death. Ruth knew that both children were lucky to be alive. Those types of incidents weren't uncommon in South East London.

Ruth looked down at the case files on Mark Fisher. 'According to the notes, Donna Fisher died from a brain haemorrhage sustained in the crash. Her family had to be restrained at the court during Mark Fisher's trial,' she said as she thumbed through the documents.

'It would certainly give them motive,' Nick said.

Buzzing down the window, Ruth lit a cigarette and gazed out at the autumnal countryside.

'Sian doing okay, is she?' Nick asked.

'Coming back to work has really tired her out. But given that a few months ago we didn't know if she would walk ever again, I think she's grateful to be up and about,' Ruth explained with a nod.

'Yeah, it's good to have her back,' Nick said. 'Even if she does take the piss out of me continually.'

'You're a soft target, Nick, that's all,' Ruth quipped.

That's one of the things that Ruth loved about Sian. Her caustic sense of humour.

Ruth squinted as Nick revved the engine and took the Astra up to seventy miles per hour.

'You don't have to drive like a seventeen-year-old boy racer, Nick,' Ruth protested.

Nick grinned and gestured to his forehead. 'In here, I am a seventeen-year-old boy racer. Thought you'd be used to my driving by now?'

'Nick, I will never get used to your driving for as long as I live. And sometimes I worry how long that might be,' Ruth said with a dark laugh.

Indicating right, Nick pulled the car into a long gravel driveway. At the end was a new-build executive-style house. Donna Fisher's family, the Harrisons, had money.

Someone from CID had called ahead. Ruth and Nick wanted to know about where the Harrisons were at the weekend and what their feelings were towards Mark Fisher. He had robbed them of their daughter while drunk at the wheel of a car. If anyone had a motive to wish Mark Fisher harm, or even death, Ruth assumed it would be Donna's parents.

Turning the engine off, Ruth and Nick sat and looked out at the three-storey house. There was a silver Jaguar F-type and a white Range Rover Evoque Sport on the driveway. A black Labrador trotted out, gave a quick bark and then disappeared.

A man in his seventies came out of the house to see what was going on. He was dressed in dark corduroy trousers and an expensive-looking navy sweater.

Nick looked at the house and said, 'Nice house, smart cars …'

'According to our records, Derek Harrison was a GP but is now retired,' Ruth explained as she got out of the car. She pulled out her warrant card.

'Dr Harrison?' Ruth asked.

'Yes,' the man replied in a confident voice.

'I'm Detective Inspector Ruth Hunter from Llancastell CID. This is my colleague, Detective Sergeant Nick Evans. I believe you're expecting us?' Ruth said.

'Yes, yes …' Derek nodded with a solemn face and ushered them inside.

The house was newly decorated and it still smelt of

fresh paint. The artwork hung up on the hallway walls was tasteful as Derek led them through to a living room.

'Please. Take a seat,' he said, gesturing to a long cream sofa. Behind that was a grand piano topped with photographs. Did anyone actually play it or was it there just for show? At the centre, there was a large framed photograph of Donna.

'Would you like some tea or coffee?' Derek asked in a way that implied it wasn't really an offer.

'We're fine. Thank you,' Nick replied as he sat down.

'You've come about that man, I expect,' Derek said wearily as he sat in a large armchair opposite.

It was clear from the outset what Derek thought of his late son-in-law.

'Mark Fisher?' Ruth said as she shifted back on the sofa and crossed her legs.

'Yes,' Derek said sharply.

'I'm afraid that we believe that Mark Fisher was murdered at the weekend,' Nick said.

Derek shrugged. 'I can't pretend to be anything but happy at that news — he killed my daughter.'

'As part of our investigation, could you tell us where you were last Saturday night and Sunday morning?' Ruth asked.

Derek said, 'I was with my wife at the theatre on Saturday night.'

He's clearly already thought about this, Ruth thought.

'Could you tell us where that was?' Nick asked, clicking his pen so he could write down the details.

'That theatre over in Mold.'

'Theatre Clwyd,' Nick said, prompting him.

'Yes. It was some kind of musical thing. Not my cup of tea,' Derek explained.

'Can anyone apart from your wife vouch for you?' Ruth asked.

Derek shrugged impatiently. 'I don't know. I doubt it. But they have CCTV in theatres, don't they?'

'We would have to check,' Nick said.

'Check away. I have nothing to hide.'

'And what about early on Sunday morning?' Ruth asked.

'Took the dogs out over the fields for a couple of hours. Went out about five-thirty – I wake up early. Medical school messes with your sleep patterns,' Derek explained.

'Can anyone vouch for that?' Nick asked.

'Yes, as a matter of fact. Jim Bird. Runs the dairy farm down the road. He was out moving his herd, so I saw him a couple of times. The local dairy is closing down, so we stopped and talked about that. I'm sure he would confirm what I've told you.'

'Thank you. I know this is a very difficult time for you, Mr Harrison,' Ruth said with her best empathetic expression.

'We told Donna not to marry him,' Derek said as he sat forward, looking wistful. 'It was all that music business stuff. He flew her out to America to be on tour with him when they were first together. I guess she was blinded by all that. Until he drank and drugged it all away …'

Casting her eyes up to a family photograph, Ruth could see that they had a son who was younger than Donna. That would put him in his forties now, Ruth calculated, although maths was never her strong point.

'I see you have a son?' Ruth said, gesturing up to the family photograph.

'Craig,' Derek said with a slightly grim tone.

'Do you know where Craig was at the weekend, Mr Harrison?' Nick asked.

'No. I have no idea,' Derek said in a withering tone.

'Where would we find Craig at the moment, Mr Harrison?' Ruth asked.

'He works up at the saw and timber mill. Sanderson's.'

'Was Craig close to his sister?' Ruth asked.

Derek nodded. 'Yes. Very close. Craig is only eighteen months younger than Donna. They did everything together. They went travelling around the world together in their early twenties.'

'So, Craig must have taken her death extremely hard?' Nick asked.

'We all took it very hard, Sergeant. She was our daughter. It was just that Craig seemed to use it as an excuse to go completely off the rails. He hasn't been the same since Donna died,' Derek explained, sounding frustrated.

Ruth looked at Derek. 'Thank you for your help, Dr Harrison.'

AFTER TEN MINUTES DRIVING, NICK PULLED THE CAR OVER to the side of the road. Ruth could see he was frustrated that Sanderson's Timber Yard wasn't where he thought it was – he needed to check the satnav.

Nick and Ruth agreed that Craig Harrison was a significant person of interest. They just needed to see if he had a decent alibi.

'I Am, I Said' by Neil Diamond was playing on the radio. Ruth loved the song. It didn't help that the song was all about a man who felt lonely and a long way from the city where he grew up and called home. It was her go-to maudlin drinking song. When she was full of pissed-up self-pity, this was the song that could take those feelings to a whole new level. It had been a long time since she had listened to that type of music, which she took as a good sign. She was in a happy place and getting on with living her life with Sian. The 'misery music' of her past was currently gathering dust in the garage.

Checking his phone and satnav for the address of the Sanderson's Timber Yard, Nick snapped off the radio.

'Hey, I was listening to that!' Ruth said in mock annoyance.

'Really?' Nick said, arching his eyebrow mockingly.

'What? Neil Diamond? Please don't tell me that you don't like Neil Diamond. Everyone likes Neil Diamond … don't they?'

'Sorry, I forgot you were born in the sixties,' Nick quipped sharply.

'Oi, I was born in the sixties by a matter of months. And I regret ever telling you that,' Ruth said, shaking her head. To be honest, she really didn't care. She had embraced being fifty with hardly a bat of her increasingly wrinkled eyelid. Other women seemed to have some kind of breakdown.

'I know you struggle with simple maths, but I think I could have worked out when you were born. You're fifty and the year is 2019,' Nick said.

'Piss off, smart arse. Have you found out where we're going yet, or are you going to get us lost again?'

'I've got it here,' Nick said as he put up his hands defensively, now breaking into a smile.

God, they really were like a bickering old married couple, Ruth thought to herself.

Ruth grabbed the patched-in Tetra radio, 'Control from three-six. I need a PNC and background check on a Craig Harrison. Aged early forties. Lives in the Barford area of Snowdonia, over.'

'Three-six from Control, received,' the Computer-aided Dispatch controller, CAD, replied.

Starting up the engine, Nick pulled away with his usual forceful burst of speed, and within ten minutes they were pulling into the uneven and pot-holed area beside a large blue Portakabin. A rusty metal sign that had seen better days read *Sanderson's Timber Yard and Sawmill.*

A large, bald man came out of the Portakabin. He was wearing ear defenders around his neck, thick work gloves, goggles and an orange high-vis jacket. It appeared that a timber yard and sawmill was not the safest place to work.

She flashed her warrant card and got the formalities over with.

'We're looking for Craig Harrison?' Nick said.

'What's he done this time?' the bald man said, shaking his head with a wry smile.

'Craig in trouble a lot then, is he?' Nick asked.

'Jesus. Drugs, women, fighting. You name it. You would have thought he'd have grown out of it by now,' the bald man said as he gestured to them to follow him. 'Come on, he should be over here.'

The wind picked up and the autumn leaves that peppered the high trees surrounding them whooshed noisily. From somewhere, someone was cutting wood with a machine that wailed and growled.

Ruth stepped over a couple of deep puddles that were half-hidden by fallen leaves. She didn't want to spend the rest of the day with wet feet again. The air smelt of damp wood and the chemicals it had been treated with – preservatives, waterproofing and staining.

A bearded man with long hair was at a circular saw cutting lengths of wood. He looked a little dishevelled, in an attractive Kurt Cobain way, Ruth thought.

'That's your man,' the bald man shouted over the noise of the saws.

No wonder they have ear defenders. It is bloody deafening!

Ruth watched as the bald man went over and tapped Craig on the shoulder and pointed over to them.

Turning off the saw, Craig lowered his large safety glasses as the bald man explained who Ruth and Nick were. He nodded as he took off his gloves.

Then suddenly he turned and sprinted through the long shed and disappeared.

'Are you bloody kidding me?' Nick said to Ruth as he took off after him.

'He's such a dick!' the bald man said as Ruth went back the way they had come to see if she could intercept Craig.

From the look of it, the other end of the shed backed onto the approach road to the yard. Breaking into a jog, Ruth's right foot went straight into the puddle that she had so carefully avoided only minutes earlier.

For fuck's sake!

Treading carefully over the next watery pot-hole, her attention was then directed away by the sound of shouting. Still running, Craig Harrison came back into the yard from the direction of the road. It was almost comical.

Moving swiftly, Ruth turned and blocked the small walkway that ran between the huge piles of wood. She was now barring his escape route. Looking around, she grabbed a sawn offcut of wood that was about two feet in length and held it like a baseball bat. She wasn't sure what she was doing.

Seconds later, Craig rounded the corner and ran halfway down the walkway before he noticed Ruth. He stopped in his tracks when he saw Ruth wielding her makeshift weapon. He then looked at Nick who had just appeared behind him. He was trapped.

Taking a step forward, Craig raised his eyebrow.

'Stay there!' Ruth thundered.

'Get out of my way,' he growled.

'Take another step forward. I dare you. Because I will happily wrap this around your skull, put you in intensive care and claim it was self-defence,' Ruth snarled, looking directly at him.

Craig stayed where he was. Something about the way she had said it must have convinced him she wasn't kidding.

Still out of breath, Nick stepped forward, read Craig his rights, then handcuffed him and took him over to the car.

'What the hell did you run for?' Nick asked as he pushed Craig down into the rear seat.

'I see coppers, I run,' Craig mumbled with a shrug.

Nick closed the door behind him and then looked over at Ruth.

'What did you say to him? He just stopped dead,' Nick asked with a raised eyebrow.

'I persuaded him that trying to move me out of the way wasn't the way to go,' Ruth said with a wry smile.

'You threatened to smash his bloody head in, didn't you?' Nick grinned.

'Yeah …' Ruth said as she got into the car. 'I stepped in a puddle and it really pissed me off.'

BACK AT THE NICK, RUTH SAT AT HER DESK CHAIR WITH only one shoe on. She stretched out her back and checked the shoe that was drying on the radiator. Still wet.

Nick knocked on her open door and gestured with some printouts.

'What have you got?' Ruth asked, looking at the printout.

'PNC and background checks on Craig Harrison,' Nick said.

'Anything interesting?' Ruth asked.

'Assault, ABH, petty theft, bit of dealing. Craig Harrison is a bit of a local scumbag.'

'Doesn't fit when you go to that house and meet with his father,' Ruth said, thinking out loud. That kind of behaviour wasn't always dependent on socio-economic background, but Ruth knew it was a major factor.

'Not really, no,' Nick said as he flicked through the pages. 'You know, most of the offences have been committed in the last decade, which is unusual with this pattern of behaviour. In fact, in my experience, they normally decrease with age, not increase.'

Ruth shot Nick a look. 'Maybe Donna's death really did send her brother off the rails.'

'You think it could have been him that we chased up by the Berwyn River?' Nick asked.

Ruth shrugged. 'It's hard to tell. Where is he now?'

'I put him in Interview Room Two to calm down. He's got a solicitor even though I've told him it's a voluntary interview,' Nick explained.

'Let's see what he has got to say for himself,' Ruth said as she got up from her chair, grabbed her jacket and her shoe. Even though it was damp, she put it on.

A FEW MINUTES LATER, THEY HAD SETTLED DOWN OPPOSITE Craig Harrison and his solicitor. Harrison sat back with his legs stretched out, but Ruth wasn't buying the whole arrogant-rebel thing. *Harrison isn't comfortable enough in his own skin to pull that off*, she thought.

'Why did you run?' Nick asked as he pulled his chair from under the table.

'I've told you already,' Harrison said with a smirk.

'Well, if you could refresh our memories, Mr Harrison,

that would be useful,' Nick said with more than a hint of sarcasm.

'When I see police officers, my instinct is to run. It's always been like that,' Harrison said with a shrug.

Ruth shuffled through his PNC record. 'Except it hasn't, has it?'

Harrison frowned and shot a look at his solicitor. 'Eh?'

'You haven't always been in trouble with the police, have you? In fact, as a teenager, you were never in any trouble at all,' Ruth said, gesturing to his record.

'What are you getting at?' Harrison said with a confused snort and then looked at his solicitor as if to say, 'What are they on about?'

Ruth and Nick let the silence play out for a few seconds to build a bit of tension.

Ruth leaned forwards and softened her voice. 'Craig …? Can I call you *Craig*?'

'I've been called worse by you lot,' Harrison said attempting to make a joke.

Frowning as if she was trying to remember something, Ruth then looked over at Harrison again. 'We spoke to your father, Craig. He says that you were very close to Donna. Is that right?'

Craig shifted uncomfortably in his chair, sat up and then crossed his legs defensively. Ruth knew enough about body language to know when someone was feeling anxious and uncomfortable.

'Yeah. Of course. She was my sister,' Harrison said cautiously.

'So, it must have been difficult for you when she died?' Ruth asked.

Harrison blinked and looked down at the floor. 'Yeah, it was …'

Letting the emotion of the question settle with Harrison, Ruth looked down at the folder in front of her for no particular reason other than to apply pressure.

Pause.

'You must have been upset?' Ruth asked.

'Yeah …' Harrison said, sitting more upright.

Pause.

'And I would guess, you were angry about how she was killed?' Ruth said.

Harrison rubbed his face awkwardly and then ran his hand through his long hair.

'Is that right, Craig? You must have been *furious?*' Ruth asked.

'Yeah … I don't want to talk about what happened to Donna, all right?' Craig sneered over at her.

'How did you feel about Mark Fisher, Craig?' Nick asked.

'Didn't you hear me? I don't want to talk about this,' Harrison protested.

'Would it be fair to say that you blamed Mark Fisher for your sister's death, Craig?' Ruth asked.

Harrison just looked at the floor.

'I mean, if Mark Fisher hadn't been driving drunk, your sister would be alive today?' Nick said.

'Yes …' Harrison muttered under this breath.

'I'm guessing that you might even wish Mark Fisher harm if he was to blame for your sister's death?' Nick asked.

'What?' Harrison furrowed his brow and looked over at his solicitor as if to say 'Can they ask me this?'

Ruth lowered her voice again. 'Craig, did you want to get revenge against Mark Fisher for killing Donna? It would be understandable.'

'No one would blame you, Craig,' Nick said.

Harrison's face changed as if he'd had a lightbulb

moment. 'Why are you asking me all this? Did something happen to him?'

'You tell us, Craig,' Ruth said.

'What? What do you want me to say? Yeah, I wanted Mark Fisher to be dead for what he did to Donna! He killed her.'

Harrison's solicitor leant over and whispered something to him. Ruth knew that the solicitor was telling him to be more cautious about his answers. He was incriminating himself.

'You wanted to kill him, didn't you?' Nick asked.

'That's not what I said!' Harrison said. 'Why, is he dead? Is that why I'm here?'

'Craig, where were you between ten o'clock Saturday night and seven yesterday morning?' Ruth asked.

'Is he dead?' Craig asked.

'Just answer the question, Craig,' Nick snapped at him.

'At home. Asleep. Like most other people.'

'Alone? Can anyone verify that?' Nick asked.

'Nope. Sorry. That doesn't make me guilty of anything though,' Harrison said with a shrug. 'What's happened?'

Ruth pulled out local newspaper reports of Mark Fisher's trial.

'I understand there were threats of violence and a skirmish at Mark Fisher's trial. That doesn't look good for you, Craig. No alibi and threatening behaviour at Mark Fisher's trial,' Ruth said.

'I wasn't at Mark Fisher's trial,' Craig said.

'Where were you?' Ruth asked. His answer had wrongfooted her slightly.

Harrison shook his head and muttered, 'I just wasn't there … I couldn't face it.'

Ruth gestured to the newspaper. 'What about the newspaper report?'

'All that trouble? That was Kathleen Taylor. It wasn't our family,' Harrison snorted defensively. 'The papers got it wrong. She went mental apparently.'

Ruth shot Nick a frustrated look.

Who the hell is Kathleen Taylor and why didn't we know about her? What have we missed?

FIFTEEN MINUTES LATER, AND RUTH AND NICK WERE BACK in the lift to the sixth floor of Llancastell Police Station. Nick had already messaged French to look into who Kathleen Taylor was and why she was relevant.

Although Ruth wasn't normally claustrophobic, the lifts in the building unsettled her. They were old and painfully slow. When inside, she felt them jerk and clank into life. The ceilings and walls were lined with metallic sheets. They were no better than the lifts in the seventies housing estates in South East London. Well, except for the smell of piss, graffiti and the crack vials that usually crunched under her feet.

'What did you think?' Ruth asked.

Ruth wasn't sure how she felt about Craig Harrison as a murder suspect by the end of their interview. Did Nick think the same as her? He usually shared her initial instincts.

'Not sure, boss. On paper, Craig Harrison is a perfect fit as our prime suspect. But something didn't feel right when we interviewed him,' Nick explained.

It was exactly how Ruth felt too. *Why was that?* And then it came to her.

The doors to the lift opened slowly. They came out and walked down towards the CID office.

'I'll tell you what it was. Either Craig Harrison is a BAFTA-winning actor, or he genuinely had no idea that

Mark Fisher was dead. It's not something that's been reported widely in the press yet,' Ruth said, thinking aloud.

'Hard to murder someone and then be one hundred per cent convincing that you know nothing about it,' Nick said.

'Unless you're a socio- or psychopath,' Ruth added.

'And I don't think Craig Harrison is either of those.'

'No. Instinct says he wasn't hiding anything,' Ruth said. And then her mind turned to Harrison's revelation. 'And who the hell is this Kathleen Taylor woman?'

Nick shrugged. 'I thought she was an actress.'

'That's Kathleen Turner, you plank,' Ruth said as they entered the CID office. 'What does she have to do with the case?'

'What have you got, Dan?' Nick asked as he spotted French tapping away at his computer.

'We know who Kathleen Taylor is now,' French explained.

Ruth and Nick approached and looked at a newspaper front page on French's computer. It was a back copy of the *Llancastell Leader*.

'Go on, Dan. Don't keep us in suspense,' Ruth said.

'Kathleen Taylor was driving the car that Mark Fisher hit in the accident in which Donna Fisher died,' French explained.

'I thought that Donna Fisher was the only casualty of that crash?' Ruth said, thinking out loud.

'That was how it was reported. But Kathleen Taylor's eight-month-old son, Charlie, was a passenger in the back of the car. The specialists diagnosed significant brain damage as a result of the accident. He now has severe learning and coordination difficulties,' French explained.

'And what's this?' Nick asked of the newspaper front page.

'Kathleen Taylor took out a private prosecution against Mark Fisher four years later, while he was in prison. Fisher's insurance company claimed that their liability had gone past the time allotted for the statute of limitations as it was a civil case. The judge agreed and as Mark Fisher had no income, savings or property, the case was dropped.'

Ruth looked at Nick. 'I'm guessing that Kathleen Taylor was an angry woman after that?'

French pointed to the screen. 'When she gave a statement after the prosecution was dropped, she said that she hoped that Fisher died in prison, and that when he was released, he would need "to watch his back".'

Ruth and Nick shared a meaningful look.

There was someone else who seemed to want Mark Fisher dead.

Chapter 6

Slotting the silver key into the lock with a wiggle, Ruth opened the front door to her house and kept it open so Sian could follow her in.

'There you go, Hopalong,' Ruth said with a grin. Sian gave her a playful death stare as she manoeuvred herself over the threshold.

'Is it me, or is it chilly in here?' Sian said as they came into the hallway.

Ruth went over to her and gave her a hug. 'I'll warm you up.'

'Aww, thank you. It's just a shame you smell of cigarette smoke,' Sian said, rolling her eyes. 'You were meant to be giving up.'

'You know the best thing about not living with a man?' Ruth said.

'I can think of a few,' Sian said, raising an eyebrow.

'Not that silly. You can put the heating on whenever you want and not be told to just wear a jumper.'

'And the toilet seat,' Sian said.

'Yeah, and the toilet seat,' Ruth said.

Striding into the kitchen, Ruth headed into the narrow utility room and clicked on the heating. She heard the deep rumble of the system crank into life.

'Wine?' Ruth called to Sian who had settled in the living room.

'Please!' Sian called back.

'Two large glasses of Rioja coming right up.' *Perfect.* Ruth passed the window that looked out from her kitchen, across the garden and then the fields that swept away and kept going as far as the eye could see. What she would have done for a view like that when she was a kid. She and her younger brother would have been out in the garden and the fields in all weathers. What a sense of freedom it would have been.

Ruth remembered the concrete walkways and stairwells of the Battersea estate that she grew up on in the eighties. It was horrendous. The fall of the Shah in Iran and the Iranian Revolution in 1979 had led to the opening up of new supply lines of heroin running from the so-called 'Golden Crescent'. In the early eighties, a smack epidemic gripped deprived areas of Britain. Battersea was no exception. Ruth's Uncle Ray – who was, in fact, a second cousin – lived in a squat on the estate next to them and used to deal small amounts to locals. He even tried to rope Ruth and her brother, Chris, into delivering the drugs until their dad found out and beat him up. She remembered all the 'junkie jargon' that seemed part of everyday speech, even at school. Every kid, however old, knew what *chasing the dragon* and *smackhead* meant. When Zammo, a character from her favourite television programme, *Grange Hill*, got addicted to heroin, the cast released an anti-drugs single called 'Just Say No'. Everyone used to sing it at school, as if it were the latest hit by Spandau Ballet.

As the wind picked up outside, a large beech tree

bowed and waved, its leaves shivering and flickering. The sky was a uniform gun-metal grey and Ruth began to long for the heat of summer again.

Looking over at the immaculate cooker, fridge and work surfaces, she saw Sian's various magnetic slogans and plaques: *This kitchen is seasoned with love*, *Today's Specials – eat it or starve!* and *Pass me the prosecco and watch me get fabulous.*

It was Sian's sense of joy and humour – she loved her for it.

Ruth was lucky to have found Sian, and having promised to put Sarah's disappearance behind her, Ruth had managed to start to live in the present and future, enjoying their blossoming relationship. She and Sian were building a life together and it felt amazing.

Kicking off her shoes by the bottom of the stairs, Ruth went into the lounge, handed Sian her wine and slumped into the large armchair. She could feel the tension in her shoulders and neck.

'I need a massage,' Ruth said as she stretched.

'I'm the one with the serious back problems, thank you very much,' Sian said with a smile.

'We can trade massages tonight?' Ruth said.

'You're on,' Sian said and they looked at each other. 'I got us lasagne for tea,' Sian said as she gestured to her shopping. 'I thought I'd cook for once. Well, use the oven or the microwave at least.'

Ruth looked at her. *God, I love her. What have I done to deserve someone like Sian?*

Putting down her wine, Ruth went over and took Sian by the hand.

'Come on, we can eat later,' Ruth said.

'Oi, cheeky. What's all this in aid of?' Sian said with a grin as she climbed gingerly to her feet.

'I thought you had a sore back?' Ruth said.

'Oh, yes. I do. Very painful, actually,' Sian said, playing along.

They came out into the hallway and Ruth began to lead Sian up the stairs.

'So, you'll need a long massage,' Ruth said playfully. 'Then I'll run you a hot bath.'

'Right, what have you done wrong? Have you broken a vase again?' Sian said with a laugh.

'No. Do I need a reason to be nice to you?' Ruth asked.

'No. I love it. Long may it continue,' Sian said with a beaming smile.

They stopped on the landing and kissed before collapsing into giggles.

BY THE TIME NICK AND AMANDA PULLED UP OUTSIDE THE small building that housed the AA meeting, it was pattering with rain. Amanda was fed up with being pregnant and Nick could sense the tension in the air as they sat quietly in the car park. Chewing on yet another heartburn tablet – Amanda's acid reflux was causing her a lot of pain. And that was on top of being about to give birth – Amanda was staring into the distance.

'You okay?' Nick asked uncertainly. *What did you ask her that for, you dick? She's clearly not all right.*

'No ...' Amanda said wearily.

'Sorry ... I was just ... Actually, I'll be quiet.'

The volume of the rain began to increase as if to signify Amanda's mood. Wincing, Amanda unclipped the seatbelt and looked up at the grey cloud cover.

'I need to go and see my dad this week. And I need you to drive me round there,' Amanda said.

Nick nodded. 'Yeah, of course.'

Amanda's father had recently got out of an open

prison after serving a sentence for drunk driving, but he was dying from cancer. Even though Amanda hadn't said as much, she was desperate for her father to see his grand-child before he passed away.

'Shall we just go home?' Amanda groaned.

Nick knew he had to handle this sensitively. 'I can drive you home, but I'll come back. I really need to keep up my meetings. I only went to one last week and I feel a bit out of sorts.'

'*You* feel a bit out of sorts?' Amanda snorted.

Nick didn't reply. He had broken his promise to himself not to complain about how he felt while Amanda was in the latter stages of pregnancy.

'They'll all be cooing around me. Getting me a chair, cups of tea. Asking me questions.'

'Yes, I can see that having lots of caring women looking after you might be a horrendous experience,' Nick said dryly.

Amanda rolled her eyes, turned and smiled at him. 'You really can't help being a sarcastic twat, can you?'

'Nope. But I am the sarcastic twat that you're marrying and having a baby with.' Nick opened the car door. 'Come on.'

Snapping open an umbrella, Nick covered Amanda as they wandered across the car park, their feet splashing in the surface water.

Once inside, Nick watched as the older women in the AA group bustled around Amanda, with kisses, hugs and a cup of tea. He smiled to himself. She was in good hands.

Sitting near the back, Nick took some time to be quiet and reflect. Even though he was feeling anxious and a little out of sorts, his need and desire for alcohol had now gone. Working the twelve-step programme, coming to meetings, talking to his sponsor. Somewhere in there was the key to his sobriety and he didn't want to unpick it to try to work out how he was remaining sober. He just was. And that was a bloody miracle.

As he sipped his coffee, Nick was aware that someone to one side was trying to catch his eye. It was Peter the Artist – as was his AA moniker. Peter was in his early fifties, small, with a round balding head and quick blue eyes. Nick remembered him from years ago, before Peter disappeared for a five-year relapse. He had been back in the rooms for about six months now, and Nick could see that he already looked physically much better. However, Peter often cut a rather doleful and sad character. He wore his self-pity and neediness on his sleeve. After a drunken bicycle accident, Peter had lost the use of his right arm. It had happened over ten years ago, but it was something he still seemed to struggle with. He could no longer paint and even found teaching painting difficult. Nick knew that Peter used the injury as an excuse to feel sorry for himself, which would lead to terrible depression to which his go-to cure was alcohol.

Peter was still prone to small relapses at the weekend, which he was very open about. He would arrive at meetings unshaven, with a corduroy barge cap pulled down low, and admit he had been drinking for a few days. It wasn't a surprise to anyone. He only wore the hat when he had relapsed. But no one judged him either. That's how AA worked.

In recent weeks, Nick and Peter had been chatting quite often about what had happened, but Peter simply had no idea why he would wander to the nearby petrol station at six in the morning to buy a litre of vodka. All Nick could do was try to explain his own experience of drinking, and how he had kept sober for a decent amount of time.

Getting up from his seat further along the row, Peter smiled and came to sit down next to Nick. He didn't mind. Peter was an intelligent man who just needed some help. At the weekend, Peter had dropped the fact that he was gay into the conversation. It didn't matter to Nick. But in the wider community of Llancastell, attitudes were still old-fashioned and homophobia was common.

'Nick, good to see you,' Peter said as they shook hands.

'Having a good week, Peter? No hat and clean-shaven is a good sign,' Nick quipped.

Peter chortled as he ran the back of his left hand over his chin as if to confirm that he had indeed shaved that day.

'There's been something I've been meaning to ask you, Nick. And I've been feeling a bit awkward about it,' Peter said as he shifted uncomfortably in his seat.

What does that mean? It wasn't the greatest opening gambit to a conversation.

'Fire away,' Nick said casually but actually worried about what Peter was going to say. Maybe he was prejudiced after all. *Not every gay man wants to sleep with you,* Nick said to himself.

'I wanted to ask you to be my sponsor,' Peter said. 'I've really enjoyed our chats. I like what you have to say and how you say it.'

Nick could feel his pride swell. It was the first time he had ever been asked. Had he come that far in his own sobriety journey that he appeared as an example to someone? However, his initial small pleasure at the implied compliment was short-lived. He was about to become a father, he worked as a police officer; he had too much on his plate.

However, helping other alcoholics to stay sober would also help Nick stay sober himself. The theory was that if you were thinking about and helping others, you would be less consumed by yourself. It also wasn't the done thing to respond with a resounding no.

'What do you think? I know you're having a baby and have a busy job. But you're the only person I feel any real affinity to,' Peter admitted. 'It's not as though I'm going to be ringing you every five minutes.'

Now he's put it like that, how can I refuse?

'Okay. I will act as your sponsor for as long as it suits both of us,' Nick said.

Peter had been around long enough to know that it was a two-way street. If the sponsor felt his sponsee just wasn't able or willing to do what they were being told, it could be time to move on. Similarly, if the sponsee didn't think they were getting what they needed from their sponsor, they could find another one. There were never any hard feelings.

'Great. That's great,' Peter said with an obvious sense of relief.

Nick remembered when he had asked Dundee Bill to be his sponsor. It had been nerve-wracking because you were making yourself vulnerable to rejection, usually at a time when you were feeling emotionally fragile.

'I've got your number. I'll text you and we'll go for a coffee in a couple of weeks. Any problems, give me a ring,' Nick said, feeling the glow of actually helping someone in AA.

Peter shook his hand as Amanda returned from her cluster of mother hens and sat beside Nick.

'Intense conversation with Peter?' Amanda said as she let out an audible sigh once she was off her feet.

'Yeah. He asked me to be his sponsor,' Nick admitted, still feeling pleased with himself.

'I assume you said no,' Amanda said immediately.

Nick didn't say anything.

'Please tell me you said no, Nick? Now is not the time, is it?' Amanda said in disbelief.

'No, of course I said no,' Nick said.

And there it was. He was back to his motto: if in doubt, lie, and then lie again.

Chapter 7

Ruth had been at work for an hour when DC Dan French came and knocked on her open door.

'Boss, call from the desk downstairs. There's a Lucy Parsons asking to see you. She says she knew you when you were working in London. Something about an old case,' French said with a shrug.

French had just come to the end of his time as a probationer and Ruth had been impressed by his professional attitude to the job. He was going to make a great detective.

'Okay, tell them I'm on my way,' Ruth said. Ruth couldn't remember a Lucy Parsons, but if she was a copper, she hadn't gone through the official channels if it was regarding an old Met case.

A few minutes later, Ruth walked into the canteen where the duty sergeant had told Lucy Parsons to wait. If what she wanted to talk about was serious in nature, they could then move to one of the interview rooms beside the custody suite.

Spotting her immediately as the well-dressed woman in

her mid-forties sitting at a table, Ruth approached and smiled.

'Mrs Parsons?' Ruth said, shaking her hand and sitting down opposite her. The first thing Ruth noticed was her blonde hair that was cut with layers and moved and swished as if she had just walked out of the hairdressers only moments earlier.

How the bloody hell is that fair? Ruth thought, unconsciously touching her own slightly greasy brunette hair that was full of split ends and greying roots.

'It's Lucy. And you're Detective Inspector Ruth Hunter, is that right?' Lucy asked hesitantly. She had a perfect middle-class English accent.

'Yes?' Ruth had no idea who this woman was. She had never seen her before in her life. 'Sorry, have we met before?'

'No. We haven't,' Lucy said as she put her hands around a mug of black coffee.

'I assume you're on the job. Are you with the Met?' Ruth asked.

'Oh, I'm not a police officer,' Lucy said, looking a little nervous.

What the hell could this be all about then?

'I'm confused. I got a call from my duty sergeant to say that you knew me from London and that you wanted to talk to me about an old case?' Ruth asked. Was Lucy Parsons going to waste her time needlessly? She was also annoyed with the duty sergeant who technically should have checked her need to talk to Ruth more thoroughly. It wouldn't have happened in the Met.

'That's not strictly true. Sorry … this is quite difficult,' Lucy said, taking a breath. Ruth could see that she was anxious.

'I'll do my best to help if I can …' Ruth said, trying to

reassure her but also wanting her to get to the bloody point. She looked at Lucy's carefully manicured French-tip nails. She wasn't wearing a wedding ring. *Interesting*, Ruth thought. Definitely divorced. More than once possibly. She had that air about her.

'There was an article in the *Daily Mail* a couple of months ago …'

Lucy's words struck a chord. She was talking about the article that had appeared in the *Daily Mail* back in the summer. 'The Curious Case of Sarah Goddard.' It was written because on 25 August 2019, Sarah should have turned forty. The article had rehashed most of the evidence that was known about Sarah's disappearance. It was more of a human-interest piece, but Ruth thought there was an unpleasant tone and slant to the article. The journalist had portrayed Sarah's lifestyle and sexuality as if putting her on the darker fringes of society. The article implied that Sarah was more likely to vanish off the face of the planet because she liked to live life a little and was gay. It was both homophobic and simply not true. Ruth had wanted to track down the journalist, but Sian had persuaded her that it could make things worse.

Ruth's heart sank. It seemed that Lucy Parsons was another crank, journalist or mystic who had latched onto Sarah's disappearance and wanted to use it to their advantage. It wasn't the first time. There had been nearly a dozen people with various motives for wanting to talk to her about Sarah. All of them had proved to be a waste of time and she had a new murder case to run.

'The article about Sarah's disappearance?' Ruth asked in a withering tone. Lucy didn't, however, look like your usual crank who had come to tell her that she had been contacted by Sarah from 'the other side'. Ruth had been approached by two 'mystics' who claimed to have spoken to Sarah and have vital clues about what had happened to her. Both had been horribly wrong about almost every detail Ruth had asked them.

'Yes. Sarah Goddard. She was your partner, wasn't she?' Lucy asked gently.

She's a fucking journalist! Ruth could feel the anger rising and knew she needed to protect herself.

'It's not something I'm going to talk to a stranger about, I'm afraid. And I don't talk to the press,' Ruth snapped as she rose from the table. If Lucy Parsons had anything of any use, she would have to declare it now. But Ruth knew she didn't.

Fuck her! Digging around in other people's lives.

'You don't understand …' Lucy said, sounding distraught. 'I'm not a journalist.'

'I'm very busy. Please don't waste my time again,' Ruth said angrily.

Beginning to walk away, Ruth's mind was already back on Mark Fisher, how and why he was killed and who had done it.

'My husband had an affair with Sarah Goddard in the summer of 2013,' Lucy said.

This time her words did more than strike a chord. They seemed to hang like a corrosive darkness in the air.

Time stopped for a few seconds. Ruth's legs stopped working as she took a few moments, still facing away from Lucy, to even hear what she had just been told before she rationalised it.

'That's not possible. Sorry. In the summer of 2013 … Sarah was living with me. She didn't have an affair. I would have known,' Ruth explained as her mind whirred with what Lucy had said. It didn't seem real.

No, not possible! Why is she saying this?

Ruth turned and Lucy looked up at her. Something

about the sadness but certainty in her eyes struck terror in Ruth. What if she was telling the truth? It was ridiculous. No …

'Sorry, that's not possible,' Ruth said, but she was completely rattled.

Just walk away, Ruth. Now! Do it!

'I'm not lying,' Lucy said as she took out her phone. 'I need you to look at something.'

Ruth's stomach was clenching with the rising anxiety. Did she have some kind of proof? If she did, Ruth didn't think she could bear to even see it.

'My husband, Jamie, left his phone unlocked one evening. I took a picture of a message …' Lucy explained as she slid the phone over.

Ruth looked at the phone. Her pulse was racing and she was feeling sick to her stomach.

Turning the phone, Ruth looked at the screenshot:

I can meet you at 5 p.m. at The Grapes by Victoria Station. Sarah xxx

The world didn't feel real. Ruth detached from reality. The Grapes pub was around the corner from where Sarah used to work. And Sarah used to drink there. And she signed off every text with three kisses.

Oh please, God, don't let this be true.

'Did you confront your husband?' Ruth asked as she fought back a tear.

'Yes. He said it was a colleague from the bank. We were living in Dubai at the time and he flew back and forth to London,' Lucy explained.

'How did you link the Sarah from the text to Sarah Goddard?' Ruth asked, trying to think straight.

It's just a coincidence, that's all this is.

'I didn't. But I knew Jamie's password for his Instagram account. I went on it and I found this on his direct messages,' Lucy said as she took the phone, tapped it and turned it again for Ruth to see.

On the direct message page there was another message:

Look what you're missing tonight! Looking forward to Saturday night. Sarah xxx.

Attached to the message was a photograph taken in a candlelit bath of the person's wet legs covered in bubbles. Ruth thought it could be anyone in a bath.

Then she saw the candles, the wall at the far end and the shampoos and conditioners. It was the bath from the flat they had shared in Crystal Palace. She felt sick.

Oh God, please … This can't be happening, can it?

As Ruth turned the phone back, she saw that her hands were shaking a little. Inside, she felt utter pain and confusion. Taking a breath, she sat back in her chair. Feeling her heart thumping, she tried to swallow but couldn't. She was on the verge of a panic attack.

Lucy looked at her. 'I'm so sorry …'

'Why now?' Ruth whispered as she felt a tear roll down her cheek. She couldn't help herself.

'I saw the article. It mentioned you. It felt like the right thing to do. If it was me, I would have wanted to know …' Lucy explained apologetically.

There was a huge part of Ruth that could have done without knowing. She wasn't sure how to process any of it.

I don't want to know. I don't want to even think about it!

'What did your ... husband say?' Ruth asked.

'I didn't ask him. He left us that September ... I never said anything,' Lucy explained, looking distraught.

'Was that all you ever found?' Ruth asked.

'Yes. That was it. For what it's worth, Jamie left us for his secretary. Fucking cliché. I guess whatever happened between him and Sarah was just a fling that summer.'

Ruth nodded. 'Yeah ...', but she wasn't really listening.

That doesn't help me! Ruth wanted to scream at her. But it wasn't this woman's fault.

'I am sorry.' Lucy looked at her watch. 'You know, I should get going. I don't know if I've done the right thing by coming to see you today. And I'm sorry that finding this out has caused you so much pain. But you're grieving for someone and so you should know everything about them – good or bad,' Lucy said.

She was right. It hurt like hell, but she had done the right thing. Ruth needed the full picture.

'Thank you, Lucy ... I know it was difficult for you to come to see me today. But ... I do want to know everything about Sarah,' Ruth said, giving her a reassuring nod, but her words sounded hollow, even to her, as she held back more tears.

'Thanks. I didn't know how you were going to react. I thought you might scream at me,' Lucy confessed as she stood up and got her things to go.

Ruth shook her head. She was still in shock.

'Where's ... your husband now?' Ruth asked, taking a breath to steady herself. She had no idea if she was going to track him down, but she needed the information if she did.

'He lives and works in London.'

'Where does he work?' Ruth asked.

'A German merchant bank called Commerzbank LDN in London. Guildhall in the City,' Lucy explained.

'Thank you,' Ruth said as they shared a look. They had both been betrayed and hurt by the affair.

Watching her go, Ruth processed what she had been told.

Then it came to her in a dark, sickening twist, like a punch to the head. She reached out to steady herself against the table.

When Sarah disappeared, Jurgen Kessler had also been working for Commerzbank in London.

Two hours later, Nick and Ruth pulled off the main high street in Llancastell. The unmarked black Astra they drove had been cleaned by the carpool overnight and now had a zesty smell. However, Ruth had only just noticed. She was still in complete shock over what Lucy Parsons had revealed to her about Sarah. It was hard to take it all in.

Ruth knew she had to come clean and tell Sian what had happened. However, that would then go against everything Ruth had promised in the summer – that she would make a concerted effort to find some closure when it came to Sarah and her disappearance. It had been driving such a wedge between her and Sian that Sian had even left her for a few days. Would the discovery of Sarah's affair drag everything back into the open? She didn't know whether her and Sian's relationship could weather it. Should she just keep quiet until she decided what to do?

'You okay, boss?' Nick asked, his forehead wrinkling.

'Yeah, miles away. Sorry.'

Should she come clean? She and Nick knew all of each other's dark secrets and skeletons, and, even though he pretended to be a juvenile, Nick often had wise words when it came to her problems. It was his own demons and darkness that he often lacked judgement on – although she had to give him his due, he was doing bloody well at the moment. He had got his life back now he was sober.

'You haven't said a word for ten minutes. Which, of course, is a complete relief,' Nick quipped, 'but very unlike you.'

Ruth rolled her eyes. 'Ha, ha.' She sighed. 'I had a visitor this morning.'

'Yeah. I saw you come back from the canteen and you didn't look yourself. In fact, you looked a bit rattled. Who was it?' Nick asked.

'A woman called Lucy Parsons …' Ruth said and then stopped.

'I don't know the name,' Nick said with a shrug.

Ruth was finding the right words. She hadn't said it out loud to anyone yet and it was painful.

'No, you wouldn't … She claimed that her husband had an affair with Sarah in London in the summer of 2013,' Ruth said. For some reason, it felt a relief just to say the words.

'Christ … Did she have any proof?' Nick asked as his brow furrowed further.

'Unfortunately, yes. She had a text,' Ruth said.

'Bloody hell. That's not good …'

'Worse than that. She had a photo that Sarah had taken in our bath and sent to him. It was definitely from her,' Ruth explained.

'God … I'm really sorry to hear that. That's horrible,' Nick said.

'Sorry. I just needed to tell someone, that's all.'

'Don't apologise. You've listened to me enough times. Christ, you picked me up from rehab not that long ago,' Nick said.

'I don't know what to do with it,' Ruth said.

Ruth sucked the last bit of her ciggie, tossed it out and buzzed up the window.

'What can you do?' Nick asked.

'I could go and find this Jamie Parsons. The husband.'

'And say what?'

'That's the thing. I don't know what I'd say. Weird thing is, he worked for Commerzbank in London at the same time as Jurgen Kessler.'

Nick took in what she had said and glanced over at her. 'What? That's way too much of a coincidence, isn't it? It's a bit creepy ...'

It confirmed to Ruth that there was something dark and unexplained about that fact.

'That's my instinct ... They employ hundreds, if not thousands, of people. But it just didn't sit right with me,' Ruth said and looked over at Nick. He gave her a reassuring nod.

'It doesn't ... Whatever you decide to do, today is not the day. Otherwise, you'll make a decision that you might regret.'

Ruth nodded. Nick was right. Nothing good came out of knee-jerk reactions. She needed time to process everything. But she wasn't sure how long that would take.

A news bulletin started on the local radio station.

'*The body of a man that was found on the banks of the Berwyn River has been identified as that of Mark Fisher. A spokesperson for North Wales Police confirmed that their investigation into Mr Fisher's death is now a murder enquiry. North Wales Police have appealed for any witnesses who were in the area on Sunday morning or have any information to contact them on the investigation hotline.*'

Nick glanced over as Ruth turned the radio down. 'Short and sweet.'

'The less we say, the less Norman No-mates or freaks we get ringing in, trying to get attention,' Ruth said sardonically.

Ruth had fielded a call earlier that morning from the North Wales Police media office in St Asaph. News had leaked about Mark Fisher's murder from somewhere. It hadn't taken long for newspapers, radio and television to start sniffing around. Ruth had discussed a press release with just the basic details.

Nick turned left as they rounded the corner and slowed along the narrow street. Ruth looked out. These Victorian streets really weren't designed for cars. She spotted parents and children as they passed a primary school. The children looked so small, so innocent. It made her heart flutter to see them smiling, running and playing as soon as they were through the gates and on the playground. Would she ever be a grandmother? She would like to be. It would be a chance to make up for being such a fuck-up as a mother to Ella. After the dysfunction of her marriage to Dan, there had been some stability when she first met Sarah and they lived together. But Sarah's disappearance had turned hers and Ella's worlds upside down just when Ella was an impressionable teenager doing her GCSEs. Ruth was amazed that Ella, who was now in her early twenties, was such a grounded and thoughtful adult. *Far more than her mother*, Ruth thought ruefully.

Pulling up outside a small fitness studio, they stopped and Nick turned off the ignition. They had arranged to meet Kathleen Taylor at ten. She taught Pilates classes there every morning. Unclipping her seatbelt, Ruth finished off her coffee even though it was tepid – she needed the caffeine. She would wait until after they talked to Kathleen for her next ciggie.

The pavement was wet from the overnight rain, and dark brown autumn leaves littered the road. She forgot that autumn started a few weeks earlier in Snowdonia.

'I'd better sign Amanda up here for after the birth,' Nick said as they went to the door where a class called 'Bums and Tums' was being advertised.

'Jesus, give her time! She's still pregnant, Nick,' Ruth said.

'Yeah, but giving birth plays havoc with your pelvic floor,' Nick said.

Ruth raised an eyebrow. 'Oh Jesus! Did you actually just say the phrase "pelvic floor"?'

'I've been reading a book on pregnancy,' Nick said boastfully.

'Bloody hell. I feel like I'm in a parallel universe,' Ruth quipped.

They arrived at the reception, flashed their warrant cards and were shown to a small café on the first floor that smelt of freshly ground coffee and herbal teas.

A tall, muscular woman dressed in yoga gear came striding across the café and offered her hand. 'Hi. I'm Kathleen Taylor. You must be DI Hunter? Shall we sit down?'

Bloody hell. She's uber-confident, Ruth thought.

'Is it that obvious that we're police officers?' Ruth asked.

'Well, in a place like this it is,' Kathleen said with a smile as she sipped from her bottle of water.

Was that an insult? Or was it just the way it was delivered?

'We're not really regulars at "Bums and Tums",' Nick joked.

Kathleen ignored him.

'We wanted to ask you a couple of questions as part of an ongoing investigation,' Ruth explained. Kathleen's manner had made Ruth feel a little insecure. It wasn't surprising that she was feeling a little sensitive after the events of the morning.

'Mark Fisher?' Kathleen said with a knowing nod.

She must have been listening to the radio this morning.

'Yes … Mark Fisher,' Ruth said.

'Christ, am I a suspect?' Kathleen said with a slightly pompous snort.

Ruth shifted in her chair. She wasn't warming to Kathleen. It was rare to meet someone so unfazed and direct when talking to police officers.

'We are following various lines of enquiry regarding Mark Fisher's death. And to help us with those enquiries, we would like to ask you a couple of questions. If that's okay?' Ruth said.

'I suppose you've been reading the newspapers from the civil trial?' Kathleen said.

Ruth and Nick looked at each other. *We'll be leading the questioning, not you, Mrs Perfect Yoga-pants!* Ruth thought.

Opening his notebook, Nick began. 'Mrs Taylor, could you tell us where you were at the weekend?'

'Well, that's easy. I was in Prague with a friend. Flew out of Manchester Friday lunchtime, came back late on Sunday night.

'Okay, thank you,' Nick said as he scribbled down the details.

'I guess that puts me out of the frame then?' Kathleen asked with more than a hint of sarcasm.

Unfortunately, it did make her an unlikely suspect, unless she had somehow arranged the murder. That wasn't impossible, but in Ruth's experience, it was very unlikely.

'You have made your feelings for Mark Fisher very public, haven't you?' Ruth said.

'The man was very drunk, smashed into my car and gave my baby severe brain damage. He never apologised or showed any remorse. How would you feel about someone that did that to your child?' Kathleen asked.

She has a good point, Ruth thought. If someone had done that to Ella, how would she feel about that person? She had met plenty of evil psychopaths in her line of work. But if someone had recklessly ruined her and Ella's lives like that, what would she think and do? She wasn't sure, but would it stretch to murder?

'So, you are admitting that you hated Mark Fisher for what he had done?' Nick asked.

'Yes, of course. I've never hidden that,' Kathleen said with a shrug.

'And you might be quite happy that someone decided to murder him?' Nick asked.

'It's not a great loss to the world. And I'll admit that when he was released from prison, it made me extremely uncomfortable and angry. He got his life back to live how he wanted to. I have to take my son to a special school every morning because he can't speak or walk properly. And that breaks my heart,' Kathleen said.

Nick looked over at Ruth. They could both see that her anger was simmering away.

'And just to clarify, you were in Prague the weekend that Mark Fisher was murdered?' Nick asked.

Kathleen raised an eyebrow. 'You say that as if I planned it. I didn't hire a hitman if that's what you are suggesting.'

'I'm not suggesting anything, Mrs Taylor. I'm just making sure we get all the facts straight,' Nick said.

Kathleen glanced at her watch. 'I'm really sorry but

I've got a class that starts in about five minutes so you'll have to excuse me. Is there anything else?'

'That's it for the moment, thank you,' Ruth said with a forced grin.

Grabbing her bottle of water, Kathleen left them and bounded downstairs.

'Well, that was a waste of time,' Nick said as he got up and pushed in his chair.

Ruth arched her eyebrow at him with a smile. 'Don't underestimate the value of TIE, Nicholas. I know it would all be car chases and action if you got your way, but the boring stuff gets more results.'

TIE stood for trace, investigate and eliminate and was the backbone of any decent police investigation.

'Not very Starsky and Hutch though, is it?' Nick said rolling his eyes.

Ruth gestured to the café counter. 'Fancy a camomile tea for the road?'

'No, ta. Tastes like old socks. I need a strong, sugary coffee and an artery-thickening bacon bap.'

As they started to go down the stairs, they looked over into the studio where Kathleen Taylor was demonstrating a shoulder stand, with her legs pointing directly up to the ceiling.

Ruth smiled as she looked at the women in the fitness studios. 'Bacon, coffee and a fag. Now that does sound perfect. Life's too short for all this nonsense.'

BY THE TIME RUTH AND NICK GOT BACK TO LLANCASTELL nick, French and Sian had finished updating the scene boards in Incident Room One. CID only ever really used Incident Room One when there was a murder or a missing person. The last time they had been in here was at the beginning of the summer when Rosie Wright had gone missing. It was a case that Ruth would never forget, especially its outcome.

On one side of the room, there were scene boards that featured a new photo of Mark Fisher along with his name, date of birth and time and place of death written in blue ink. There was a detailed map of the area with a red pin to show where the murder had taken place.

As Ruth entered, she realised that she far preferred Incident Room One to the CID office that they normally worked in. It had a different energy. It felt more focussed and sharper. She couldn't really define what was different. The ceilings were higher and the room was more spacious – maybe that was it? She also associated it with high-pressured cases where everyone buzzed with adrenaline to get the right result.

Ruth went over to the small office in the far corner that she would now use as she was the senior investigating officer, SIO. She went in, sat at her desk and logged on. She had called a late-morning briefing as they needed to get together as a team.

However, what was really weighing on her mind was far more personal: the idea that Sarah had had an affair with a married man. How could Ruth not have known? Why wasn't being with Ruth enough for Sarah? After the last six years, the betrayal really hurt. What was Ruth going to tell Sian about the conversation she had had with Lucy Parsons? Sian had enough to deal with just getting to work, plus all the physio she was doing to see if she could eventually walk without a stick. It was the last thing either of them needed. Ruth decided that she would wait before talking to her about what had happened; she couldn't burden her with this.

Before she realised it, Ruth had started to type Jamie

Parsons's name into various social media accounts. Within seconds, she had found his Instagram page. In front of her, the man who had an affair with Sarah only months before she had disappeared. Did Jamie Parsons have anything to do with it? She couldn't rule that out now. And there was also the crushing thought that if Sarah had kept an affair from her, what else was going on in her life that Ruth didn't know about?

From his profile, Ruth could see that Jamie Parsons was handsome, with a greying beard and an angular face. He looked like he could have been a Hollywood actor from the forties or fifties – old-fashioned handsome. She could see the attraction. Parsons ran marathons, liked windsurfing, and seemed to be permanently travelling the world with work.

A knock on the door broke her train of thought. Closing down the profile page quickly, Ruth spun on her chair to see Nick.

She could see from his face that he had already spotted what she had been looking at. That was Nick. As her old dad always said, 'sharp as a tack.'

'Is that a good idea, boss?' Nick asked as he gestured to the computer screen.

'I don't know. I can't help but be curious,' Ruth said with a shrug.

'Yeah, just don't go torturing yourself, eh?' Nick said with a kind smile. 'Everyone's here for the briefing, boss.'

'Right, great,' Ruth said, trying to focus, grabbing her files, and then heading out into the incident room. DCI Drake spotted her and came over. In the Met, Drake would have been her *guv'nor* or *skipper*. In North Wales CID, Drake was just *boss*.

DCI Ashley Drake was muscular and always well

dressed. Since he took over at Llancastell CID, he had been an excellent line manager.

'How was Ruby's interview, boss?' Ruth asked. Drake's youngest daughter was having an interview and audition for a music scholarship to a prestigious school in Cheshire. Clarinet, singing and piano, if she remembered correctly.

'She thought it was a disaster. But then again, Ruby thinks everything is a disaster and then she does really well,' Drake said with a beaming smile. Every time he talked about his daughters, his face lit up. He was a proud dad, and it was lovely to see.

'She'll be fine. I once played "Three Blind Mice" on the recorder and my dad threw it in the bin,' Ruth joked. 'How's Paula doing?'

Drake's wife, Paula, had been diagnosed with cancer earlier in the year and it had been pre-occupying him.

'Test results any day now, so fingers crossed.'

'I'll be thinking of you both,' Ruth said.

'Thank you, Ruth.' Drake then gestured to the assembled murder team of half a dozen CID detectives. 'Mind if I sit in?' He didn't really need to ask her permission, but that was what he was like. His man-management was spot on. He didn't suffer fools, but he was comfortable enough in his own skin not to have to swing his dick around to show that he was in charge.

'Help yourself,' Ruth said, gesturing for Drake to sit where he wanted.

She had heard rumours that a detective superintendent position had become available up in Cumbria Police. It was the next rank up for Drake, but she was praying that he didn't take it. His wife and kids were now settled in North Wales after all. He was an excellent boss – one of the best she had worked for. And that could make or break the experience of being in CID. She should know. She had worked for some right bastards and there was nothing worse than dreading a day at work or not trusting your line manager not to stab you in the back.

Added to that, Ruth knew that if Drake left, Superintendent Jones would come to her and ask her to take over the position of DCI in Llancastell CID. It was arrogant thinking, but she was the obvious choice. However, she had come to North Wales for a more peaceful way of life. It hadn't worked out like that though; there had been several high-profile cases that had proved just as challenging as anything she had ever tackled in South London. Moving up to DCI was never in her plans and even though she was only fifty, she had planned a downward trajectory for her career – not promotion.

Grabbing her files, Ruth walked to the centre of the room. 'Morning, everyone. I don't know if you've had a chance to have a look at this photograph, but this is Mark Fisher who was murdered on the banks of the Berwyn River sometime in the early hours of Sunday morning. Our killer attempted to make it look like Mark had taken his own life by cutting his wrists, but the evidence tells us that he was murdered. And we owe it to Mark and his family to do our best work for him and find out who killed him.' Ruth said and thought of Eileen Fisher and all that she had been through over the years. 'Nick?'

Getting up from his chair, Nick went over to the computer and clicked a photograph of Mark Fisher as they had found him, slumped dead under a tree beside the river. 'Mark was discovered like this by two canoeists at around eight o'clock on Sunday morning. The PM tells us that he was killed between midnight and two o'clock on Sunday morning.'

'Do we have anything more specific on that, Nick?' Drake asked sitting forwards in his chair.

'It was very cold early on Sunday morning, boss. So the chief pathologist says that a more precise time of death would be dependent on knowing how long Mark Fisher's body was out in the cold or whether he was murdered inside and the body moved, as we suspect,' Nick explained.

'What's our baseline for time of death?' Drake asked.

'Midnight, if he was killed in situ,' Nick said.

'Those woods would have been pitch black,' Drake said, thinking out loud. 'Whoever did this would have needed a torch or torches.'

'We've had SOCOs looking through the woods where we pursued our mystery person. They've come back with nothing so far,' Ruth explained.

'Footprints?' Drake asked.

'Too many to narrow it down with any certainty,' Ruth explained.

'You think this person was connected to the murder?' Drake asked.

'They had to be, otherwise what were they doing there and why did they run?' Nick said.

Clicking on the computer again, a close-up photograph of the wounds on Mark Fisher's wrists during the post-mortem showed on the wall-mounted screen. Ruth could see that they were so deep that the flaps of skin either side of the cuts were visible.

'These are the wounds on Mark Fisher's left wrist that led him to bleed to death. We are waiting for the toxi-cology report, but there was an empty bottle of vodka beside the body when it was found.' Nick looked down at his notes. 'The Chief Pathologist concluded that the wounds he found on Mark's wrist were unlike any other. He said it was highly unusual to see the ulnar artery severed rather than the radial. His conclusion was that it made the death suspicious.'

'But he didn't rule out suicide?' Drake asked to clarify.

'Not at the preliminary PM. But later that day, he examined the lividity of Mark's body which proved that it had been moved after he was dead,' Nick explained.

Drake nodded. 'And so he was murdered.'

Ruth moved to the board and pointed to a picture. 'This is a photograph of Mark Fisher's right hand. This is the hand that he is supposed to have made the deep cuts into his left wrist with. Except you can see from this photograph that the bones around the knuckles and joints are swollen and twisted out of shape. Mark Fisher had terrible arthritis in his right hand as a result of decades of playing the guitar. It's relatively common, apparently. When we spoke to Eileen Fisher, his mother, she said that Mark couldn't cut up his food and sometimes he couldn't even hold a pen to write. The chief pathologist confirmed the severe arthritis in Mark's right hand and concluded that he couldn't have made the deep cuts in his left wrist.'

Drake nodded. 'Any suspects?'

'Mark Fisher was in a DUI accident that killed his wife Donna in 2013. He got a prison sentence and was released three months ago. Donna Fisher's family blame him for her death. And that could make them suspects,' Ruth explained.

'What did they say?' Drake asked.

'The father, Derek, claims he was out walking his dog early on Sunday morning and spoke to the local farmer a few times. It's all a bit vague,' Nick said.

'Derek's son Craig has a police record as long as your arm. He was in bed asleep on his own all morning,' Ruth explained.

'And no one can verify that?' Drake asked.

Ruth shook her head. 'No. But Nick and I thought that

his reaction to learning of Mark Fisher's death was one of genuine shock.'

'Maybe he's just a very good actor?' Drake suggested with a shrug.

'Maybe. We're not ruling him out. It was just our instinct when we interviewed him, boss,' Ruth said.

'Anyone else?' Drake asked, looking at his watch and getting up to go.

'Kathleen Taylor was the driver of the car that Mark Fisher hit in the accident. Her son was only a baby at the time and was diagnosed with traumatic brain injuries due to the crash. He now has severe learning difficulties. She brought a civil case against Mark Fisher but it failed. At the end of the case, she made a very public threat against him.'

'And what does she have to say for herself?' Drake asked.

'She was in Prague all weekend. She made a joke about her hiring a hitman,' Nick said.

'I've seen stranger things than that,' Drake said.

Ruth knew that Drake had a point but her initial instincts were that Kathleen Taylor didn't have anything to do with Mark Fisher's death. Her focus was going to be on Derek and Craig Harrison.

French came into the incident room, holding some printouts.

'Boss, I've found out what the interview with Mark Fisher was about in 2015,' French explained. 'And why it wasn't made clearer on his police record.'

'Go on,' Ruth said, her mind jumping to all sorts of conclusions.

'Fisher was interviewed by detectives as part of Operation Yewtree.'

Ruth remembered when Operation Yewtree had

started in 2012. It was led by London's Metropolitan Police, who investigated historic allegations of sexual abuse against children. It became notorious because many of those investigated were television and media celebrities with the allegations dating back to the seventies and eighties. As more and more allegations came out, the operation had been scaled up and by 2015 there were nearly a hundred police officers working on it.

'Any details?' Drake asked.

'One allegation of rape and three of sexual assault and underage sex while touring and working as a musician in the UK in 1997 and 1998,' French explained.

'I'm assuming the victims were granted anonymity?' Ruth asked, knowing that they would be covered by the Sexual Offences Act of 2003, and to get their identities would require an identity warrant from a judge. She didn't even know if they had sufficient grounds for one of those yet.

'A Detective Inspector Graham Kosminski was the lead officer on the case,' French said as he scoured the case report.

'His name doesn't ring a bell. Where is Kosminski now?' Nick asked.

'He retired in 2016,' French explained and then he frowned as he looked at the documents. 'Actually, he only lives a couple of miles from Ceiriog, where you found Fisher.'

Drake looked over at Ruth and shrugged. 'Might be something in it? Go and have a chat with him.'

Ruth caught Nick's eye and gestured that they were going.

Nick turned to get his coat and made a face. 'I know the drill,' he said as he pulled out the car keys.

. . .

As they drove out of Llancastell, Nick and Ruth headed for the A5. Nick was in charge of the music today and Ruth was having to listen to the new Pixies album, which wasn't doing much for her mood.

The A5 was the same route that Ruth's dad would take when driving them back to London after their summer holidays on the Welsh coast. She remembered the sense of deflation that the end of their trip always brought her and her brother, Chris. Sometimes the thought of returning to their tiny flat on the concrete estate in Battersea was over-whelmingly gloomy. Why didn't they move to North Wales? Her dad was always saying how much cheaper everything was, particularly a pint of beer. And everyone was so much friendlier, even if they did speak Welsh sometimes.

Ruth's Uncle Charlie, who had become known as 'Charlie the Cockney' in the local village since his move up from South London, tried to teach her and Chris a smattering of Welsh words. The only two phrases she could ever remember were *Iechyd da*, which everyone knew meant 'cheers', and *mae yna lawer o ddefaid*, which meant 'there are lots of sheep'.

Turning off the main route, Nick and Ruth entered Ceiriog Valley. The striking landscape rolled away down into the basin of the river, which snaked away into the distance. Following the flowing water with her eyes, Ruth's mind was drawn back to Sarah and her affair with Jamie Parsons. The initial shock and numbness were wearing away and being replaced by raw pain. And questions. So many questions. Why someone like Jamie Parsons? Sarah hated those types of public-school rugger-buggers that worked in the City. From what she could see on social media, Jamie Parsons was one of those men. What did Sarah get from Parsons that she wasn't getting from her at home? It was a thread that she kept pulling at but didn't really want to unravel. If it came loose, it might reveal a series of dark, uncomfortable truths.

Ruth looked at the small cottages and narrow roads as they slowed and arrived in the village of Llansantffraid Glyn Ceiriog. Nick pointed to the old bridge that traversed the River Ceiriog.

'The Devil's Bridge,' Nick remarked.

Ruth prepared herself for some more local history that she pretended to find tedious but they both knew she actually enjoyed. She pulled a face as if to say, 'Here we go.'

'According to legend, the Devil visited here in the eleventh century...,'

'The Devil?' Ruth asked dryly.

'Just listen. The Devil struck a bargain with a local woman whose cow was stranded across the river. In an attempt to buy her soul, the Devil said he'd build her a bridge in exchange for the soul of the first living thing that crossed it. When the bridge was built, the woman threw a loaf of bread across it, which her dog then chased. The Devil was never seen in Wales again, too embarrassed at being outwitted by the old lady.'

Ruth smiled and shook her head. 'Typical man. Can't deal with the fact that women are superior, so he sods off.'

Nick smiled. 'I guess you're lucky to have me as your partner then, boss? I realised that women are superior a long time ago. It's much easier that way.'

'Bloody hell. You sound like an old married man, Nick,' Ruth said.

Ruth and Nick pulled up outside retired Detective Inspector Graham Kosminski's cottage.

Retirement seemed to suit Kosminski, Ruth thought. He looked a lot younger than his sixty-three years when he opened the door to them. His hair was still dark and swept back, and he had a bit of a Roger Moore look about him.

Casting her eye around the cottage, Ruth deduced that Kosminski lived with his wife. There were photos of them as a couple but no photos of any children. Someone was hoovering upstairs and she assumed it was Mrs Kosminski.

They followed Graham Kosminski into a large room that looked like it was used as a study. There was a masculinity to the décor with virtually no feminine touches. It smelt of books and pine polish, like one of the big old South London libraries Ruth visited on rare occasions as a child. The furniture was old-fashioned but tasteful. A huge oak table was neatly stacked with papers, folders and books.

Kosminski was clean-shaven and dressed in a dark polo-neck jumper – his angular chin finished in a neat cleft at the bottom of his face. His appearance and demeanour were a bit of a surprise to Ruth. She had visited various retired police officers over the years. The ones that seemed to have lost their purpose or zest for life far outweighed those that had embraced a joyful retirement. The statistics of PTSD, mental health problems and even addiction in retired officers made for grim reading. Ruth thought about her own future. There were plenty of officers retiring in their mid to late fifties. Unusually, Kosminski was an advert for the benefits of early retirement.

Ruth looked as Nick flicked over his notebook. She could have done with a coffee but nothing had been offered.

'How can I help?' Kosminski asked.

'You spoke to Mark Fisher as part of Operation Yewtree, is that right?' Nick asked.

Kosminski shifted and smoothed his chin. 'Yeah, that's

right. In the autumn some time. 2014, or '15, I think it was.'

'Why did you speak to him?' Nick asked.

'We'd had some reports on the historic grooming of young girls by musicians and bands from up this way. We got a directive from the Met to have a look. Mark Fisher's name kept coming up in the intel we gathered.'

Ruth shifted forwards on the leather sofa. 'What were the allegations?'

'By the time I had done some digging around, we had three allegations of underage sex and one of rape,' Kosminski explained.

'What did Mark Fisher say?' Nick asked.

'He denied it all and he didn't seem to care. Cold bastard. Seemed to think that fourteen- and fifteen-year-old girls who went to backstage parties or recording studios were fair game.'

'And the rape?' Ruth asked.

'Zoe Tardelli. She was fourteen at the time. Fisher trapped her in an under-stairs cupboard and raped her. He said he didn't know the girl or even remember being at the party. So it was her word against his,' Kosminski explained.

Ruth could feel her stomach tighten with anger. It seemed there had been several decades when celebrities and pop stars having sex with children was seen 'as a bit of fun'.

'Did you re-interview Zoe Tardelli?' Nick asked.

Kosminski shook his head. 'I couldn't find her anywhere. It was as if she had vanished off the face of the earth at the turn of the Millennium.'

'No witnesses?' Ruth asked.

'Her friend Heather Morrison. But she didn't witness the actual attack. And Zoe didn't report it until later so there weren't any forensics,' Kosminski explained.

'There were no charges brought against Mark Fisher?' Nick asked.

'No. Not enough evidence. Bastard got away with it,' Kosminski growled. Ruth could see that the case had got to him.

'You seem to have got quite personally involved in the investigation?' Ruth said. It wasn't a criticism. It's something she couldn't help doing herself on a regular basis.

'That sort of thing destroys lives. You don't get over something like that,' Kosminski said darkly.

Ruth nodded in agreement and then said, 'You know that Mark Fisher was murdered last Sunday?' She couldn't tell whether or not Kosminski thought he was still alive. He was still talking about Mark Fisher in the present tense.

'Yeah, I did,' Kosminski said, letting out a sigh of satisfaction. 'Raping Zoe Tardelli and attacking those girls was just the tip of the iceberg. I got the feeling there were dozens more who just didn't say anything … However it sounds, the world's a better place without Mark Fisher in it.'

Ruth took all this in. Were any of Mark Fisher's victims involved in his murder? They would have been left emotionally scarred. Ruth had seen it too many times. Rape and sexual abuse, especially at a vulnerable age, changed people forever.

'Do you have any details for Zoe Tardelli or Heather Morrison?' Nick asked. Did Zoe Tardelli or one of her relatives track down Mark Fisher? The fury of a damaged or ruined life could be overwhelming.

Ruth glanced over at the stack of files and paperwork on the oak desk. Her eye was drawn to three different folders that had thick, black writing on the side – judging by the case numbers on the spines, they were police case files.

'Like I say, nothing on Zoe Tardelli. And I think Heather Morrison has moved since I spoke to her,' Kosminski explained.

Although Ruth was listening, she had also spotted the police case file closest to the top of the pile: *Yewtree – Llancastell CID – Case no. 35987 DI Kosminski SIO.*

After another five minutes, they thanked Kosminski for his help and left.

MAKING THEIR WAY OUT TO THE A623, RUTH AND NICK began to head back to Llancastell.

Ruth clicked on her Tetra radio: 'Three-six to Control. PNC check, please, on a Heather Morrison. Likely to be in the Snowdonia area. Date of birth would be …'

Ruth glanced at Nick for help.

'Fourteen in 1997. So year of birth would be 1983 or thereabouts,' Nick said with a smile.

'Control, date of birth would be 1983, 1984, over.'

Nick smiled as he took the turning towards Llancastell.

'Don't you dare judge me and my numeracy skills, Sergeant Evans,' Ruth joked.

Nick shrugged. 'I'm saying nothing. I'm just amazed you passed the basic numeracy test.'

'I don't think it was very difficult in 1990,' Ruth said.

The Tetra radio crackled. 'Control to three-six. PNC check. We have a Heather Sarah Morrison, born twelfth of May 1983, living at Sallow Cottages in Tregeiriog.'

Ruth clicked her radio. 'Three-six to Control, received, over.'

Nick turned the car down the next right-hand turn, changing their destination to the small village of Tregeiriog,

Ruth glanced over. 'Kosminski had police case files on his desk.'

'What?' Nick said with a frown. 'Photocopies?'

'Not sure. They can't be originals. Unless he's never returned them to records?' Ruth said. It was highly irregular to have case files at home anyway.

'Did you see what they were?' Nick asked.

'The one near the top was marked "Yewtree",' Ruth explained.

'Why is a case file that he investigated four years ago so close to hand?' Nick said as he changed gear to overtake a caravan.

'It's definitely strange. You think he's involved?' Ruth asked uncertainly. Any allegation or suspicion of a fellow officer felt uncomfortable. But she knew from experience that police officers weren't all honest, law-abiding citizens. It was only two years ago that she had had direct experience of that in Llancastell CID with catastrophic results.

'I dunno. Mark Fisher's body was only a few miles from his house. He was clearly angry that Fisher was never convicted. But that's then a very long stretch to murder.'

'We didn't ask him where he was last Sunday,' Ruth said, airing her thoughts.

'No, we didn't,' Ruth said. Was Kosminski really a suspect? However, there was no personal involvement and, at this stage, Ruth couldn't see why Kosminski would get embroiled in something as dark as murder.

'Let's talk to Heather Morrison and see what she has to say,' Nick said.

Ruth realised that there were a growing number of people who would have liked to have seen Mark Fisher dead. Derek and Craig Harrison for starters. Neither of them had solid alibis for the time of Mark Fisher's murder. Kathleen Taylor had the perfect alibi, but she had made public comments about getting some kind of retribution. And now an unknown number of young women that Mark Fisher had attacked or raped sometime in the nineties.

'Mark Fisher was not a popular man,' Ruth said thinking out loud.

'I had a mate called Fisher. Years ago. Ian Fisher. Fairly sure they're not related. Thick as fuck, he was. And his older brother used to work as a lifeguard at the Plas Madoc Leisure Centre, so we got in free. Always surrounded by girls, he was. We were dead jealous. So, Ian goes and asks him what his secret is. And his brother told him he put a big carrot down his swimming shorts to impress the ladies.'

Ruth chortled. Nick was good at telling stories and being distracted was a welcome relief.

'So Ian says he's gonna give it a try. Next day, we go to the pool. Bombing, big water slide. I'd forgotten all about it. Then Ian's brother comes over and asks him how the carrot thing is going. Ian scratches his head and tells him it's not working. In fact, if anything, people are actively avoiding him. We look at his shorts but I can't see anything. His brother walks around him and says, "You're meant to put the carrot down the front of your shorts, not the back, you twat!"'

Ruth laughed.

'Priceless growing up in North Wales, I tell you …' Nick chortled.

Ruth thought it was nice to see Nick grinning like his old self.

'Here we go,' Nick gestured that they had reached their destination.

Pulling the car over, Ruth looked out at the neat miner's cottage. It was built from grey stone and had a black slate roof. A diminutive woman in her late thirties was hanging out washing.

'Ms Morrison?' Nick said. He pulled out his warrant card. 'DS Evans and DI Hunter from Llancastell CID.'

Heather's face whitened. 'Oh God, is everything all right?' she asked as her hand dropped from the navy polo shirt she was trying to peg to the clothesline. The polo shirt dropped to the grass and she leant down to get it.

'It's nothing to worry about, Ms Morrison. Just a few routine questions, that's all,' Ruth reassured her. Maybe her previous experience of the police had made her anxious.

'Actually, it's Mrs Morrison. And it's Heather,' she said nervously.

'Just checking that you are the Heather Morrison who spoke to a DI Kosminski back in 2015?'

'Oh, God. Yes, come inside,' she mumbled, a little flustered, and beckoned them inside.

She wasn't the first person Ruth had seen completely thrown by the arrival of police officers but she was clearly rattled.

Inside the cottage was neat, tidy but small. They exchanged some chit-chat as Nick and Ruth sat at the long pine table that filled the narrow kitchen.

Taking out his notebook, Nick clicked his pen. 'We're looking into some historical allegations of sexual abuse from the nineties,' Nick explained.

Ruth could see that Heather's whole demeanour dropped. 'Not this again,' she said wearily.

'We understand that you spoke to a Detective Inspector Kosminski as part of Operation Yewtree?' Ruth asked.

'Yes. And I told him I wasn't interested in taking things any further. I was just a kid, you know?' Heather said.

'The allegation of sexual assault and underage sex was against Mark Fisher, is that correct?' Nick asked as he took notes.

'Yes. I told the detective back then, I wasn't interested,' Heather explained.

'We have statements from you and Zoe Tardelli from 1997 where you allege that you had underage sex with several musicians and that you were sexually assaulted by Mark Fisher,' Ruth said.

Heather leaned forwards and looked nervously around as if someone might hear. 'Does my husband have to know about any of this? I've never told him.'

Ruth shook her head. 'Anything you tell us today will be in the strictest confidence. If a crime has been committed, however, then we will have to follow the appropriate legal procedure.'

'Me and Zoe were groupies. We got to know some of the bands in the area. We were fourteen, but we both looked much older. We told people we were twenty-one. And there were parties backstage and then at hotels or the tour bus. Sometimes we'd hang out at the recording studios for days on end. It was such a laugh ...' Heather explained. Ruth thought that Heather seemed to be making excuses for her reckless behaviour.

'And what happened at these parties, Heather?' Nick asked.

'You know. Lots of drinking ...'

'Drugs?' Nick asked.

'Yeah, drugs.' Heather said but Ruth could see she was feeling uncomfortable.

'And presumably sex?' Ruth asked in a very matter-of-fact tone.

There were a few seconds of silence – Heather clearly didn't want to answer the question.

'Yeah ...'

'You had sex with members of the band?' Ruth asked.

'Sometimes ... '

'Were you forced to?' Ruth asked.

Heather considered her answer for a second. 'No …
We knew what we were doing. I was fourteen and I was in
bed with the lead singer who I'd seen on *Top of The Pops*
the week before. Or on the front of a magazine in the
corner shop. He was nineteen or twenty, and lots of girls
would have killed to be doing stuff like that,' Heather
explained, now more confident that what she was saying
wasn't that bad.

Ruth thought she had a point. When she was fifteen,
she and her mates would have given anything for a night
with John Taylor, Martin Kemp or Andrew Ridgeley. The
lines of legal consent and legality felt a little blurred when
she looked at it like that.

'What about Mark Fisher?' Nick asked.

'No. He was different. Creepy. He was very quiet, a bit
older and spent a lot of time looking at the girls. And if
anyone got with him, he was rough,' Heather explained.

'Was he ever rough with you?' Ruth asked in a gentle
voice.

Heather nodded. The memory of it clearly made her
feel uneasy as she blinked nervously. 'Yeah … One night,
he woke me up. He told me that I couldn't just pick and
choose who I slept with. And …'

Ruth could see Heather was struggling with what she
was telling them.

'It's all right, Heather …' Ruth said very quietly.

Heather took a breath. 'He … made me do stuff. I
didn't sleep with him but it made me feel sick.' Her recollection of the event had made her physically shake.

'He sexually assaulted you?' Ruth asked.

'Yeah …' Heather nodded and looked down at the
floor.

'Was that the only time?'

Heather shook her head and she pursed her lips. 'No … It happened … three times.'

'And you reported it to the police?'

'Yeah. There was a female officer who was really nice to me, but she said because I was drinking and taking drugs, it would be very difficult to get a conviction against him.'

Ruth saw the tears welling in Heather's eyes. Twenty years ago, that was probably true. It was only in recent years that the definition of consent had been tightened in the eyes of the law.

Nick looked over at Heather. 'I don't know if you've seen the news, but we believe that Mark Fisher was murdered last Sunday.'

Heather's eyes widened. 'What? Oh, God. No, I didn't know … Do you know who did it?'

Ruth could see that Heather's reaction was genuine. She seemed to have no idea that Mark Fisher was dead.

'I'm afraid we can't discuss the details of the case with you, Heather,' Ruth explained.

'Just for our records, can you tell us where you were between midnight Saturday and six o'clock Sunday morning?' Nick asked.

'Erm … I would have been asleep here,' Heather said, her eyes moving anxiously as she tried to remember.

'Was there anyone else in the house?' Nick asked.

'My husband. But he was asleep too …' Heather asked nervously. She sounded terrified.

'It's just routine, Heather … Zoe Tardelli was a friend of yours at that time, wasn't she?' Ruth said.

'Yeah. We were best friends.'

'And you were there the night she alleged that Mark Fisher raped her?' Ruth asked.

'Yeah. It was in some big posh house,' Heather explained.

'And where was that?' Ruth asked.

'Middle of nowhere. Near the coast by Abergele, I think.'

'Can you tell us what happened?' Nick asked.

'Everyone was drunk or off their heads. And then Zoe came in screaming. She said that Mark had trapped her in the under-stairs cupboard and raped her. No one seemed to believe her at first. Everyone was too wasted.'

'But she went to the police?' Ruth asked.

'Yeah. It was about a week later. They were nice, but they said all the evidence had gone, so it was just her word against his. She never got over it though,' Heather said darkly.

'Why do you say that?' Ruth asked.

'She went completely off the rails. Drugs, fighting, stopped going to school. Then she got excluded and disappeared.'

'Do you still see her?' Nick asked, his pen hovering over his notebook.

'No. Not for a long time,' Heather said sadly, shaking her head.

'We're trying to track her down. Do you have any idea where she is?' Ruth asked.

Heather thought for a moment. 'Someone told me she had moved to Australia but got put in prison. Then someone said she was dying from breast cancer … but …'

Ruth could see that Heather had thought of something.

'Go on … However small, it might help us,' Ruth said.

'There were some photos on Facebook last week. An old classmate of ours, Danny Elder, was having a party over in the next village. There was a woman there that looked just like Zoe. Older, but you know … She had dyed red hair. Zoe had dyed red hair since she was at school and I could see it was her. She was tagged as "Nicole Lace". I found the profile for Nicole Lace but it's definitely Zoe. She must have changed her name. There were just lots of photos of her partying,' Heather explained with an air of sadness.

Ruth gestured to the laptop on the table, 'Think you could show us?'

'Yeah, of course,' Heather replied as she reached over and flipped the laptop open.

Chapter 8

I t was early evening. Nick and Amanda were sitting with her father, Tony. He had recently been released on licence from an open prison in Cheshire. Amanda had pulled a few strings with her connections in social services to get him temporary housing in Llancastell.

Nick could see that the cancer was taking its toll on Tony. His face was gaunt and grey. His limbs were stick-thin and bony. Tony had revealed to Nick earlier in the year that he had terminal pancreatic cancer and then, eventually, he had told Amanda.

Tony was rolling yet another cigarette. Nick could see that his forearms were sinewy where he was rapidly losing weight.

'Do you have to?' Amanda asked, gesturing to the cigarette.

Tony rolled his eyes with a smile and then looked at Nick. 'It's all right. I'm going out in the garden. I'm sure Nick will keep me company and stop me getting into trouble.'

'I didn't mean that, Dad. I meant it's not good for you,' Amanda said.

'Yeah, I think that ship has sailed, love,' Tony said as he started to seal the cigarette paper.

Nick calculated that Tony was on his third cigarette since they had got there. Given his diagnosis, he didn't blame Tony for chain-smoking.

There was a buzz on his phone and Nick looked down. Peter the Artist was calling him.

I'll call him when I get home. Probably just wants a chat, Nick thought.

'It's not going to make you feel better, is it?' Amanda reprimanded, looking at Tony.

Tony pushed himself slowly up from the armchair and got gingerly to his feet. His trousers flapped around his diminutive legs. 'That's the thing. They do make me feel better. And I'm too old and too ill to try to stop now.'

Nick caught Amanda's eye. He could see the sadness in her face. Once in a while in recent weeks, Amanda had just started to cry. Something on the television or the radio just brought home the fact that her father was dying and it became too much for her to bear.

Nick's train of thought was broken as his phone buzzed again in his pocket – Peter must have left him a voicemail. Nick felt mildly annoyed at the interruption. *Why doesn't he just text? What is so important?*

'Come on,' Tony said to Nick, gesturing for him to come outside while he smoked. Tony then looked at Amanda. 'And don't start tidying up. Not in your condition.'

Amanda smiled. 'Condition? Jesus, you're so old-fash-ioned, Dad … And this place is a pit.'

Nick gave Amanda a reassuring wink as he followed Tony outside into the tiny back garden of the ground-floor flat. The patio was uneven and lined with moss and weeds. The air smelt of a bonfire and a handful of leaves skittered noisily close to their feet.

'You know where the playing fields are over there?' Tony said, pointing north from the garden.

'Yeah. Used to play rugby there,' Nick said.

'My dad always told me that Owain Glyndwr camped out there for weeks during the war of independence,' Tony said. 'Not sure if there was any truth in it, mind.'

This was right up Nick's street – he loved history and Owain Glyndwr was his hero.

'Makes sense. There was fighting in Chester and that moved down to Corwen. Llancastell would be on the way,' Nick said, smiling. He'd never heard that Owain Glyndwr had been in his hometown. He hoped it was true.

Tony lit his cigarette, took a long, deep drag and then looked over at Nick as he let the bluish smoke out slowly.

'Thank you, Nick,' Tony said narrowing his eyes.

Nick shrugged. 'What for?'

'For looking after her,' Tony said, gesturing to Amanda inside.

Nick could see that Tony didn't find conversations like this easy.

'She means the world to me,' Nick said. 'You don't need to worry. I'll always look after her.'

'I know. I can see that. And that … puts my mind at rest, you know?' Tony said a little awkwardly.

Nick nodded to reassure Tony he knew exactly what he meant. Men of Tony's generation found opening up incredibly difficult.

'I'll put the kettle on, shall I?' Tony said, breaking what was becoming an uncomfortable silence.

'Yeah, good idea,' Nick said and then took the phone

out of his pocket. 'Just need to pick up a message,' he said as he put the phone to his ear.

'I'll see you inside.' Tony nodded as he walked back to the kitchen door.

The phone connected to the voicemail service.

'Nick, it's Peter here … I'm just calling … erm …'

Peter was hammered and his voice slurred. Nick was about to get annoyed before remembering the number of times he had been drunk and phoned people.

Peter continued. *'Just to say I'm very, very … pleased … you're going to be my sponsor. But I've had a drink and I'm feeling upset, you see? And I'm not sure I can keep doing this … Maybe I won't … Maybe I'll just stop …'*

The message stopped mid-sentence and Nick put the phone away, feeling uneasy. What did Peter mean? He sounded desperate and sad. The booze would just heighten that.

Nick tried to ring Peter back. The phone rang out.

He phoned again. Nothing.

Going on his instinct, Nick knew he needed to go round and see Peter to check that he was all right. 'Maybe I'll just stop' was ambiguous and he didn't like the uncomfortable feeling it had left him with.

Making his way inside, Nick looked at Amanda. She could already see that he had his car keys in his hand. She didn't look happy.

'Going somewhere?' Amanda asked.

'Peter's left me a message. He's hammered. Now he's not answering his phone,' Nick explained.

'I thought you turned him down to be his sponsor?' Amanda growled.

'I did! You know that!' Nick said, lying through his teeth. He didn't want to stress Amanda out.

'So why is he ringing you?' Amanda asked sharply.

Nick shrugged. 'He's just a mate. And I want to make sure he's all right.'

He saw that Amanda was about to protest, but something stopped her. Instead, she nodded. 'I'll walk back from here in a bit.'

It was only a five-minute walk to their house, but Nick gave her a frown.

'Sure? I can pick you up?'

'It's fine. Just don't be late,' Amanda said with a withering look. 'And tell him to ring someone else next time.'

By the time Ruth got home, Sian was resting on the sofa. A glass of red wine stood half-drunk beside her. The mixture of alcohol and the pain medication for her back always made Sian very drowsy.

'You're back late,' Sian mumbled in her sleepiness.

'I just had some things that I wanted to get off my desk before tomorrow,' Ruth said.

Sian moved up the sofa to look at Ruth properly. 'Are you all right?' Sian asked in a tone that implied there was a subtext to the question.

'Yeah, why?' Ruth asked. Nothing had been all right since her conversation with Lucy Parsons.

'It's just I saw you a couple of times at work today and you looked like you had the weight of the world on your shoulders,' Sian said.

'No. Well, no more than usual. I'm going to get some wine. Want a top-up?' Ruth asked, eager to change the conversation.

'Please,' Sian nodded and then shifted again to lie back on the cushions.

By the time Ruth had been to the kitchen to collect the bottle of wine and returned, Sian had fallen asleep. Ruth watched her. Her chest moving slowly up and down. There was such beauty in her stillness. The exquisiteness of her face. The shadows that fell across her cheeks and mouth from a nearby lamp. Why had someone like Sian decided to be with her? Ruth felt slightly bewildered at the thought of it.

And then the guilt came. She had promised Sian that she would move on from what had happened with Sarah. Their relationship couldn't survive the dark spectre of Sarah and the uncertain grief of what had happened to her. Ruth assured Sian that she could move on and find closure.

However, Lucy Parsons's visit and the revelation of Sarah and Jamie Parsons's affair had thrown a hand grenade into the middle of that new beginning. If she came clean to Sian and told her, she feared that would be the final straw. But what was she meant to do? Ignore the information? Whatever Ruth told herself, she wouldn't get any meaningful kind of resolution until she found out what had actually happened to Sarah. And her affair with Jamie Parsons was another significant piece in that jigsaw. The connections with Jurgen Kessler were chilling.

Going to the kitchen, Ruth poured a glass of wine. She looked in the fridge, but she wasn't really hungry. Returning to the living room, she took the laptop and slumped quietly into the large armchair. She didn't want to disturb Sian. It was time to research Jamie Parsons a little more. She felt far less guilty if Sian was out for the count.

Paramount in Ruth's mind was the connection between Jurgen Kessler and Jamie Parsons. Kessler was the last person Sarah had been seen talking to on the train and was now wanted by Berlin police for two murders but had seemingly vanished. Kessler had worked for Commerzbank in Guildhall in the City of London. Jamie

Parsons, who Sarah had had an affair with just before she went missing, also worked at Commerzbank.

At first, Ruth had dismissed this as sheer coincidence. She focussed her well-honed mind – she didn't believe in quirks of fate. So, what was the connection between Jurgen Kessler and Jamie Parsons? How did Sarah fit into that connection?

Typing into various search engines, Ruth managed to find a brief overview of Jamie Parsons's education and employment on a recruitment and head-hunting website. Parsons was educated at St Paul's School in London and then did an economics degree at the University of Exeter, where he gained a first.

And then she saw it. In fact, she read it twice to make sure she hadn't misread what was in front of her.

Jamie Parsons had studied for a Masters' degree in finance and banking at the Berlin School of Economics in 2003. Was there a connection with Jurgen Kessler here too? Wasn't Kessler from Berlin? Could she find out if Kessler went to the Berlin School of Economics?

Finding the website for the *Hochschule Fur Wirtschaft Und Recht Berlin*, Ruth tapped into the alumni network. However, she needed a passcode to gain any kind of access to previous students. Scanning to the left, she saw a drop-down list for scholarships and prizes. Had Jurgen Kessler been a high-achieving student? Working her way to 2003, she could then see a list of names for prizes and scholarships awarded by the school. It was a long shot.

However, there it was. Halfway down the page.

Joint prize winners for Masters' in Economics and Finance: Birgit Tecklenberg and … *Jurgen Kessler*.

Parsons and Kessler had been there at the same time.

. . .

Nick had managed to gain access to Peter's house by scaling the garden fence and opening the kitchen door, which had been left unlocked. Nick knew that Peter lived alone with his two cats, Titian and Turner, that often featured on his social media posts. Peter told him that they were named after his two favourite artists, but Nick wasn't sure he knew paintings by either.

The kitchen was cluttered with washing-up, glasses, half-eaten food and empty vodka and wine bottles. Peter had clearly been on a proper bender over the last few days.

'Peter? Peter?' Nick called as he began to look around the house. The other rooms on the ground floor were tidy and clean.

'Peter? It's Nick,' Nick shouted again. The silence was beginning to unnerve him. There were some alcoholics that just couldn't stop relapsing. Their desperation to stop drinking allowed them days, even weeks, of sobriety. However, this often meant that the despair of another relapse after a period of recovery was too much to bear. They thought the only solution to their addiction was to end their lives. The coroner would record the death as suicide. But in truth, that person had died from alcoholism.

As Nick began to climb the stairs with a sense of urgency, there was a moan. Someone was mumbling somewhere.

The noise was coming from a bedroom at the end of the landing. As Nick went in, he saw Peter curled up in a ball on the bed, dressed in a T-shirt and underpants. The room stank of stale urine and alcohol. A pillow, covered in regurgitated red wine, had been thrown to the floor.

'Peter? It's Nick. You okay, mate?' Nick said, approaching him.

Peter looked up, but he didn't know what day it was. 'Nick? My dear friend Nick. There you are …' he slurred.

'Come on, mate. We need to get you cleaned up,' Nick said.

Nick helped Peter off the bed, got him standing and eventually took him to the bathroom. There he took off his clothes, helped Peter into the shower cubicle and began to shower him down.

Jesus, this is not what I signed up for when I agreed to be your bloody sponsor, mate, Nick thought. But actually, it was.

Ten minutes later, Nick had managed to dry Peter off with a towel, led him to the spare bedroom, and had put him into a clean bed. He stripped the piss-soaked bedclothes and put them into the washing machine downstairs. Having tidied the kitchen, Nick then went on the hunt for any booze. It reminded him of the times he had frantically searched his own home, praying that he had put booze somewhere and forgotten.

Sliding back the small sofa in the living room, Nick saw a new two-litre bottle of vodka on the carpet underneath. He picked it up and put the bottle on the table. For a moment, he sat and looked at it. He was hit by a flashback of the excitement and buzz the sight of a new bottle of vodka would give him. Liquid silver. The calm and peace it would bring to him. All the anxiety of becoming a father would melt away for a few hours and that would be a relief.

What would actually happen if I took a couple of glugs? No one would know. I'd feel better and no one would be the wiser.

And then Nick played the scenario forward in his head. He would wake the next day and start to think about booze. He might plan to drink again. The thoughts and cravings for alcohol would become overwhelming. And in a few weeks, he would be drinking for breakfast and would have lost everything that was dear to him.

Standing up, Nick took the vodka, marched into the kitchen and poured it down the sink. He felt angry but also anxious about what had just passed through his head. However, the main thing was that he hadn't taken a drink.

By the time Nick got home, Amanda had gone to bed. He made himself a cup of tea and thought about what had happened at Peter's home. Peter wouldn't remember any of it.

Nick wondered how he had gone from being a chronic alcoholic to someone who could help another alcoholic in trouble and, despite a momentary temptation, pour two litres of perfectly good vodka down the drain?

Somebody up there likes me, Nick thought to himself.

Chapter 9

Placing the cups and mugs neatly into the cupboard, Mary Doyle moved them so that they all faced outwards. Something about the uniformity and order made her less frustrated. She had a touch of OCD, but what the bloody hell was wrong with wanting things to be neat and in their proper place? Her husband, Gerry, didn't see it like that. He said she was a nag and controlling.

Mary took pride in their three-bedroomed home in one of the more upmarket suburbs of Llancastell. Nothing wrong with that. It mattered to her what the neighbours thought or to feel house proud on the rare occasions that they had guests. Gerry didn't seem to understand that.

Carole King's *Tapestry* was playing and Mary hummed along. They had been to London to see Carole King a year or two ago in Hyde Park. It was the last time she could remember her and Gerry doing anything fun. They used to go to gigs all the time, back in the day. He didn't want to do anything these days.

Returning to the dishwasher, Mary took a glass and

then recoiled. It was still very hot from the dishwasher. She shook her hand until it cooled. It bothered her when things were left overnight in the dishwasher. She felt uncomfortable until everything was put away where it should be.

Where the hell is Gerry? Mary thought to herself. He said he was only popping out to the garage for a moment. He was always bloody 'popping' somewhere. He seemed to want to spend increasing amounts of time in the garden, his shed or the garage. There was always a radio playing cricket or football. He seemed to have lost his love of music. And it was as if he had also grown tired of spending time with her. And when she confronted him about it, he told her she was being bloody daft.

Now the glasses had cooled slightly in the room temperature of the kitchen, Mary put the last few things away. As she did this, however, she became increasingly aware of a low droning noise coming from somewhere. Closing the door to the dishwasher, she could still feel the heat on her hand. She noticed the knuckles on her right hand were slightly bruised. *At least the swelling has gone down*, she thought.

The incessant low hum was beginning to annoy her. It sounded like a car was waiting out on the street. That might be it. On the very rare occasions that they got a taxi into Llancastell, that was the same sound as the waiting taxi. *But we haven't ordered a bloody taxi*, Mary thought as she began to get annoyed and frustrated again. *And where the bloody hell is Gerry?*

With an impatient huff, Mary went out to the utility room where the tumble dryer was in full motion. The low hum wasn't that though.

'Gerry? What are you doing?' Mary yelled, almost like a mother talking to a child. 'Where are you?'

As she opened the door from the utility room, she felt

the cold air rush unabated down the side passage of the house. The door to the garage was slightly ajar. The smell of exhaust fumes was thick and the engine of their car was running. Maybe Gerry was tinkering with the engine; he liked to pretend that he could fix and repair cars, but she was aware that he was full of shit. But then again, that was Gerry for you. Full of shit most of the time.

'Gerry?' Mary called as she pushed open the door to see what he was doing.

Scouring the garage from the doorway, she couldn't see him anywhere. Then something caught her eye. A green plastic hosepipe that stretched along the length of the car.

Oh God! No! Please …

Scuttling inside the garage, she raced to the driver's window where the pipe went inside and had been shut tight into the window.

Gerry's body was slumped forward against the steering wheel.

'Gerry! Gerry!' Mary yelled, hoping that he was just unconscious and might rouse.

Pulling at the hose feverishly, Mary realised it was stuck tight. The fumes choked her as her pulse raced in panic.

Banging on the window again, she pounded the glass with her fists.

It was no use.

Gerry Doyle was dead.

Chapter 10

The day was colourless with a tepid wind, and, away to the east, the sky looked threatening. Ruth had dropped Sian at work. It was going to be at least another eight weeks until she could drive.

Pulling over in a small residential cul-de-sac, Ruth parked her car. She was supposed to be meeting Nick here for some observation work and a possible arrest. Ruth reached into her bag and pulled out a ciggie. Fumbling for the lighter, she buzzed down the window and the wind brushed her face. She clicked the lighter and got that lovely hint of lighter fluid as she lit the ciggie and then took her first deep drag. She rested her arm on the car door where the window was open. As the wind picked up, it scattered a cluster of deep orange leaves violently across the road. Their movement made a skidding noise on the tarmac. It made her jump momentarily.

Across the road, a small two-storey detached house faced her. It had two windows on the first floor, two on the ground and the front door in the middle, much like those of a child's drawing. She remembered when Ella had drawn pictures like that and decorated them with brightly coloured flowers with her crayons. If she looked back and took stock, that was a perfect time in her life. She had set up home with

Sarah and the three of them seemed like a beautiful, loving 'modern' family unit. Sarah had taken to being Ella's 'other mummy' like she was born to it. There were no resentments or tiffs that Ella was Ruth's child from a previous marriage. It was made easier that Ella's dad, Dan, had moved to Australia and had little to do with her. There was no need to negotiate who had Ella on what day or which weekend. Ella had two 'mummies'; they lived together and that was that. It was simple and it was perfect.

Ruth's train of thought was broken by the sound of a car engine slowing. From the juddering sound, she could tell the car had a diesel engine. Glancing in her rear-view mirror, Ruth spotted a smart black Discovery Sport come past her. The windows were tinted. The car pulled up onto the pavement further down the road. Something about the car's appearance spooked her. Where the bloody hell is Nick? she thought as she glanced at her watch.

Both front doors of the Discovery opened and for a couple of seconds, the driver and passenger made no appearance. Then, slowly, two men got out of the car and looked around.

To her horror, she instantly recognised the two men. The man who had been in the passenger seat and was now standing in the middle of the road was Jamie Parsons. He was taller than photos suggested and was wearing a green wax jacket.

The driver was tall, with blond hair and glasses. Jurgen Kessler.

Ruth's stomach lurched as sheer panic swept through her body. What is going on? Jesus! What are they doing on a small side road in North Wales?

Now Ruth had to decide what to do. Get out and confront them? Or start the car and drive off.

Turning her ignition key, the car engine crunched and then stopped. A red battery light clicked on the dashboard.

Fuck! How is the battery flat, for God's sake?

The sound of the engine had alerted Parsons and Kessler to her. They were pointing and shouting to her.

'She's in that car over there!' Kessler bellowed.

They began to run towards her.

Ruth couldn't get her breath. She tried the car again. Nothing. Glancing up, the two men were only a matter of yards away.

What the hell am I going to do?

There was an electronic beeping that nagged away in her head. Was it the battery? What the bloody hell is it?

Coming to, Ruth registered that the alarm from her phone was sounding. It was six-thirty. She could feel her pulse drumming in her chest and neck. Sucking in a breath, she sat up in bed. There was sweat on her top lip. Sian stirred next to her and opened her eyes.

'Bloody hell, you were restless last night,' Sian said as she yawned.

'Was I? I couldn't get comfortable,' Ruth said.

'And you were talking in your sleep. Actually, you shouted at one point,' Sian said, smiling and shaking her head.

'Did I? Sorry. I can't remember,' Ruth said. 'Time to get up. I'll put the kettle on.'

This was one anxiety dream she couldn't share with her.

By the time Ruth arrived at Incident Room One, it was alive with the buzz of a murder case. She was still carrying the emotional hangover of her dream. She could feel it in her stomach and her shoulders. Sipping from her latte as she walked, Ruth spotted Drake coming her way.

'Morning, boss,' Ruth said, trying not to show how she actually felt.

Drake had grown a very neat goatee in recent months. She wasn't usually a fan, but it seemed to add to his quiet authority.

'Ruth. Thought I'd sit in on the briefing and get up to

speed. From what I hear, Mark Fisher had given quite a few people motive to harm him?' Drake said as he loosened his collar a little. That was one drawback of Incident Room One – it could get stuffy even in the depths of winter.

'Yes, boss. He seems to have damaged quite a few lives.'

Taking off her coat, Ruth watched as Drake went over and sat on a desk and sipped from his bottle of water. She was trying to suss out whether he was acting differently. Had he made a decision on the vacant detective superintendent position in Cumbria? If he had, Drake wasn't giving anything away.

Ruth grabbed her files and headed for the front of the room and scene boards. 'Morning, everyone. If we can get going please.'

She finished her coffee and could still taste the faint remnants of her last cigarette in her mouth. The room had quietened and the murder team were now focussed on her. She swelled with pride as she looked at them; they had all come a long way since she had taken her first briefing over two and a half years ago. Having just arrived from London, Ruth had been made SIO on what became known as the Dinas Padog Murders. Standing here in the same incident room, Llancastell CID now felt like home.

'Okay, developments in Mark Fisher's murder. Nick and I spoke to retired Detective Inspector Graham Kosminski. He questioned Mark Fisher as part of the Met's Operation Yewtree in 2015. The allegations were that Mark Fisher had raped a fourteen-year-old girl, Zoe Tardelli, and sexually assaulted another fourteen-year-old girl, Heather Morrison, back in 1997. The girls were essentially groupies and were caught up in backstage parties, hotels and touring.'

'Was this reported?' Drake asked.

'Yes, boss. But it was a week later and so it was explained to them that it would be Mark Fisher's word against theirs,' Ruth said.

'The girls had been drinking and taking drugs and were in hotel rooms and houses with the band voluntarily. It was made clear that any prosecution against Mark Fisher would be difficult,' Nick explained.

Drake shifted and leaned forward. 'And this was 1997. Before the word "grooming" became part of our vocabulary.'

'And it's pre-Yewtree and pre-Rotherham,' Ruth said, thinking out loud.

Rotherham had been a case where a group of men had used alcohol and drugs to groom, rape and abuse over two hundred teenage girls over three decades. Rotherham was now a byword for this kind of grooming and child sex abuse.

'So, we think these victims are now suspects in Mark Fisher's murder?' French asked.

'They have to be,' Nick explained.

'We interviewed Heather Morrison yesterday. She has an alibi of sorts – she was at home with her husband but he was asleep,' Ruth said.

'Unless he's lying too,' Drake pointed out.

'I didn't get the feeling that either of them were hiding anything from us. But yes, that's a possibility,' Ruth replied, before walking to the scene board where a recent photo of Zoe Tardelli, dark red hair and looking drunkenly at the camera, was pinned. 'Dan, what did we get on Zoe Tardelli? Or her new identity, Nicole Lace?'

'Nothing really, boss. I checked the PNC. A few fines and a suspended sentence for drunk and disorderly when she was in her late teens. Nothing since,' French explained.

'Nothing?' Ruth asked. 'She must have popped up on some kind of official records somewhere'

'Seriously, boss. Nothing at all,' French explained.

'Sian?' Ruth said, looking over at her and immediately feeling a pang of guilt.

'Same. Nothing anywhere, boss. Zoe Tardelli hasn't paid taxes since 2005. No passport, no driving licence. It's as if she vanished. I'm still waiting for the local council tax records for North Wales, but I'm not holding out much hope,' Sian explained.

Ruth nodded and went back to the photo. Their inability to find any record of Zoe Tardelli was troubling. 'Heather Morrison was adamant that the woman in this photo was Zoe Tardelli. However, she was tagged as Nicole Lace. And Nicole Lace has a Facebook profile, which Heather Morrison is one hundred per cent sure belongs to Zoe Tardelli.'

'Nicole Lace. Fancy name,' Drake said, raising his eyebrow quizzically. 'Do we know if a Nicole Lace exists?'

'Working on it, boss,' Sian replied. 'Should know by the end of the day.'

'Thank you, Sian,' Drake said and then looked up at Ruth.

Heading for the other side of the board, Ruth then pointed to a series of other photos. 'Okay, our other possible leads. We know that Mark Fisher was in a car crash that killed his wife Donna. Her family blame him for her death. And that makes them suspects,' Ruth explained. 'Any word on Derek Harrison's alibi for the time of the murder yet?'

French looked over. 'We're trying to get hold of Mr Bird, the farmer that Derek Harrison claims saw him several times on Sunday morning.'

'Good. Let me know when you do. I'm not convinced

Derek Harrison is telling us the truth. And he hated Mark Fisher for years,' Ruth said.

'What about the brother?' Drake asked.

French shook his head and said, 'Nothing. He can't prove that he was on his own at home at the time of the murder.'

'What about his phone?' Nick asked.

'Claims it was out of charge, so no signal,' French explained.

'Can we check that?' Ruth asked.

Sian looked up. 'I've got the number. I'll run it past Tech and get them to check it against the local masts.'

'Anything on Kathleen Taylor?' Ruth asked.

'Got the passenger list from the airline. She definitely flew to and from Prague over the weekend,' French explained.

'Okay. That effectively rules her out. Great work, everyone. Thank you,' Ruth said, gathering up her files.

As Ruth went to have a quiet chat with Drake, a uniformed officer approached.

'Ma'am?' the PC said, looking down at a note.

'How can I help, Constable?' Ruth asked.

'Message from Dr Tony Amis, the pathologist. He said he tried your mobile, but you weren't answering,' the constable explained.

'What's the message?' Ruth asked.

'He's just left the scene of a suicide that we attended last night in Mulsford,' the PC said. Ruth knew the suburb of Mulsford that lay on the western edges of Llancastell. 'He would like you to attend the post-mortem at the hospital with DS Evans.'

Ruth frowned and exchanged a look with Drake. 'Did he say why?'

'He said that he doesn't think it is suicide. He thinks it's suspicious.'

Ruth shot Nick a look – two suspicious suicides in three days?

AMIS HAD BEEN EXAMINING GERRY DOYLE'S BODY FOR over an hour when Ruth and Nick arrived at the Llancastell University Hospital mortuary. Ruth immediately felt the chill of the room as they came quietly through the double doors.

As if on cue, Amis turned on an electric saw, which then squealed as it hit the body's breastbone. Not only did it grate on Ruth's teeth, but it made her stomach churn.

You're an experienced SIO, Ruth –sort yourself out!

Christ, she remembered that when she first joined the Met, officers used to smoke at the back of the morgue to hide the smell of the bodies and stop them retching.

Turning her mind back to the case in hand, Ruth questioned what Amis had meant exactly. She had returned his call, but he had clearly been in the middle of the post-mortem by that point.

Turning off the saw, Amis noticed Ruth and Nick approach the gurney. He pulled down his green surgical mask to reveal his boyish and clean-shaven face.

'Ah, the cavalry have arrived,' Amis said with a winning smile.

'Problem, Doctor?' Ruth asked, aware that all she could now hear were the chiller cabinets that housed dead bodies at just the right temperature. She wasn't sure what was worse.

Bloody hell! Why do people take the piss when I admit I don't like PMs? she thought.

123

'Yes. And utterly bizarre to have two of these almost back to back,' Amis said.

'Report said that the deceased was found in his car with the engine running. Likely suicide. Uniform notes said that a hose had been fitted from the exhaust pipe to the inside of the car,' Nick said.

'That's right. I assumed that this time it was a suicide by carbon monoxide poisoning. Relatively common when it comes to this kind of case. I think I've examined quite a few such suicides in the last few years,' Amis explained.

'But it's not a suicide?' Ruth asked.

'No. His post-mortem lividity should have been cherry-pink,' Amis said, pointing to the cadaver's marble-white skin. 'There's no congestion in the lungs and brain macroscopically. In my histological examination of the heart, there was no partial disarrangement or necrosis found in the myocardium. The liver cells showed no derangement and no degenerative changes,' Amis explained, but Ruth was now lost. She just needed to know whether a crime had been committed.

'So, what killed him?' Nick said with a wry smile. Ruth knew that he had picked up her frustration. Maybe it was the distracted way she had shuffled her feet a moment earlier.

'Asphyxiation,' Amis said.

Ruth frowned. She couldn't see any marks around Gerry Doyle's neck. She had been a copper long enough to know what to look for. 'He was strangled?'

'No, not strangled. Suffocated,' Amis said.

Ruth shot Nick a look. How had Gerry Doyle been suffocated? Most cases of suffocation that she had dealt with had been some kind of smothering.

'Any idea how?' Ruth asked.

'We did a preliminary blood test. There is a high

concentration of diazepam in his blood. In fact, at that dose, the victim was in danger of death before he was suffocated.'

Ruth knew that diazepam was a powerful benzodiazepine that would have rendered Doyle drowsy or, as Amis was suggesting, unconscious.

'Gerry Doyle was drugged, suffocated and then his body was placed in the car so that it looked like he had committed suicide,' Ruth said, connecting the dots.

'That's what my preliminary post-mortem suggests. There is virtually no carbon monoxide anywhere in his body, which means he wasn't breathing when he was in the car. He was dead before he was placed in the car,' Amis confirmed, and then went over to a small stainless-steel dish. Dipping tweezers into the dish, he showed them a small piece of transparent plastic.

'We found two pieces of this wedged between his teeth,' Amis said.

'What is it?' Nick asked.

'Polyvinyl chloride,' Amis said.

'Which is?' Ruth asked.

'At a guess, clingfilm,' Nick said.

Ruth turned to him with an arched eyebrow. 'How on earth do you know that?'

'It was on *The Chase* the other day,' Nick explained with mock superiority.

'Yes, it's just bog-standard clingfilm,' Amis confirmed.

Ruth put her hypothesis together and said it out loud. 'Gerry Doyle was drugged and then clingfilm was wrapped around his face and mouth so he couldn't breathe. He suffocated and died before someone put his body into the car. The murderer isn't aware that the lack of carbon monoxide is a complete giveaway that the suicide was staged.'

She looked to Nick for confirmation that he was impressed by her instant Sherlock-like deduction. However, Nick was more interested in looking at Gerry Doyle's body around the side and the hips.

'That looks like bruising,' Nick remarked as he crouched a little to get a closer look.

He was right. There were a series of small bruises behind the ribcage, the pelvis and the upper thighs. Ruth didn't know how she hadn't spotted it.

'And a whole rainbow of colours,' Ruth said. The bruises ranged from black to purple to green and then faint yellow. And that meant they were historic and not just from one attack.

'Yes. That was going to be my next observation. Mr Doyle has been the victim of long-term physical abuse that goes back years. He has three cracked ribs that have partially healed. A fracture to the pelvis. And this ...' Amis pointed to the back of Doyle's hand. It was a deep, nasty-looking cigarette burn.

'Jesus. What the hell was going on at home?' Nick said.

'If it was home,' Ruth said.

She didn't want to jump to any conclusions yet. But she also knew the likelihood was that this was the result of domestic violence. She had seen enough injuries to know what that kind of abuse looked like. And even though a man being domestically abused was less likely, Ruth knew that two in five reports were of a man being abused by his partner – much higher than most of the British general public would have guessed.

It was mid-morning by the time Ruth and Nick arrived at the modern cul-de-sac in Mulsford where the Doyles lived. It had started to spit with rain. Outside number seven was a patrol car and a SOCO forensic van. As they pulled up outside, Ruth caught some of the neighbours at their windows, having a look at who else was arriving. It was that kind of cul-de-sac. Everyone knew everyone – and that was always useful in getting a detailed picture of the victim.

Making their way over, Ruth and Nick were shown through a slatted wooden gate, down the side of the house and into the garage where a team of SOCOs were going over the car and the garage.

Walking into the kitchen, Ruth could see that it was fastidiously clean and tidy. Nothing was out of place. It was in complete contrast to the garage, which had been untidy and lacking order. That told Ruth immediately that this was Mrs Doyle's domain and she liked order and control. That didn't make her guilty of domestic abuse, but Ruth knew that the two could often go hand in hand. Had that then escalated to murder? Had Mary killed her husband and made a botched attempt to pass it off as suicide?

Mary Doyle was washing mugs at the sink until she noticed their presence.

Ruth gave her a sympathetic smile and showed her warrant card. 'Mrs Doyle?'

'Mary … Yes,' she said as she took a tea towel and began to dry the mugs as though her life depended on it.

If Mary had nothing to do with her husband's death then she still assumed that Gerry had killed himself. She might have been full of self-recrimination about how she hadn't noticed his mental state. That was the usual reaction. And that was what Ruth and Nick were looking for: Mary Doyle's reaction to the news that her husband had been murdered. If she had killed him, then she would have to fake the surprise and shock of that news. However, the body and mind have a habit of reacting instinctively to emotion before the more rational part of the brain takes over. And that was what Ruth and Nick would be looking for.

'DI Ruth Hunter and DS Nick Evans from Llancastell CID. I'm so sorry for your loss,' Ruth said. She was trying to suss Mary Doyle out. She looked at her height and build to start with. Did she have the strength to pull her husband's dead body into a car and get it sitting in the driver's seat? Ruth wasn't sure.

Mary took the mugs to the cupboard and gestured for them to sit down at the kitchen table.

'I did tell the other officers everything I know,' Mary said quietly.

'Yes, of course. Could you come and sit down?' Ruth said. She didn't want her holding crockery when she broke the news that her husband had been murdered.

Pulling the chair out from under the table with a noisy judder, Mary sat down. Ruth looked at the rings on Mary's fingers. They were gold and a little too tight so that the flesh of the finger bulged a little. Maybe she was a bit heavier than when she first put them on. The nails on both hands were cut neatly to the tips with no polish. They could have easily been the hands of a man. Ruth then noticed some bruising on the knuckles of her right hand. Did they have anything to do with the bruises they had seen on Gerry Doyle's body?

As Ruth looked over at her, there was something slightly asexual about Mary Doyle.

'Mary, I'm very sorry to have to tell you this, but we don't think that Gerry's death was suicide. It's our belief that he was murdered,' Ruth said in her well-rehearsed gentle tone.

The final word hung in the air and Mary blinked as though she hadn't actually heard anything Ruth had said.

And then her forehead wrinkled and her eyes closed as she took a breath.

'What? I'm sorry. I … I don't understand … I found Gerry in the car in the garage,' she said quietly. Her utter confusion seemed genuine.

Nick shot Ruth a look. It looked like Nick had also seen an authentic reaction.

'The evidence from the post-mortem suggests that Gerry was already dead and then someone put him in the car to make it look like suicide,' Ruth explained.

'What? Don't be ridiculous,' Mary said, shaking her head. 'No … I mean I was here. He was out in the garage … I … This is ridiculous …'

Nick got out his notepad and pen. 'How long had your husband been out in the garage before you found him?'

'What? … Half an hour. Actually, maybe a bit longer,' Mary said. Even though her voice was steady, Ruth could see that her hands were trembling with the shock of what she had been told.

'And did he say what he was going to do?' Nick asked.

'Stuff …' Mary said with a slightly ironic shake of her head.

'Sorry …' Nick said as he looked up from his notepad.

'He always had "stuff" to do. In the garage or the garden,' Mary muttered.

'And there was no one else in the house?' Ruth asked.

'No. No one.'

'Did you see anyone around? Neighbours?' Nick asked.

'No. I'm sorry but it was very quiet.'

'But you didn't hear anything?' Ruth asked.

'I had music playing. But I did notice this low hum when I'd finished with the dishwasher. I thought it was the tumble dryer, so went to the utility room to check. That's when I noticed it was the sound of a car's engine and that it was coming from the garage.' Mary explained. The recollection of that moment got to her and she pursed her lips and let out an audible breath. 'Sorry …'

'Please, don't be sorry. This must be incredibly difficult for you. It's just the more information we have, the more likely it is that we can catch whoever did this to Gerry,' Ruth explained gently.

Mary nodded. 'Yes. Thank you.'

Nick shifted in his chair and leaned forwards a little. 'Do you know anyone that might want to harm Gerry?'

Mary shook her head. 'No, no. There's nothing like that.'

'We're still waiting for our checks to come back, but had Gerry ever been in trouble with the police or anything like that?' Nick asked.

Ruth noticed Mary's facial expression change as something significant dawned on her and she nodded.

'Yes … Actually, there is something,' Mary said and then stopped.

'Go on,' Ruth said.

'Gerry went to prison in 2015,' Mary explained.

'What was he convicted of?' Ruth asked. Was there something in his past that might provide a clue?

'Manslaughter. He was involved in a fight and a man was killed,' Mary explained but clearly felt uncomfortable.

'How long did he serve?' Nick asked.

'Eighteen months,' Mary said.

'And what about the dead man's family?' Ruth asked. 'How did they react to his sentence?'

Mary nodded as if filling the gaps. 'Yes. They were livid with the sentence. They said it was a disgrace.'

Ruth looked over at Nick. They were on familiar ground.

Chapter 11

Gazing out of the sixth-floor window, Ruth looked across Llancastell as the first innocuous drops of rain began to fall and appear silently on the glass. The wind shook the chocolate-coloured leaves of a nearby tree.

Ruth tapped a pen against her teeth; she should have been preparing to go and brief the CID team. But she turned back to her computer and began checking her personal emails, just for a second, then she'd get on with briefing the case. She was lost in thought about what she ought to be doing rather than browsing the latest nonsense newsletters she'd been sent and offers from companies she'd never buy from. Casting her eyes down her inbox, she saw a new email.

Sender: Jamie Parsons.

Ruth nervously opened it.

Hi Ruth.

I have monitoring software and I see that you've been looking at my social media accounts. I know who you are. I wondered if you would ever contact me. There are some things you should know and I guess that means we should arrange to talk – either on the phone or face to face? Your call.

Best wishes,

Jamie Parsons

OH MY GOD! WHAT THE HELL? WITH HER MIND NOW whirring, Ruth reread the email just to make sure she wasn't imagining things. Her pulse quickened. Her breathing was laboured. She didn't know what to do. The beginnings of a panic attack?

'Boss, we're ready for you,' Nick said, knocking on her door.

Bloody hell! How am I meant to do a briefing now?

Ruth tried to get her head together as she grabbed her files and her coffee and marched out into Incident Room One where the CID officers had gathered. Drake agreed that the focus of the Mark Fisher investigation might have changed with the murder of Gerry Doyle and had wanted to discuss it with the wider team.

'Okay … Can I have everyone's attention please?' Ruth said as she reached the centre of the room.

She needed to focus. Parsons's email would have to wait. *Get it together, Ruth,* she said to herself.

'If you weren't already aware, we are now treating Gerry Doyle's death as murder, not suicide.' Ruth went to a photo of Gerry Doyle. He had short grey hair, black eyebrows and piercing blue eyes. 'The PM conclusively shows that Gerry Doyle was dead before he entered the car. He was drugged with diazepam, then suffocated, possibly with clingfilm, before being placed inside the car with the hose and the engine running. It was staged to look like a suicide,' Ruth explained.

French frowned. 'Boss, am I missing something here? We've got two staged suicides in three days that are, in fact, murders,' French said, his forehead furrowed.

'Yeah, well, I don't believe in coincidences. And in twenty-five years of policing, I've only ever worked one other murder that had been made to look like suicide,' Ruth said.

'You're saying the murders are linked, boss?' Sian asked.

'I think we have to look at that being a serious line of enquiry … Nick, what have we got on the victim?'' Ruth said.

Nick got up and pointed to the photo. 'Gerry Doyle, originally from Cork, aged sixty. In 2015, Doyle was convicted of manslaughter after a Max McCarthy was killed in a fight outside a pub in Llancastell. Doyle served eighteen months of a four-year sentence.'

'Do we have any more details on that?' Ruth asked.

'Not yet, boss. I'm waiting for the case files to come up from the "salt mines",' Nick explained.

'Max McCarthy's family?' Sian asked.

'There is an older sister, Helen, who lives in Llancastell. She's a nurse at the hospital. According to Mary Doyle, Helen McCarthy was furious that Gerry Doyle only served eighteen months for killing her brother,' Nick explained.

'Got an address?' Ruth asked.

Nick nodded. 'Over by the aqueduct. But she's working at the hospital today.'

'Me and you can go and talk to her after this.' Ruth looked out at the team again. 'The PM showed extensive and historic evidence of violence on Gerry Doyle's body. Broken ribs, pelvis.'

'I checked University Hospital's admissions database. No record of a Gerry Doyle and the database goes back ten years,' Sian explained.

'Which means that Gerry Doyle didn't go to hospital with these injuries. Why?' Ruth asked.

'Domestic abuse?' French suggested.

'I noticed that Mary Doyle had bruised knuckles the other day. With the bruising on Gerry Doyle's body, that makes me suspicious. And normally I would think that if a partner who is being violently abused, ends up being murdered at the family home, the suspicion has to fall on the abuser. But I'm not convinced with this one,' Ruth said.

'You don't think it's her?' Sian asked, picking up on Ruth's hesitation.

'Not sure. When we told her that Gerry had not committed suicide but had been murdered, she seemed genuinely shocked. Nick's and my instinct after our interview was that Mary Doyle had no idea that her husband had been murdered,' Ruth explained.

'Are we ruling her out?' French asked.

'Not yet. And we've got stuff coming back from Forensics that might prove us wrong,' Ruth explained, but her gut instinct was almost always right.

Ruth sipped her coffee that was now room temperature. She couldn't get the email from Jamie Parsons out of her head. Attempting to plough on, Ruth pointed at the two crime boards.

'We have two murder victims in the space of three days. Both are murders that have been staged to look like suicides. Both victims have served prison sentences for manslaughter. And in both cases, our killer has made some basic mistakes.' Ruth then looked out at her team. 'So our job is to find out what links our two victims.'

· · ·

As Ruth and Nick made their way to Llancastell University Hospital, Ruth took a ciggie, lit it and buzzed down the window.

Ruth worried that, somehow, she had misremembered how things had actually been with Sarah. If Sarah had had an affair, there must have been signs. She must have been unhappy. Did Ruth *really* know Sarah? The real Sarah? Or had she spent the last six years looking back at their relationship with rose-tinted glasses?

The faces of Jamie Parsons and Jurgen Kessler from her dream came flooding into her mind. And then the email. What was she going to do about that? Was she going to meet Jamie Parsons? *God, what a day.*

Taking a final drag on her cigarette, Ruth buzzed up the window and sat back in her seat.

Nick glanced over at her. 'You all right, boss?'

Ruth thought for a second and then said, 'No … not really.' She was close enough to Nick not to have to pretend.

'The stuff with Sarah?' Nick asked.

Ruth nodded. 'I did some digging around.'

'And?' Nick asked.

'Jurgen Kessler and Jamie Parsons were both at the Berlin School of Economics at the same time,' Ruth explained.

'You think they knew each other?' Nick asked, sounding surprised.

'They went to the same university at the same time. They both then went to work for the same German bank in London. Parsons had an affair with Sarah a few months before she went missing. Kessler was the last person seen talking to Sarah before she disappeared,' Ruth said.

Ruth could feel that her body was tense and an uneasy chill had run through her. There was some dark secret between those three people that was the answer to what had happened to Sarah. And it was making her incredibly unsettled.

'Jamie Parsons sent me an email,' Ruth blurted out.

'What?' Nick said, his eyebrows skyrocketed in amazement.

'You know I was digging around on social media? Parsons has some kind of software that can flag that up. So he emailed me.'

'Well, tracking software's a bit creepy … Bloody hell. What did he say?' Nick asked.

'He said he wasn't sure if I would ever contact him.'

'Did you reply?' Nick asked.

'Not yet.'

'Are you going to?' Nick asked.

'I have to, I suppose. He said there are a few things I should know and that we should talk,' Ruth said.

'You're going to meet him?' Nick asked.

'I don't know. I should do. There are lots of things I want to ask him.'

'Are you going to ask him about Kessler?' Nick said.

Ruth hadn't quite got that far in her thinking.

'I don't think I could meet him and not ask about Kessler,' Ruth said.

For her own peace of mind, she knew she needed to go and meet Jamie Parsons.

HELEN MCCARTHY, DRESSED IN HER DARK BLUE NURSE'S uniform, sat opposite Ruth and Nick in the hospital cafeteria. She had both hands wrapped around a white mug of tea and looked nervous.

Ruth had done all the formalities. Helen's face was thin

and angular, and her blonde hair was pinned back on her head.

'And can you tell us what kind of man Max was?' Ruth said with an empathetic look as Nick took notes.

'Lovely. Kind. He worked here as a paediatric nurse. Life and soul,' Helen said, her face saddening from remembering her brother.

'Our case files show that Max got involved in a fight—' Nick said.

Helen shook her head and interrupted. 'No, no. He wasn't in a fight. He was attacked.'

'There are some witness statements that suggest that Max was in a fight,' Nick said, treading carefully.

'My brother was gay. He was having a drink with his boyfriend. That … man,' Ruth could see that Helen couldn't bring herself to say Gerry Doyle's name. 'He called him a "faggot". They got into an argument and then my brother was attacked. He was defending himself. They knocked him unconscious … When he fell, he hit his head on the kerb …' Helen took a breath as a tear rolled down her face.

Ruth passed her a tissue from her pocket. 'Here you go.'

'Thanks,' Helen said as she sniffed. 'I won't have anyone say my brother was killed in a fight. It's just not true. He was attacked and murdered because he was gay. And this fucking town is so backward, it still thinks that's some terrible crime.'

Ruth nodded sympathetically. 'I'm really sorry that we're having to talk to you about this … but we believe that Gerry Doyle was murdered two days ago.'

Helen took a breath as her eyes widened and she looked at Nick and then back at Ruth as if she couldn't believe what she had just been told. 'What? How?'

'Sorry, we can't discuss the details,' Nick explained.

Helen let out an audible sigh and shook her head. 'He's dead?' she said, almost to herself.

'Yes. It's not been in the local press, so you wouldn't have known,' Ruth explained. It was pretty clear that Helen had no idea.

Having composed herself for a second, Helen nodded. 'Good. Good. I'm glad someone killed him. He only served eighteen months in prison for killing Max, you know? It was a fucking joke!'

'Helen, can you tell us where you were last Saturday night, midnight, through to Sunday morning,' Ruth said gently.

Helen snorted. 'Bloody hell! You think I killed him? … I wish I had, but I was in Glasgow all weekend with friends.'

'And they'll verify that, will they?' Nick said as he made notes on his pad.

'Yeah, of course,' Helen said.

As they made their way back towards the centre of Llancastell, Ruth's phone buzzed and she answered it.

'Boss?' said a voice. It was Sian.

'Hi, Sian. You okay?' Ruth asked. The sound of Sian's voice hit Ruth with a fresh wave of guilt.

'Yes, fine. We've had a report back from Traffic that Craig Harrison's car was caught on several ANPR cameras between five and six last Sunday morning. Didn't he tell you that he was fast asleep in bed?' Sian explained.

'Yes … We'd better go for a chat,' Ruth said.

'It gets worse. An hour ago, Craig Harrison broke into the family home and stole his father's shotgun and ammunition. He told Derek Harrison that he was going to be with his sister, Donna,' Sian said.

'Have we any idea what that means?' Ruth asked, as her mind ran through a variety of scenarios. It didn't sound good.

'Donna Fisher is buried at St Stephen's Church in Llancastell,' Sian explained.

'Thank you, Sian,' Ruth said, now on high alert. They could be dealing with a possible suicide.

'See you later, boss,' Sian said and then hung up.

Ruth turned to Nick. 'Back the way we came, Nick.'

Hitting the brakes harder than he needed to, Nick slowed the car. The seatbelt yanked against Ruth's shoulder. 'Where are we going?'

'Know St Stephen's Church?' Ruth asked, deciding not to comment on Nick's excessive use of the brakes.

'I should do. My parents got married there,' Nick said as he turned the car. 'Blues and twos?'

Ruth nodded and Nick flicked on the lights and sirens.

'Craig Harrison has stolen a shotgun and was heading to the graveyard where Donna Fisher is buried. His car was picked up on an ANPR on Sunday morning in the Ceiriog Valley area when he said he was at home,' Ruth explained.

'You think he murdered Mark Fisher?' Nick asked.

'He had motive, means and opportunity,' Ruth said.

'And no alibi,' Nick said.

FOR THE NEXT TEN MINUTES, THEY TORE UP THE A328 AND Ruth set about organising for an Armed Response team to meet them there. She was taking no risks. If Craig Harrison had a shotgun and was planning on taking his life, he was also a major risk to others. They already had Harrison's car and registration.

The road swung out to the west and the teak-coloured hills sloped away to the left. A minute later, a sign signalled that they were entering Llancastell.

Ruth clicked her radio. 'Three-six to Control. We are two minutes from St Stephen's Church, over.'

'Three-six received,' Control responded.

'Three-six, to Control. Do we have an ETA for the ARU to be in attendance, over?' Ruth asked. Sometimes Armed Response Units could be miles from where they were needed.

'Three-six, will advise,' Control responded. Ruth replaced the Tetra radio – she was feeling unsettled.

Nick turned left onto a quiet residential road. It led them to a large playing field. St Stephen's Church was on the far side. Half a dozen boys played football nearby. Ruth immediately registered their presence – there might be an armed and desperate man nearby and she didn't want innocent bystanders getting hurt.

Nick slowed the car. Ruth could see that the small, grey slated church building looked a little dilapidated. The dark arched windows had been fitted with chicken wire. It was a rough part of Llancastell.

'Here we go,' Nick said, gesturing to the parked white BMW X5.

'Craig Harrison's here,' Ruth said under her breath. Her pulse quickened slightly.

Getting out of the car, she and Nick scanned the grave-yard for anything out of the ordinary.

Peering again, Ruth thought she saw a figure in the hedges behind the fence. Or was it her imagination? It was about a hundred yards away.

It could be a shape made by leaves and branches, she thought.

Ruth squinted and peered again, trying to focus.

CRACK!

The air filled with the thunderous sound of a gunshot. The windshield of their Astra shattered, the glass collapsing noisily.

'Fuck!' Nick shouted, as he flinched and ducked.

Ruth hit the ground instinctively and bellowed, 'Bloody hell!'

What the fuck is he shooting at us for?

'All right, boss?' Nick came scurrying over. They both glanced at the fence and hedges that lined the churchyard.

Harrison had disappeared.

'I think so,' Ruth said, her heart banging like a drum in her chest. 'You?'

'Brilliant,' Nick said with a sardonic smile. 'He wasn't joking about hating the police.'

Down on their haunches, they scuttled behind the Astra for protection. Its engine was still clicking as the hot metal of the engine cooled.

'Control from three-six, officers under fire. We have a Code Zero situation. Request armed officers immediately,' Ruth gasped into her radio.

'Three-six, received.'

'Nice of the cavalry to take their time,' Nick quipped sarcastically.

'Don't worry. They're having a nice coffee. They'll be along in a bit,' Ruth quipped.

Suddenly, there was movement from the thick hedges over to their left. Leaves shook. Then the faint sound of rustling.

Assessing the situation, Ruth knew this wasn't good. Harrison was inside the graveyard, hiding behind the hedgerow, feeling suicidal with a shotgun. *And* he had them pinned down.

'Boss,' Nick said, pointing out where the branches had swayed. It was closer than before. 'He's coming this way.'

Shit! What do we do now?

Ruth felt her stomach lurch. Peering over the bonnet, she caught sight of a figure behind the dark wooden fence.

She could see him clearly now. It was Craig Harrison.

BOOM!

A flash from a gun muzzle. Ruth ducked as the metal shotgun pellets cracked noisily against the car's bodywork.

Jesus, that was a bit too close for comfort, she thought.

'For fuck's sake!' Nick growled. 'Stay there, boss!'

'Where the hell do you think you're going?' Ruth asked.

'Haven't you seen the end of *Butch Cassidy and The Sundance Kid?*' Nick joked.

'Erm, yes I have. And they both get shot,' Ruth said with a raised eyebrow.

'Oh yeah. Well, you know what I mean?' Nick said with a shrug.

Before Ruth could say anything, Nick was up and sprinting towards the far end of the fence.

He really is a reckless twat, she thought.

It was, however, no more than she had come to expect from DS Nick Evans. In moments like this, he seemed to have no fear, which was both admirable and terrifying. And perhaps a little stupid for a soon-to-be father.

Ruth waited and braced herself. *No gunshot. Thank God!* She watched as Nick disappeared over the fence and dropped out of sight.

Where is that bloody Armed Response Unit?

Crouching forward, Ruth felt the rhythmic pounding of her pulse in her neck. When she had gone into situations like this in Peckham, she had been wearing her Kevlar bulletproof vest. It might have been heavy and restrictive, but she could have done with having it to hand now.

She looked over at the old black gates that marked the entrance to the churchyard. They were about twenty yards away. Her thigh muscles were starting to burn from crouching down too long.

Bloody hell! Getting old isn't fun, is it?

She wasn't prepared to wait for Craig Harrison to come and shoot her like a sitting duck. She straightened and stood up. With her eyes fixed on the fence, she made a dash for the gates and a wooden archway. Her feet clattered noisily on the ground.

Bracing herself for a gunshot, she instinctively hunched her shoulders as she ran.

She scanned the graveyard for signs of movement. Nothing. Ruth took a breath and looked at her next target. A large grey gravestone, about thirty yards away.

That was twice now that Harrison had had the chance to shoot at them but hadn't. Maybe he didn't have any more cartridges. If he wasn't expecting the police to arrive, he would have only needed one to blow his head off.

Ruth sprinted again, shoulders and back hunched. She wasn't taking any chances.

As she hit full speed, there was the thunderous crack of a shotgun that seemed to reverberate across the sky and back again.

Jesus fucking Christ!

Diving for the floor, Ruth scrambled behind the simple headstone. She banged her knee heavily on a stone grave border.

Bollocks! Bang goes that theory about having no more shells! And that really bloody hurt! she thought at the delayed realisation that her knee throbbed in searing pain.

Gritting her teeth, she took cover behind the dark grey

headstone. The inscription was faded and yellow lichen had grown into the letters so that they were hard to read.

Drawing breath, Ruth peered around the cold stone. She could smell its dampness.

Craig Harrison made his move. He came out of the undergrowth and began to run towards the church, weaving in and out of the gravestones like a rugby player in full flight.

Before Harrison was halfway across the graveyard, Nick appeared from the right, as if out of nowhere. Nick sprinted full pelt at him as if he was on the opposing team and was going to take him out with a rugby tackle.

Harrison spotted him and stopped. He swivelled the shotgun around.

Oh, Jesus, he's going to shoot him!

Ruth ran towards them. 'No!' she screamed.

Harrison tried to shoot but there were no shells left.

Now frustrated, Harrison smashed the butt of the shotgun into Nick's face and sent him reeling to the gravel path.

Glancing up, Harrison saw Ruth approaching, tossed the shotgun away onto a grass bank and ran into the church.

Sitting up with a groan, Nick put his hand to his bloody face as Ruth got to him.

'You okay?' Ruth yelled with a gasp.

'Think so …' Nick said, looking at the blood on his hand that he'd wiped from his nose.

'Three-six to Control. Suspect, Craig Harrison, now inside St Stephen's Church. As far as we know, he is no longer armed. *But* I still need a bloody ARU here. Now!' Ruth said, fuming.

'Three-six, received. ETA of ARU ten minutes.'

Ruth clicked off her radio angrily. 'Ten bloody minutes! They're having a laugh, aren't they?'

Ruth could see that Nick was unsteady on his feet. 'Stay there for a minute.'

'Why? Where the hell are you going?' Nick asked.

Ruth indicated the church. 'Confession.'

If Craig Harrison had murdered Mark Fisher, then it was likely he had something to do with Gerry Doyle's death too. She didn't want Harrison to kill himself before she had time to ask him. If he was planning suicide, then he would have little to lose and might well come clean about what had happened.

However, Harrison no longer had a gun. If he was going to kill himself, then he would have to find another way. Gazing up at the high church tower, Ruth realised where Harrison might be heading.

With her feet crunching on the gravel path, Ruth ran to the enormous arched wooden door that was studded with rusty iron bolts and went in.

The inside of the church was dark and freezing. It smelt of wood and the musty pages of an old book. Rushing through the nave, her heeled shoes echoed.

She scanned left and right, Harrison was nowhere to be seen. He could be crouched behind a pew. Ruth stopped and strained her hearing. Nothing except the thud of her pulse.

Then the sound of movement over by the gold lectern. There was a dark wooden door that had been left open. Inside, a stone staircase leading up.

Harrison was heading for the bell tower. She needed to stop him from flinging himself off the top.

Feeling her shoes slip on the polished wooden floor, Ruth ran towards the doorway. A glint of green light flashed across her face from the stained-glass window as she went.

Ruth started to dash up the narrow staircase. There was definitely movement from above. She could feel fresh air coming down the staircase and onto her face.

Taking it two steps at a time, she climbed the sharp stone stairs. She placed her left hand on the cold, rough stone wall to keep her balance. The noise of her movements echoed up the stairwell, amplifying and rebounding off the stone walls.

There was another noise from above. She hoped she got to Harrison in time.

Getting to the top of the staircase, Ruth was out of breath. There was no time to lose. She rushed through a room where thick burgundy striped ropes hung in a row like nooses; the ropes that sounded the church bells overhead. Above her loomed a dark red stained-glass window.

Glancing up, Ruth could see half a dozen dark metal bells of differing sizes. The largest had to be over six feet long. Above that, the internal wooden structure of the church tower itself stretched up for another thirty feet. It made her feel momentarily dizzy.

Moving quickly, Ruth looked around. *Where the hell is he?* All she could hear was the rhythmic thud of her pulse and heart.

She didn't want to panic him into jumping.

'Craig?' Ruth said in a gentle voice. 'Craig? It's Ruth Hunter. Remember?'

Harrison must know who she was and why she was there. But he was suicidal and clearly didn't care about what he did now. There wouldn't be any consequences. He would be dead.

'Listen, Craig, I know why you're here. I know it's

where Donna is,' Ruth said quietly, as if trying to coax a small child.

There was silence.

Ruth felt a brush of icy air on her face. As she leant to one side, she could see a small door that was slightly open.

It must lead out to the roof, Ruth thought.

'Don't talk about her!' Harrison shouted.

Ruth moved gingerly to the door. 'I'm coming out, Craig.'

Stepping out of the door and over the wooden lip, Ruth squinted as her eyes adjusted to the daylight.

Harrison was sitting on the parapet wall, with one leg dangling down. Below was a one-hundred-and-fifty-foot drop to the gravel pathway.

'Stay there!' Harrison barked at Ruth.

This wasn't Ruth's first suicide. She needed to keep Harrison talking and let the emotion of the situation die down a little. Time was crucial.

Ruth held up her hands in an open gesture. 'I'm not going to do anything you don't want me to do, Craig. Okay?'

Silence as the wind buffeted around them, flicking a wisp of hair into Ruth's face. She recalled her police negotiator training. Her ultimate goal was to influence Harrison's state of mind very slowly. She needed to build rapport. And not interrupt him. Maybe try to find a way in or a hook.

'Your dad told us that you came here to be with Donna?' Ruth said.

Harrison shrugged. 'Yeah … I don't want to live anymore. What's the point? It's too painful.'

'What about your father and mother?'

'What about them?' Harrison sneered. Ruth had seen

that kind of self-pity plenty of times before: suicide victims were usually full of pain and self-pity.

'They've lost Donna. They don't want to lose you too now, do they?' Ruth said.

Harrison snorted. 'They don't care. Seriously. I embarrass them. My dad wanted me to be a solicitor or something like that. Private school, tutor, everything. Now I'm the village drunk and work at a timber yard. He can't tell his friends at the golf club that, can he?'

'If your father didn't care, why did he ring us and say that he was very worried about you?' Ruth asked. 'He was really concerned. He didn't want you to harm yourself because he cares. Because he loves you, Craig.'

Ruth had no idea if that were true, but she could see a small chink in Harrison's despair. His face and expression had changed.

'I can't stop you killing yourself, Craig. But maybe you owe it to your mum and dad to talk to them. If you still want to kill yourself tomorrow, there's nothing I can do to stop you, is there?' Ruth suggested. She had seen this tactic work before too.

'They'll just try to talk me out of it,' Harrison said.

'Of course they will. They love you,' Ruth said.

'Really? Is that why they packed me and Donna off to boarding school while they lived it up all over the world. They won't tell you that.'

'I can see you're really upset. What do you think Donna would say if she knew you were doing this to yourself?' Ruth asked in a hushed tone.

'I told you. I don't want you to talk about her!' Harrison growled.

'Okay, okay. I'm sorry. We can talk about something else.'

The light of the day had been snuffed out by a series of

large, metallic-grey clouds and there was the first hint of rain in the air.

Harrison looked back and directly at Ruth. 'You know I did it, don't you?'

Something about his expression was unsettling. What was he talking about?

'Sorry, Craig. I don't know what you mean by that. What did you do?'

Harrison's eyes lit up and he smirked. 'I killed him. You do know that?'

There was something unnervingly cold about the look on Harrison's face.

'I killed that man.'

'Mark Fisher?'

'Yeah. *Mark Fisher*.' Harrison virtually spat the words out of his mouth as if it made him sick to say them out loud.

Up until now, Craig Harrison had been low down on her list of possible suspects. They also now believed that whoever killed Mark Fisher also killed Gerry Doyle. What was Harrison's connection to Doyle? What was his motive to kill him? Could it really be just a coincidence?

'You murdered Mark Fisher, Craig?' Ruth asked.

'Yes! I just said that! Jesus!' Harrison snapped and then wobbled and nearly lost his balance.

'Okay. Well, thank you for telling me that, Craig. That's a very brave and honest thing to do. Why don't you come off that wall, and you can tell me all about it?' Ruth suggested.

'I don't think so.'

Ruth wasn't sure what she thought now. Harrison's head was all over the place. Maybe he just wanted the attention of claiming to have killed Mark Fisher?

'Could you tell me how you killed Mark Fisher, Craig?' Ruth asked with no hint of the gravity of the question.

'No. That's between me, him and God,' Harrison said.

'Now that you've told me that, I'm guessing that you know about Gerry?' Ruth asked.

Harrison looked at her and sneered. 'Of course. Of course I know Gerry. Jesus …'

Was Harrison just playing along with her?

'Gerry McCarthy?' Ruth asked, seeing if Harrison would go along with this.

Harrison shrugged. 'Don't know his surname. Sorry.'

Suddenly the distant sound of sirens. The ARU was arriving with blues and twos as it was an emergency.

Now they turn up? Shit! I wish I'd had time to radio for them to come silently!

Harrison looked in the direction of the sirens and then back at Ruth. He looked startled and grabbed the wall with both hands.

'It's all right, Craig. No one's going to hurt you. We just want to hear what you've got to say,' Ruth said with an empathetic look.

Harrison's eyes flicked as his anxiety built and he shifted on the wall. Ruth could see that he wasn't sure what to do now and it was making him volatile.

'Craig, look at me. I want to hear what you have to say,' Ruth said.

But Harrison was no longer looking at her. He was looking out across the fields that swept away to the west.

Then Ruth saw Harrison's face and body relax in a moment of sheer relief.

Oh, Jesus, no …

'Craig, look at me!' Ruth yelled as she lurched forward.

Harrison swung his other leg over the wall, leant over

and let himself fall as he vanished over the side of the church.

'No!' Ruth yelled and rushed to the parapet.

Gazing down, she saw that Craig Harrison's body lay in an unnatural twisted pose on the pathway below. Already there was dark blood coming from where he had cracked open his skull.

He was dead.

Nick raced over and then glanced up at Ruth peering over.

'You okay, boss?' he shouted.

'Not really,' Ruth whispered.

Chapter 12

I t was gone eight and Nick and Amanda were sitting in an AA meeting at the Llancastell Detox Unit. There was an unusually large amount of people there as a nearby rehab centre had brought around ten of their patients to listen. They sat with their counsellor in the back row, as they did about once a month.

Nick looked at their faces. It was clear that some of them had only been in the rehab centre for a day or two as they were still sweating and shaking. There was such a clear contrast between them and those who had been there for a few weeks. They looked fresh-faced, well dressed and wore an expression on their faces that was a mixture of relief and growing happiness. Nick remembered that feeling. He also remembered when he had first come to this meeting about ten years earlier. One of the old-timers had told him in no uncertain terms that it wasn't a long way between where he was sitting to those in the back row. Nick could recall how angry he had been at the suggestion that he could ever end up in rehab. He was a police officer and therefore a respected member of society. How dare anyone insinuate that he was anything like the chronic alcoholics that sat at the back. At the time, he thought he just had a drink problem. Of course, just as the man had said, within two years Nick had been to the local rehab and the detox centre that was just down the path from the meeting that they were sitting in. Alcoholism could happen to anyone – it didn't discriminate. And it had taken a host of creative geniuses with it. George Best, Amy Winehouse, Peter Cook, George Michael, Richard Burton – the list went on.

A voice from over by the door broke his train of thought. 'Hi, my name's Peter, and I'm an alcoholic.'

'Hello, Peter,' said everyone in the room.

Nick knew the voice. Looking over, he saw that Peter the Artist had crept in and was sitting on a table. He didn't look well but, having seen him twenty-four hours earlier, Nick was amazed that he had got himself to a meeting.

Fair play. Maybe he's going to take his sobriety seriously now, Nick thought.

'I have to be honest. I've had one of my little slips, yet again. Two days, but it doesn't really matter how long. And I can't tell you why, except that I'm an alcoholic. But I've got a new sponsor who, for some reason, has said he will help me. He's in this room. And I'm incredibly grateful to him. And this morning, I had some kind of epiphany. I know that I have no defence against the first drink. If I put alcohol into my body, I will need another drink and I won't be able to stop until I pass out. So this morning, I looked up to whoever it is that is looking out for me up there, and I said, "I give up. I surrender. I cannot do this anymore. I won't get away with having a drink ever again." And that's okay. And something has changed. But I'm not stupid. I know this only works a day at a time. But I just wanted to share that I'm feeling grateful today, and I'll leave it at that,' Peter said.

'Thanks, Peter,' said the room.

Peter looked over at Nick, smiled and gave him a thumbs-up.

Nick could feel Amanda already glaring at him.

'I thought you said that you hadn't agreed to be Peter's sponsor?' Amanda whispered with a frown.

'Did I?' Nick said, trying to put on his winning cheeky smile.

'You're such a dick, Nick Evans,' Amanda said shaking her head.

'I know.'

'You don't have time to look after someone else's sobriety,' Amanda said.

'Do you remember when you came to your first meeting?' Nick asked.

'Yes. Of course. I was terrified,' Amanda said.

'Imagine if I hadn't taken the time to talk to you and listen to how you felt. Imagine if some of the friends you've made in here had decided they just didn't have time to answer your questions or support you. We're recovering alcoholics. If someone asks us for help, then we have to say yes. That's the deal,' Nick said.

Amanda looked at him, processing what he had said. 'Hang on. You only helped me because you wanted to get in my knickers,' she said with a grin.

Nick gave her a look and raised an eyebrow.

'Okay. Point taken,' Amanda said with a smile.

Ruth sat at the small dining table with a glass of red wine. *Moon Safari* by Air was playing quietly from the living room. Sian was at the gym doing some of her stretching and strengthening exercises that her physio had given her.

Looking at her watch, Ruth realised that she had twenty minutes before her daughter Ella arrived. After the Andrew Gates case, Ella had lived with Ruth and Sian for months and Ruth had got used to having her around. Ella had finally moved out a month ago to a small cottage right on the border between Wales and England, but she usually came over for dinner once a week.

Ruth sipped her wine. In front of her was a box of newspaper cuttings, printouts and notes about Sarah's case. Ruth wanted to use the time on her own to look through the research she had on Jurgen Kessler that she'd collected before she'd promised Sian to try to move on. Were there any more links between Kessler and Jamie Parsons? Was there something else that she had missed?

Turning over a magazine article, Ruth saw Sarah's face beaming back at her from the page. And suddenly she was overwhelmed by emotion. Taking a breath, she allowed herself to look at the photograph and take it in. It wasn't the right thing to do. She should have turned it over. But she couldn't help herself.

It was a photograph from Ruth and Sarah's last holiday before she disappeared. A girls' weekend to Ibiza. Sarah had posted the image on social media and so the magazine had easily found it. They had been sitting at the Café Mambo beach bar in the late afternoon. Sarah was wearing her trademark seventies Carrera sunglasses. That night they had been to the terrace bar at Space and danced until dawn. However, that memory now seemed to be tainted. It was likely that Sarah was having an affair, sending clandestine messages to Parsons, when they went to Ibiza and the thought of that was hideous.

Ruth heard the crunching of gravel and saw someone coming up the drive out of the corner of her eye. Shovelling as many of the notes and articles into the box on the table as she could, Ruth went to the door as the figure knocked.

Opening the door, Ruth saw it was Ella.

'Hiya, Mum,' Ella said, giving her a massive hug.

'Oh, you're early,' Ruth said, trying to hide how flustered she was.

'Charming. I can come back later if you like!' Ella said in mock offence.

'Sorry, no. Lovely to see you,' Ruth said as they went in. 'I'll get you a drink.'

Ruth watched as Ella glanced through the archway to the small dining room and spotted the box on the table. She knew what it was. And Ella was aware that Ruth had promised Sian – and Ella to some extent – that she would put what had happened to Sarah to one side and get on with her life.

'What are you doing?' Ella asked quietly.

There was an awkward silence as Ruth went over to the box and tidied away the last few bits of paper.

'Mum?' Ella said.

'It's not what you think, darling,' Ruth protested, knowing that she had to come clean.

'How is sitting here on your own, drinking and looking through all that stuff, getting on with your life? I know it's difficult, Mum, but do you want to still be doing this when you're seventy?' Ella asked firmly.

'No. And you're right. But something happened. And it's sort of changed everything,' Ruth tried to explain.

'What are you talking about?' Ella said.

'Sarah had an affair. With a man,' Ruth said.

'What? When?' Ella said, her eyes widening in disbelief.

'The summer before she went missing.'

Ella shook her head. 'No. You would have known. One of us would have noticed.'

'I'm really sorry, but it's true. I've seen the evidence,' Ruth said.

'Bloody hell … That's horrible. I'm so sorry,' Ella said.

'Yeah, it's a bit of a shock,' Ruth admitted.

'Who the hell did she have an affair with?' Ella asked, starting to sound angry.

'The man's name is Jamie Parsons. He's sent me an email and suggested that we talk,' Ruth explained.

'What are you going to do?'

'I'm going to meet him. I need to know what happened.'

'What about Sian? Does she know?' Ella asked with a frown.

Ruth didn't answer the question as she walked out of the dining room with the box, heading for the garage.

'Mum!' Ella said loudly.

Ruth stopped and put the box down. 'No. I can't tell her after everything we went through in the summer.'

Ella shook her head, frustrated. 'Bloody hell! You can't lie to her! Look, if Sarah had an affair while she was with you, that's even more reason to move on with your life. Don't fuck up what you've got with Sian, Mum. Please.'

'I need to know what happened.'

'Why?' Ella let out a frustrated sigh. 'Why do you need to know the details of an affair Sarah had six years ago?'

'I just do. It's hard to explain.'

'I think I'm going to go.'

'What? Don't go,' Ruth said, feeling hurt.

'Because you're going to lose Sian. And then you're going to expect me to pick up the pieces again. And I've been doing that for the last six years,' Ella said.

'That's not fair,' Ruth said.

'Isn't it? Mum, I love you. But you've got to realise that you're not the only person who has ever had tragedy or loss in their life. You have to move on,' Ella said, going to the front door and opening it.

'You don't have to go,' Ruth said.

'I do. Otherwise I might say something I'll really regret. I'll give you a call,' Ella said as she slammed the front door.

Chapter 13

I t was morning and the team were assembled in Incident Room One as Ruth came out of her office. She spotted the photo of Craig Harrison up on the scene board – a holiday snap where he was wearing a big hat and just as big a smile. The contrasting image of his twisted body lying on the path below the church tower was still burnt into her mind's eye.

Drake came in, caught her eye and gestured to a seat at the back of the room where he sat down. She hadn't had a chance to debrief Drake after the dramatic events of the previous day but had got a message to him that Harrison had committed suicide – but that was all.

'Right, everyone. Let's get you all up to speed with this,' Ruth said as she walked up to the front of the room and the whiteboards. 'As some of you are aware, Nick and I were called to St Stephen's Church yesterday. We had reports that Craig Harrison had broken into the family home, stolen a shotgun and intended to be with his dead sister, Donna. When we arrived, Craig Harrison shot at us and hit Nick with the gun. I pursued Harrison to the bell tower, where he told me that he had killed Mark Fisher. He wasn't willing to give me any more details than that. I also asked him if he knew "Gerry". Harrison claimed he did but said he didn't know his surname.'

'What did you think?' Drake asked, sitting forwards in his chair.

'You know what? I couldn't tell if he was bullshitting or not. At first, I thought he was lying, but he had this look on his face. I don't know, boss,' Ruth said.

'Anything to link him to Gerry Doyle's murder?' Drake asked.

'Nothing yet.' Ruth walked over to the board and pointed to the photo of Mark Fisher. 'Both Derek and Craig Harrison have motive to murder Mark Fisher. They blamed him for Donna Fisher's death. Where are we with Derek Harrison's alibi?'

'Boss, we've finally tracked down the farmer that Derek Harrison claimed he saw early on Sunday morning. We're going there today,' French said.

'Good.' Ruth then pointed to a blurred photo that had been taken off Facebook. 'This is Zoe Tardelli, who we think now goes by the name Nicole Lace. She was allegedly raped when she was fourteen by Mark Fisher in 1997, although charges were never brought.'

'What about Heather Morrison? The woman who Fisher sexually assaulted at that time?' Drake asked.

'We're going to see the husband today as well,' French said.

'Anything on Zoe Tardelli or Nicole Lace?' Drake asked.

Sian looked up. 'Nothing yet on either name, boss. I'm trying to track her through friends on Facebook. Council tax came back as a blank, as did work and pensions.'

'Okay. It looks like if she is working, it's cash in hand.

Let me know how you get on.' Ruth could feel herself getting frustrated. They seemed to be making no progress at all in the case. She pointed to another photo of a woman. 'And we've established that Kathleen Taylor was in Prague for the whole of that weekend?'

'Yes, boss,' Sian replied. Their eyes met and Ruth lost concentration. Her conversation with Ella was still floating around her mind. Maybe she just needed to bite the bullet. Forget about Parsons and the affair. Accept that Sarah was gone and build a life with Sian.

Focus, Ruth. Deal with that later!

Ruth pointed to another photo. 'And now we have Gerry Doyle. Another murder that has been dressed up to look like a suicide. Mary Doyle, the wife, claims that she was in the kitchen while her husband was murdered in the garage and saw or heard nothing.'

'Do we believe her?' Sian asked.

'Not sure. She seemed upset,' Nick said.

'And tidying the kitchen on your own is a terrible alibi if you're going to kill your husband,' Ruth said.

'Anything back from Forensics?' Drake asked.

Nick shook his head. 'Not yet.'

'Max McCarthy's sister, Helen, has an alibi that needs checking. She claims that she was in Glasgow with friends. Anything else on Gerry Doyle?'

No one said anything, so Ruth had her answer.

'Come on, everyone! You're a good team but it's like walking through treacle at the moment,' Ruth said, unable to hide her frustration at the lack of progress.

Ruth saw Drake stand and walk casually to the front of Incident Room One, his right hand in his pocket. She was glad that he was going to chip in – the homicide team needed some guidance and his experience was invaluable.

Drake looked at them for a second. 'Both murders were

planned and pre-meditated. And both were botched. Simple stuff was missed. We have to go on the assumption that they were carried out by the same person or people. Why? What links our two victims? That has to be the key to this investigation.'

Ruth nodded as she looked out at the team. 'Who had a motive to kill both these men? And why?'

Nick was now holding a computer printout and gestured to it. 'Boss, this came through a few minutes ago. Gerry Doyle worked for years as a sound engineer.'

Nick's tone was clearly meant to imply that this was some kind of clue.

'Sorry, Nick. I don't really know what a sound engineer is.' Ruth said with a shrug.

Oh God, does that make me look old and out of touch?

'They work with record producers and artists when they're recording songs, albums,' Nick explained with an expression that said, 'Why don't you know this?'

'And Mark Fisher was a musician,' Ruth said. The penny dropped.

'According to this, Gerry Doyle worked at The Mill Recording Studios, outside Mold from 1987 through to 2010,' Nick said, reading aloud.

'The Mill?' Drake said. He had clearly heard of it.

'And we know that Mark Fisher worked as a session guitarist, as well as doing his own stuff,' Sian said.

'No one else has heard of The Mill?' Nick asked, shaking his head. 'Everyone's recorded there. Queen, Simple Minds, Radiohead.'

'Radio who?' French said.

Nick shared a withering look with Drake, who smiled back at him.

'That's all right, Dan. You were in nappies when Radiohead produced their last decent album,' Nick said.

'Right, thank you, everyone. Let's get going, eh?' Ruth said with some urgency and then looked at Nick. 'We need to talk to Mary Doyle again.'

Maybe this was the breakthrough they had been waiting for.

Sitting at the kitchen table, Ruth and Nick were drinking coffee as they re-interviewed Mary Doyle. Ruth could see that the stress of her husband's death was taking its toll. The skin under Mary's eyes was dark and baggy – she wasn't sleeping. Ruth knew that kind of turmoil and grief. When Sarah had gone missing, Ruth didn't sleep properly for nearly a year. She just couldn't switch her brain off.

As they talked, Ruth was trying to figure out if Mary Doyle was the kind of woman who could plan and kill her husband in cold blood. If she had the wherewithal to drug him, suffocate him and get his body into the car, would she really claim to have been on her own in the kitchen at the time of the murder? In fact, in Ruth's experience, it was usually only innocent people that didn't have some kind of decent alibi.

Ruth glanced down and saw that Mary's hand was still bruised. 'That looks nasty. How did it happen?'

Mary didn't react. 'I was moving a table. My hand got trapped between it and the wall. Looks worse than it is,' she explained.

If she's guilty of domestic violence or worse, she seemed untroubled by the question.

'Mary, I asked you last time whether or not you could think of anyone that might wish Gerry harm?' Ruth said, warming her hands on the mug. The kitchen was chilly.

Mary nodded. She clearly had no idea what Ruth was talking about – or at least she was pretending she didn't.

'Yes, that's right. There is no one,' Mary said, blinking as she thought again.

Nick tapped his pen on his notepad and looked over at her. 'But your husband served a prison sentence for the manslaughter of Max McCarthy?'

'Yes. Yes, he did. And he was devastated that young man died. But it was an accident,' Mary said.

'We spoke to Helen McCarthy, his sister,' Ruth said.

Mary looked at her and frowned deeply. 'You can't think that after all these years, that one of his family came up here and murdered Gerry?'

'We have to look at everything,' Ruth said.

'Why now? It doesn't make any sense …' Mary said, her voice trailing off as she took in what had been said.

'And you're sure that you didn't see or hear anyone or anything that evening?' Nick asked.

'No, no. Of course not,' Mary said, getting a little choked. 'I would have said …'

'Gerry worked as a sound engineer at The Mill Recording Studios, is that right?'

Nick asked.

'Yes. He was there for years,' Mary explained.

'So, he worked with a lot of musicians?' Ruth asked.

'Yeah, loads. Every day,' Mary said – she didn't understand why Ruth was asking her about this.

'But he wasn't working there anymore?' Nick asked.

'No. He was getting on a bit and the hours were long. He'd be there for days on end so he packed it in,' Mary explained.

'Did he ever mention the name Mark Fisher? He was a guitarist,' Ruth asked.

Mary shrugged. 'No. Doesn't ring a bell. Gerry would

only tell me when someone famous had been in. You know, pop stars. But I never heard the name Mark Fisher before.'

'He was a session guitarist. Played with bands in the nineties and just after the Millennium?' Nick said.

'No. Sorry. Never heard of him,' Mary said.

Ruth shot Nick a look – finding a link between the two victims wasn't going to be as easy as she had hoped.

SIAN AND FRENCH WERE HEADING OUT TO THE CEIRIOG Valley to interview the farmer, Mr Bird, who Derek Harrison claimed to have seen a couple of times on the morning that Mark Fisher had been murdered.

Shifting on the passenger seat, Sian felt a twinge in her lower back. The pain medication she was on was starting to wear off. She would have to take some more soon. Sipping her water, Sian swilled it around her mouth and under her tongue. The medication made her mouth dry.

Sian winced again, reached into her pocket and took out her painkillers and popped two into her mouth. They were opioids and made her head swim. Ruth had told her that they were called opioids because they came from the opium poppy and were the same class of drug as heroin. Sian had joked and asked if that made her a smackhead?

Sian was feeling annoyed and it wasn't just the back pain. Ruth had been acting strangely for the past day or two. She seemed distant and distracted.

'You okay?' French asked in a concerned tone, spotting her taking her medication.

'I will be when these bad boys kick in,' Sian said, still lost in her thoughts about Ruth.

French indicated to turn left as they were now close to Hazel Farm where they were due to meet Mr Bird.

'Sian, can I ask you something?' French said hesitantly.

Oh God, what's this about? I'm not in the mood this morning, Sian thought.

From his tone, Sian could sense this was going to be a personal question. Sian's relationship with Ruth was known but not spoken about in CID. She and French had never spoken about it, so it was only a matter of time.

'Yes, Dan,' Sian said slowly.

'You and the boss …' French said with a quizzical look on his face.

Oh great. Here we go.

'Me and DI Hunter? Yes,' Sian said.

'You live together, right?'

French was finding this awkward, but Sian wasn't going to make it easy for him. She was in that kind of mood.

'Do we? Who told you that, Dan?' Sian said, taking the piss.

'Oh, fuck off, Sian. Everyone knows that,' French said, slowing the car as the road curved into the large yard of Hazel Farm.

'Oh God, Dan. Have you been looking at porn again? Well, the answer is no. Me and DI Hunter don't like men and we don't want to have a threesome with you, okay?' Sian said with a wry grin, hoping to really make French squirm.

'Sian! That's not … I just wondered if it was weird working together and then going home, that's all. You didn't have to make it …' French paused as he searched for the word.

'Uncomfortable?' Sian suggested.

'Yeah …' French nodded.

'I just don't like talking about it, that's all.'

French looked suitably embarrassed. Even though part of Sian had enjoyed making him squirm, she knew she was taking out her bad mood on him.

'No, no. Sorry … I …' Dan mumbled.

Sian opened the car door and stepped out, with a little difficulty, into the main yard. It was muddy and there were potholes everywhere. And then the smell – slurry that was under a tarpaulin in a nearby barn.

As if on cue, Mr Bird came out of a nearby barn. He wiped his nose on his sleeve as he approached the car and then spat on the floor.

He's a little treat, Sian said to herself.

French showed his warrant card. 'Mr Bird?'

'That's right,' Bird said as two border collies circled around his feet.

'DC French and DC Hockney from Llancastell CID. We spoke yesterday.' French said.

'Aye. How can I help?' Bird said, hitching up his trousers.

Sian looked at his weather-worn face, which was chubby and unshaven. It was one of those faces that was hard to pinpoint in terms of age. She couldn't tell if he was late thirties or early fifties.

'We understand that you know Derek Harrison?' French asked.

'That's right. Lives up at the posh house. Been there years. Saw on the news about poor Craig. Terrible,' Bird said, shaking his head.

'You knew Craig Harrison?' Sian asked.

'Aye. Him and his sister used to come up and play with my kids when they was young. When he was a bit older, Craig used to come and do some work for us,' Bird explained.

'We're investigating the murder of Mark Fisher on Sunday up by the Berwyn river,' French said, gesturing over in that direction.

'Aye, heard about that too,' Bird said, nodding.

'Where were you on Sunday morning, Mr Bird?' Sian asked.

Bird wrinkled his nose while he thought. 'From about five, I was bringing in the herds for milking. Then I took them back out about seven, half seven, I suppose.'

'Derek Harrison said that he saw you that morning. Is that right?' French said.

'Aye, I saw Derek. Must have been about half five. Didn't see me, mind,' Bird said.

'He said he was out walking his dog on the fields and saw you a couple of times.' Sian asked.

Bird furrowed his brow. 'Eh? No. He wasn't walking his dog until the afternoon.'

'What was he doing at five-thirty in the morning?' Sian asked, confused by Bird's reaction.

'He was in the car with Craig. They drove past but didn't see me. They were in a bloody rush to get somewhere,' Bird explained. 'Going like the bloody clappers, they were.'

Sian shot French a look – Derek Harrison was lying to them.

THE MILL RECORDING STUDIOS WERE JUST OUTSIDE THE town of Mold, which was twenty miles north-west of Llancastell and whose name came from the Norman French *mont hault*, meaning 'high hill'. It was the site of vicious battles between the Romano Britons and invading Scots as far back as AD 430. These days, Mold was one of the most affluent areas of North Wales and known for its street market and regular food and drink festivals.

Ruth was having to squint as the autumnal sun glistened brightly off the windscreen. She pulled down the visor as Nick turned left at the sign for The Mill Recording Studios.

Two large white gates and stone pillars marked the long track that led down to The Mill. Ruth could see the attraction of the place. It really was in the middle of nowhere. Rolling fields stretched away on both sides and then to the west, the dark plum edges of Snowdonia.

After about a mile, they reached the converted farmhouse buildings that clearly housed the studios, living space and accommodation. Ruth could see that a lot of money had been spent on making the farmhouses modern and fashionable. A new Aston Martin and white Porsche Cayenne were parked in the yard. It seemed that the music business was still as lucrative as ever.

Having parked up and explained who they were to the young receptionist, Ruth and Nick were led down a series of corridors that had been painted a dark red and housed framed gold and platinum records. It was an impressive set-up, Ruth thought to herself.

She could see that Nick was in his element as he walked slowly, looking and reading the records and the small photo of the album sleeve that was attached to each one. She had to stop a number of times to wait for him to catch up. He did love his music.

Eventually, they arrived at studio manager Micky Rice's office. Rice looked up and smiled. He was in his fifties with a fashionable beard and smart, expensive-looking clothes.

'Come in, sit down,' Rice said, beckoning them. He had a thick cockney accent and Ruth was sure he was from the East End somewhere. When she saw a framed West Ham shirt on his wall, it confirmed her suspicions.

'Anyone offered you a drink?' Rice asked.

'We're fine, thanks,' Nick said as he took out his notepad.

'We're investigating Gerry Doyle's death,' Ruth said.

'Yeah, I heard. Horrible. Happened at his house, didn't it? Papers didn't say much more than that,' Rice asked.

'We can't discuss the details of the case, I'm afraid,' Ruth said.

'Right, course. He was a good bloke, Gerry. Liked him a lot,' Rice said.

'We understand that he worked here for a long time?' Nick said.

Rice scratched his head and nodded. 'Gerry? Christ, yeah, he was here for donkey's years. It was a shame ... when he ...you know, had to leave us.'

Ruth looked over at Nick, who had stopped writing and returned her glance. Rice's comment implied this was not the amicable arrangement of Gerry's semi-retirement that Mary Doyle had told them.

'Shame? We understood that Gerry Doyle stopped working here because the hours were too long and he was getting too old?' Ruth asked.

Rice looked visibly uncomfortable and narrowed his eyes. 'Erm ... I suppose that was part of it, yeah.'

Now you're backtracking. What are you hiding? Ruth thought.

'Why else did he stop working here then?' Nick asked.

Moving forwards in his seat, Rice looked at them both. 'It's ... a bit delicate, you know?'

'Mr Rice, Gerry Doyle was murdered,' Nick said bluntly. 'This is a murder investigation.'

'What?' Rice said with his eyes widening in surprise. 'Eh? Jesus! I thought it was suicide?'

'No, I'm afraid not ... So, we need you to tell us anything that might help us catch who did that,' Ruth said in a tone to suggest that this wasn't the time to keep secrets.

'Well, yeah. Of course … How shall I put it? Gerry had an eye for the ladies, especially the younger ones.'

'Do you mean teenage girls?' Ruth asked.

'I suppose so, yeah … We have bands up here for months on end sometimes if they're recording an album. There are parties and groupies. All sorts. And in the old days, everyone would turn a blind eye. It was just a bit of fun, you know?' Micky explained.

'Underage girls?' Ruth asked. She was trying to hide her anger at Rice's use of 'just a bit of fun'. Since when was the abuse, assault and even rape of teenage girls 'fun'?

'I dunno. No one asked. They wore make-up, looked older than they were, maybe. I'm not saying it was all right, but …' Rice stopped himself before he made another flippant excuse.

'That doesn't explain why Gerry Doyle was asked to leave,' Nick said.

'Gerry was a bit rough. Got carried away. There were complaints …' Rice explained. 'And times had changed.'

'Were the police involved?' Ruth asked.

'No, no. No one wanted the police here,' Rice said. 'But that's the way it was going, so I told him he had to go.'

Ruth's mind had already gone back to their interview with Heather Morrison. The parties that Rice had described sounded similar to what she had talked about. Was she one of the girls that Rice was talking about?

'Do the names Heather Morrison or Zoe Tardelli ring a bell?' Ruth asked.

Rice shook his head. 'Sorry, no. When are we talking about?'

'Late nineties,' Nick said.

'Zoe … Actually, yeah, there was a Zoe that used to knock about a bit. I was only a runner back in those days,' Rice explained.

'Dyed red hair,' Ruth said, remembering what Heather had told her.

'Yeah. That sounds like her. It was a bloody long time ago,' Rice said.

'Do you know if there was anything between her and Gerry Doyle?' Nick asked.

As always, Nick was following the lead.

'No, sorry. I can't remember anything like that.'

Ruth nodded as she shifted in her seat. 'What about Mark Fisher? Did you know him?'

Rice's face couldn't hide his recognition of the name. 'Yeah. Guitarist. Did a lot of session work here. Bloody talented from what I remember.'

'Did Mark Fisher and Gerry Doyle ever work together?' Nick asked.

Rice paused as he thought. 'I don't think so, but as I said, that would have been at least fifteen, twenty years ago, if not longer.'

'And did you ever see Gerry Doyle and Mark Fisher at the same parties here?' Ruth asked.

Rice shook his head. 'I'm really sorry. It's all a bit of a blur. Quite likely though. We've only got two major studios here.'

'Do you remember if there were any complaints about Mark Fisher around the same time?' Ruth asked.

'There were rumours, but nothing more than that. I've got some old photos I could dig out if that would help?' Rice said.

Ruth nodded. 'Yeah, thank you. That would be useful. Thanks for your time, Mr Rice.'

They had established a very possible connection between Gerry Doyle and Mark Fisher. Now they needed to find Zoe Tardelli, or Nicole Lace if that was the new name she was going by.

.   .   .

SIAN AND FRENCH WERE MAKING THEIR WAY TO SPEAK TO Derek Harrison about why he had lied about his whereabouts on the Sunday morning that Mark Fisher was murdered.

As Sian looked out of the passenger window, she could see a small huddle of enormous trees on the dip of the Ceiriog Valley. The light of the day was beginning to fade, and the trees stood proudly silhouetted against the sky that was now turning into a wash of pinks and plum beyond the ridges. It reminded her of being taken on holiday by her *taid* and *nain*. They stayed in a little cottage on the Wales and Shropshire borders. Sian and her brother would play for hours in the fields with their taid's dark brown cocker spaniel, Brandy. One morning, a local farmer offered to take them up to his farm to watch the cows being milked. She must have only been seven or eight, and her brother was younger. Without a care in the world, they hopped into his filthy blue Land Rover and drove away to the farm. The track had been full of bumps and dips – the jolts threw them around the car. She and her brother howled with laughter. The farmer had filthy hands and a long cut across the back of his hand that was bleeding and full of dirt. Sian remembered being amazed that the farmer just didn't seem bothered. He just chortled when she mentioned it. They watched the cows being milked by machines and even tasted some of the warm, fresh milk. Then the farmer popped them home.

Sian's taid, Owen, had gone mad at them. It was a dangerous, reckless thing to have done. Sian and her brother cried. They just wanted to go and see the cows being milked. However, she thought back on it with mixed feelings. How lovely it was to have been that innocent and trusting that they could just go and enjoy the experience with no sense of suspicion or fear. Sian also shuddered when she thought about how their little trip in the Land Rover could have taken a far darker turn.

'Where the hell were Derek and Craig Harrison rushing to or from at five-thirty on a Sunday morning?' French blurted out, breaking Sian's train of thought.

'God knows. They might have been on their way from murdering Mark Fisher?' Sian replied.

'Yeah … But how do they link to Gerry Doyle though?' Sian asked.

'No idea yet,' French said as he turned onto the drive of the Harrisons' home.

Ten minutes later, Sian and French were sitting in the well-presented living room opposite Derek Harrison. His face was drawn and grey, his eyes blue but milky.

'I'm so sorry for your loss,' Sian said in a gentle tone. Derek Harrison had lost both his children in tragic circumstances and he looked like a man who had lost all hope. She couldn't work out if he was the kind of man who could have hunted down Mark Fisher and murdered him.

'Is this really necessary?' Derek asked quietly. 'My wife has taken Craig's death very badly.'

'I'm sorry to hear that. There are a couple of things we need to clarify with you if you can,' French said.

'Yes, right. Get it out of the way. I have spoken to uniformed officers already and given a statement,' Derek said, getting short-tempered.

'It won't take more than a few minutes,' Sian said, giving him an empathetic look.

'Fine. Craig turned up here yesterday morning ranting like a madman. I think he was on drugs, but I suppose you'll be able to tell me that. He took a shotgun out of that cabinet. I tried to stop him, but he pushed me to the floor. Then he left and told me that he intended to be with his sister. And then … well, you know the rest …' Derek pursed his lips, looking upset.

Sian shot French a look – that's not why they were there. Derek Harrison had clearly got the wrong end of the stick when she had spoken to him earlier.

'Mr Harrison, we're actually here to talk to you about last Sunday's events,' French said cautiously.

'Last Sunday?' Derek said, screwing up his face. 'What about last Sunday? I told DI Hunter where I was.'

'I'm afraid we've just spoken to Mr Bird and he doesn't remember seeing you walking the dog last Sunday morning,' Sian explained.

'What? Then the man's an idiot!' Derek thundered.

'Mr Bird told us that he saw you in a car with your son, Craig, driving at speed at about five-thirty last Sunday morning,' French said.

Derek processed what had been said. Then he shook his head. 'Nonsense! That's just not true!'

'He seemed very certain about it,' Sian said.

Derek Harrison got up out of the armchair and glared at them. 'Are you going to arrest me?'

'No, sir. We just came to ask you where you were last Sunday morning,' French said.

'I've told you. If you don't believe me, then that isn't my problem. And unless you're going to arrest me, I would like you to leave my house now,' Derek growled.

Sian looked at French and they got up to go.

'I'm afraid that does mean that we will be back to talk to you again. And I do have to warn you that might be under caution,' Sian said calmly.

'Don't worry. I have no intention of talking to you again without my solicitor present,' Derek said.

'IF WE'RE LOOKING FOR WHAT LINKS OUR TWO VICTIMS, then The Mill Recording Studios is it. Gerry Doyle worked there for years. Mark Fisher also worked there as a session guitarist. They had to know each other,' Ruth explained.

Ruth had been updating Drake on the two murder cases for ten minutes, keeping him up to speed.

'And we know that both men liked teenage girls. I'm assuming that somewhere like The Mill was awash with young groupies back in the day?' Drake said.

'From the sounds of it,' Ruth said.

'How does that lead to them both being murdered?' Drake asked.

'Zoe Tardelli was allegedly raped by Mark Fisher in 1997 at a party in North Wales when she was fourteen. Micky Rice at The Mill remembers her from around then and says she spent time at the studio partying. Maybe something happened with Gerry Doyle too?' Ruth suggested. This was all speculation, but Ruth was confident that this is what linked both the victims. To her relief, she felt that they were finally making progress in the investigation.

'And Zoe Tardelli killed them both, trying to make it look like a suicide?' Drake asked.

'It's the only thing that links our two victims at the moment, boss.'

'Why now?' Drake asked.

It was a good question, Ruth thought to herself.

'We think that Zoe Tardelli might have been out of the country. She has certainly been keeping a very low profile. No taxes, council tax, benefits. And then she popped up on

Facebook three months ago with a new name, Nicole Lace. Maybe she thought it was time she got revenge for what they did to her back then?' Ruth suggested.

'Have you managed to track her down?' Drake asked.

'Not yet. But we'll find her,' Ruth said confidently.

Drake's mobile phone rang. She could see from his face that it was important but as she stood to go, he signalled for her to stay seated by raising his finger to show that he would be with her in a moment.

Gazing around the office, she spotted the large photo that featured Drake, his wife and his two daughters. They were a beautiful family, no doubt about it. Ruth wondered if she was about to press self-destruct on her own family?

Drake rubbed his hand over his shaved head and then let out an audible breath, Ruth could see that he was feeling emotional.

Nodding his head, Drake hung up the mobile phone and looked over at her.

'All clear …' Drake said with his voice breaking a little. His large fingers reached up to the corner of one eye to wipe away a tear. 'She's all clear. No cancer … It's gone.'

'That's brilliant. I'm so glad,' Ruth said as she smiled at him across the desk.

Drake took a deep breath and let it out slowly. 'Sorry … I just …'

'Don't apologise. I know how much it's been worrying you, boss,' Ruth said sitting forward.

'Thank you, Ruth,' Drake said. She could see he really meant it.

Chapter 14

Ruth and Nick had been called in to Llancastell University Hospital mortuary just after briefing. Doctor Amis told Ruth that there was something significant in the full post-mortems of the two faked suicides that she needed to see.

Both Mark Fisher and Gerry Doyle's porcelain white cadavers had been laid out on gurneys at either end of the ice-cold room. They had been sawn open and their major organs examined and weighed.

Amis beckoned them over to Mark Fisher's body and showed them a Perspex slide with tiny particles of white on it.

'Two things. Firstly, we've retrieved a few of these particles from the victim's hair,' Amis explained.

'What is it?' Ruth asked.

'Not dandruff, but I'm not sure. It's a chalk-like substance so I'll get it analysed,' Amis said.

'Right. You said two things, Tony?' Ruth asked.

'I wanted to show you this,' Amis said, pointing to an area behind Mark Fisher's ear.

Ruth peered closely, but all she could see was the milky skin that was tinged with the faintest blue hue. She could also see that Fisher's earlobe had been pierced a couple of times. 'What exactly am I looking at?'

Putting his finger on the neck, Amis pointed to a minute dot on the skin. It was virtually impossible to see.

'What is it?' Nick asked.

Needle mark, Ruth immediately thought to herself. She had seen enough dead junkies in South London to recognise the spot where someone had been injected. Heroin addicts would inject themselves anywhere to hide their habit – in between toes, under fingernails and even the scrotum.

'It's the mark made by a needle from a syringe,' Amis explained.

Knew it. Ten points for being a know-it-all, Ruth thought.

'Did he do it?' Nick said with a furrowed brow.

'I doubt it. From that angle, I can't believe that our victim injected himself,' Amis said. 'My educated guess is that someone else did it.'

'Do we know when the mark was made?' Ruth asked.

'From the depth of the mark and the lack of healing, it would have to be at a similar time to when the victim was murdered,' Amis said.

'Is the toxicology report back?' Nick asked.

'About an hour ago,' Amis said as he wandered away to his desk to grab the report. 'Couple of things that might help us.'

'We're all ears,' Ruth said.

'There is alcohol in Mark Fisher's blood. But the strange thing is that his blood alcohol concentration was only point zero seven,' Amis explained.

'What does that mean?' Ruth asked.

'Too drunk to drive but certainly not falling-down

drunk. I've also analysed the vodka that we found in the victim's stomach. It still has an extremely high alcohol content – far higher than I would expect from someone having a late-night tipple or three – which means that it hadn't been absorbed into the bloodstream.'

'Why would that happen?' Nick asked.

'My guess is that the vodka arrived in the victim's stomach after he was dead. The heart was no longer working and so the alcohol stayed where it was and was never absorbed,' Amis said.

'Someone poured it down his throat after he was dead,' Ruth said, thinking out loud.

'Make it look like he was hammered and committed suicide,' Nick said.

'What else does the report tell us?' Ruth said.

Amis gestured to the toxicology report again. 'Mark Fisher also had remarkably high concentrations of propofol and etomidate in his blood.'

'Which are?' Ruth asked.

'They are an immensely powerful combination of drugs used as a general anaesthetic,' Amis explained.

'Not available over the counter at Boots then?' quipped Nick.

'No. Whoever injected Mark Fisher had access to drugs in a medical setting and was probably medically trained,' Amis said.

'Why do you think medically trained?' Ruth asked.

'The injection went straight into the jugular vein. It would have rendered our victim unconscious in less than two seconds. It takes medical skill to do that precisely,' Amis explained.

Ruth and Nick looked at each other – at least that narrowed down the range of suspects. Helen McCarthy and Derek Harrison – a nurse and GP, respectively.

'However, if we go over to our other victim,' Amis said, ushering them down to the other end of the mortuary.

Ruth and Nick followed Amis down to Gerry Doyle's body.

'He was also injected in the neck …'

Same MO. And that establishes another direct link between our victims, Ruth thought. *That's progress.*

'Exactly the same?' Nick asked with a raised eyebrow.

'Almost. The drugs are similar. Medical-grade tranquilliser,' Amis said.

'What's different?' Ruth asked.

'The way this victim was injected,' Amis said as he pointed to the mark on Gerry Doyle's neck. 'The site of the injection is much higher. It missed all the veins and arteries and the needle tip hit the jawbone. There is also some bruising to the skin where the needle went in, which shows that it was delivered with great force but little accuracy.'

'So what does that tell us?' Nick asked.

'I can't tell you categorically, but the evidence suggests that the injections weren't carried out by the same person. So, you might be looking for two different people.'

The excitement Ruth had felt at their near breakthrough fizzled out. That's not what they wanted to hear.

A WAFT OF COFFEE AND CHIPS CAME IN FROM INCIDENT Room One as Ruth sat at her desk in the DI's office. The case was driving her mad. It felt like for every step they took forwards, they were taking two back or one to the side. The focus of the investigation kept shifting, which meant that the homicide team were feeling confused. They were looking to Ruth for guidance, but she was as frustrated as they were. They just had to stick to the basic principles of detection and at some point, they would get to the truth. At least, she hoped that's how it would work.

Ruth stared at the computer screen in front of her. As a way of distraction, she had spent the last twenty minutes writing, deleting and rewriting an email to Jamie Parsons. She didn't know what to address in the details of the email and what to leave for a conversation. She had decided to go for short and succinct.

Dear Jamie,

Thank you for getting in touch. This is obviously a very emotive subject for me. However, I do think it would be good to meet up as there are lots of questions that I need answering. I also think that meeting face to face would be more beneficial than a telephone conversation. Maybe you can suggest some dates? I can come to London if that works better?

Kind regards,

Ruth

For some reason, Ruth felt going to London to meet Jamie Parsons was preferable to him coming anywhere near her new life. Her finger hovered close to the button to send it. She stopped. She would have another read through it after briefing.

Closing the email, Ruth took her case files, came out of her office and headed for the centre of the room beside the crime scene boards.

'Right, everyone, if we can get on with this, please?' Ruth said, raising her voice above the chatter.

Glancing up, Ruth saw Drake entering. He gestured at her and sat down. She could see that the good news about his wife Paula's cancer was a huge weight off his shoulders.

However, did that mean he might be looking for a new challenge or a fresh start in a different police force?

'What we are looking for is the solid connection between our two victims,' Ruth said. 'Nick and I spoke to the pathologist this morning. Mark Fisher and Gerry Doyle were both injected in the neck with tranquillisers or anaesthetics that would have rendered them unconscious very quickly. However, the pathologist also thought that the injections were made by two different people.'

Some of the team exchanged confused looks. The recording studio had appeared to be the link, but this evidence was making things more confusing, rather than clarifying.

'And these drugs were medical grade. Not something you could have bought in a chemist,' Nick said.

'Derek Harrison is a retired GP, but we don't have anything to link him to Gerry Doyle. Any explanation about why he was driving with Craig Harrison early on Sunday morning or why he lied to us about his whereabouts?'

Sian shook her head. 'He's not willing to say anything else until he has a solicitor present.'

'That's okay. Pull him in for a formal interview. Check his bank records and see if we can get anything on his phone. He's hiding something from us,' Ruth said decisively.

'We're also getting a key so we can look around Craig Harrison's flat this morning, boss,' French said.

'Good work.' Ruth pointed up to a photo of Helen McCarthy, Max McCarthy's sister, dressed in her nurses' uniform. 'Helen McCarthy works at University Hospital and has access to all sorts of drugs. Have we checked her alibi yet?'

Dan looked up. 'Yes, boss. Alibi checks out. She was in

Glasgow.'

'Okay. That seems to rule her out.'

'Sorry, boss. But I thought Zoe Tardelli was our prime suspect because of what had happened up at The Mill Studios?' French said, looking confused.

'Are we changing the focus of the investigation?' Sian asked.

Ruth shook her head – she wished she had a simple answer.

'I'm going to level with you. There is something about these murder cases that doesn't add up at the moment. We have three lines of enquiry that we are pursuing. We have to apply methodical detective work to all of them and hope that we can start to eliminate suspects. You're a brilliant team and if we're patient, I know we're going to get to the truth of who killed these men. I know it's frustrating, but in twenty-five years as a copper, I've never worked on an investigation quite like this one,' Ruth said. She looked up at the photo of Zoe Tardelli, or Nicole Lace, as she might now be known. 'Now, what about our elusive friend, Zoe Tardelli? Please tell me we have *something* to go on.'

'Madame Nicole Lace?' Nick said in a mock sultry voice. There was laughter.

Ruth could see that her little pep talk had calmed everyone and given them a bit of a confidence boost.

Sian shook her head. 'Nothing, boss.'

Ruth took a step back to look at the scene boards. 'I'm not getting it. We have strong motives for both of these men to be murdered. And I'm convinced that someone on this board had a motive to kill the both of them. We just don't know who.'

. . .

An hour later, Sian and French were making their way out to Craig Harrison's flat for a quick search. If he and his father had been on their way to murder Mark Fisher last Sunday morning, there might be something at the flat that could help the investigation. Until there was something obvious, Ruth had told them to hold off bringing in SOCO.

As French slowed for the turning to Pontfadog, Sian realised that she had been out to the small village before. It was within the Ceiriog Valley, west of Chirk and part of the community of Glyntraian. It had been built to house workers in the nearby quarries. The name Pontfadog translated as 'Bridge of Madoc'; the village had an old stone bridge over the River Ceiriog – it was this that Sian recognised.

'I've been out here before,' Sian said. The case came flooding back to her.

'Really?' French asked, arching his eyebrow. He had a point – Pontfadog was in the middle of nowhere.

'We were called to a burglary. By the time me and the sergeant got to the house, there was no one inside. But there was a broken back window. So we go upstairs for a quick look around, and there's a neat pool of blood on the landing carpet. As we're looking at it, a drop of blood comes sailing down past my ear and lands on the carpet.'

'What?' French said, pulling a face.

'We look up and see a closed hatch to the attic. The blood is in the direct line of it,' Sian explained.

'Your burglar's hiding up there?' French asked.

'Yeah. He's cut his arm getting through the window. I turn to my sarge and say, "Looks like he's gone, Sarge. We'll call it in and get going."'

'My sarge plays along. "Yeah. Come on, we'll get back to the station."'

'So we head down the stairs, open and close the front door and wait in silence in the hallway. Two minutes later, we hear the twat open the hatch and drop down. He comes down the stairs, sees us. I say, "Hello…" He screams and tries to run up the stairs again. He's got nowhere to go. He trips over, falls back down the stairs and we cuff him,' Sian said, laughing.

French snorted. 'What an idiot!'

'I know. Most of the time, we're dealing with morons. Not like on the telly where they're all criminal masterminds.'

French nodded and pulled the car over, parking outside a small row of shops that clearly made up the centre of the small rural village. Above them, Sian could see the dark green slopes of Ceiriog Valley that rose steeply against the cold grey sky.

A cold wind zipped noisily through the nearby trees, shaking them. The painkillers had taken away the ache of her back but had left her feeling numb all over. She was finding it hard to focus.

Sian and French had collected the keys to Craig Harrison's flat from the family solicitor in Llancastell.

Pushing the brass key into the lock, French opened the door to the flat – it was stiff. The hallway was piled high with post and junk mail. As Sian pushed down on her crutch and hobbled inside, she was met by the stench of sour milk and weed.

Jesus! That's disgusting!

Suddenly, Sian heard a noise from within the flat. The sound of something being dropped and smashing.

She shot a look at French. *There's someone in the flat? Could be family or a friend?*

'Hello? It's North Wales Police. Anyone there?' Sian called out as she rested her weight on the metallic crutch.

A rapid increase in noise and commotion but no response; distinctly suspicious. French looked at her and motioned towards what she assumed was the living room.

'Hello! North Wales Police,' French said loudly.

Sian was now a little concerned.

Getting to the door, French shoved it open with a bang.

Sian and French looked in from the doorway. Two men were trying to clamber out of an open window. They wore black balaclavas and black jackets. The living room had been turned upside down and smashed to pieces.

They were definitely looking for something.

Sian was startled as her heart started to thump. 'Police! Stay where you are!'

She suddenly became very aware of how vulnerable she was with her crutch and general immobility. She wasn't so certain she'd get out of this unharmed.

One of the men had already levered himself out of the large ground-floor window. The other looked back at her as he swung his leg outside.

At least they're going to do a runner and don't want to get into a fight, she thought.

French sprinted, launched himself over the sofa and got to the window.

'Oh, God! Be careful, Dan!' Sian shouted as she tried to follow him.

'Stay there!' French yelled back as he managed to grab the jacket of the man as he tried to run.

The man swung his gloved fist and hit French on the side of the head. French fell backwards onto the floor.

'You okay?' Sian said, going over to him as French sat up, looking dazed.

Sian noticed a patio door and tried it. Nothing. She twisted the key and opened it. As a pain shot up her back and into her left shoulder, she shuffled onto a patio.

She caught sight of the second man sitting astride an eight-foot fence. Throwing his leg over, the man dropped out of sight down the other side.

'Oi! Stay there. Police!' Sian shouted, although she didn't know what she was going to do if he did.

Sian looked at the fence. *Well, I won't be getting over that, will I?*

There was the grumbling sound of a car engine starting close by. Moving a green wheelie bin that was covered with a black bin liner out of the way, Sian leaned against the fence. There was a gap between the wooden panels that she could see through.

Sian watched as the man reached a small blue Citroën. He got in, slammed the passenger door and the car did a noisy U-turn and sped away.

Bollocks! I can't even see the plate properly from here!

Sian saw French approaching.

'I should have ducked really,' French said sardonically.

'Sure you're okay?' Sian asked.

'As my nain would say, where there's no sense, there's no feeling,' French said with a smirk.

'Control from four-eight,' Sian said into her Tetra radio.

'Go ahead, four-eight.'

'All units. Suspect vehicle, blue Citroën C-three. Partial plate, Yankee-foxtrot, Yankee. Suspects in a burglary and assault. Heading away from Pontfadog. Could be going to Llancastell, over,' Sian said as she and French came back into the living room from the patio.

'Request received, four-eight.'

Looking around at the mess, it was obvious the two men had been looking for something. The fact that Sian and French had disturbed them meant it was likely that they hadn't found it.

'What the bloody hell were they looking for?' French asked to no one in particular.

They both took their purple forensic gloves from their pockets, snapped them on and began to sift through some of the stuff.

'Whatever it was, they were willing to take a huge risk trying to get it,' Sian said.

'Drugs or money?' French said as he cast his eyes around.

'Usually is,' Sian said. The more she worked with DC Dan French, the more she could see that he was going to make a bloody good detective. In fact, his instinct on various cases had made her feel a little insecure about her own ability.

However, it was in that second that Sian thought of the bin outside. Why was there a bin bag secured over the top of it?

Someone needs to keep whatever is in the bin dry!

'The bin …' Sian said as she hobbled towards the door to the patio.

'Eh?' French said as he walked beside her.

Getting to the green wheelie bin, Sian ripped away the brown masking tape that secured the plastic sheeting to the top. 'Who needs to keep their rubbish dry?'

French gave her a helping hand and a knowing smile. 'No one, unless you're keeping something else in there instead.'

Flipping the lid open, Sian peered inside and then pulled out her torch. There were objects in the bottom, but she needed to see them clearly.

In the torch's beam, Sian could see two bags, both the size of a house brick. And then she got a strong smell of what was inside.

'Weed,' French said.

Sian nodded. 'Yeah. That's about ten thousand pounds worth of cannabis.'

French looked at her. 'So that's what they were looking for.'

Chapter 15

R uth glanced out into Incident Room One, which was busy with detectives on the phone or at their computers. With her finger poised, Ruth took one last look at the email she had composed to Jamie Parsons and then pressed return to send it.

There! Done it! No going back, she thought.

She was hit by a wave of anxiety now it had been sent. She had thrown a grenade and just had to wait for it to explode. What was she going to say if they met? What was she going to ask him? Ruth knew that she needed to know everything, however hurtful that proved to be.

Ruth had a sudden realisation. Her birthday in the summer of 2013. They went out with friends to a bar in Fulham. It had been a fantastic evening full of laughter and drinks. On the way home, Ruth and Sarah had walked hand in hand along the King's Road and, even though it was gone ten o'clock, the summer sky was still a translucent blue. Cutting down to Chelsea Embankment, they walked across Albert Bridge. It was one of Ruth's favourite sights in London: a magnificent Victorian suspension bridge with four thousand lights strung across its vast structure. As they reached the middle, they stopped and looked east up the Thames. They kissed and admitted that they were blissfully happy.

Recalling this, Ruth felt a lump come into her throat. And then she wiped a tear away. Her realisation was that Sarah had been having an affair with Jamie Parsons at the time. It made her feel so let down, so angry and yet sickeningly sad at the same time. She took a deep breath and closed her eyes for a second.

There was a knock at the door, which broke Ruth's train of thought. It was Nick. She tried to compose herself, but he could see she was upset.

'You okay, boss?' Nick asked.

'Yeah, yeah, fine. What's up?' Ruth asked.

'I need your mince pies on this, boss,' Nick said with a glimmer of a grin.

'Don't use cockney rhyming slang, Nick. It sounds very weird in a Welsh accent,' Ruth said, now smiling and feeling relieved to be distracted.

Nick took her over to his computer screen. She could see he had been studying CCTV from a supermarket car park.

'What are we looking at?' Ruth asked.

'I'm trying to trace Mark Fisher's movements on the days leading up to his murder. I got one hit on the ANPR. He went to this supermarket on the Friday. And I'm trawling through when I spot this ...' Nick said as he pointed to the screen.

Ruth could see Mark Fisher leaving the supermarket with a carrier bag and heading across the car park. She couldn't see anything.

'What am I looking at?' Ruth asked.

Nick pointed to a woman in a baseball cap standing by a row of trolleys. She is clearly waiting for someone.

'This woman here. Watch what she does as Mark Fisher comes out,' Nick said.

As Nick played the footage forward, and as Mark Fisher emerges from the main entrance, the woman seems to follow him at a distance across the car park. She then takes out a mobile phone and dials it as she is walking.

'She's following him, isn't she?' Ruth said.

'Yeah. Unfortunately, we don't have any clear footage of her face,' Nick explained.

'Where does she go?' Ruth said.

Nick played the footage on for a few seconds. 'She gets into this car here and then follows Fisher out of the car park.'

Nick paused the CCTV footage to show that a dirty old Rover had pulled out behind Fisher's small Renault Clio and was now following him out of the car park.

'Can you see the plate?' Ruth asked.

'Yeah. I ran it through the PNC but it doesn't exist,' Nick explained.

'False plates,' Ruth said, thinking out loud. It was surprising as it was usually only organised criminals that used false number plates.

'Must be …' Nick said.

Ruth looked again at the footage. 'Is that the best image of the plate we've got, or can you zoom in?'

Nick clicked the mouse, the image juddered, and then showed a close-up of the Rover's plate. It was barely visible through the dirt.

FL56 WDA?

Ruth squinted. 'Foxtrot-Lima-five-six, whisky-delta-alpha?'

Nick nodded. 'That's it.'

Ruth looked again. 'What if that 'L' isn't an 'L'? I think that's dirt at the bottom there.'

'Which makes it an 'I'?' Nick said as he logged onto the PNC to do another number plate search.

'Let's see if we get a hit on that?' Ruth said.

After a second, Nick gave her a meaningful look. 'If it is an 'I', then that car is registered to a Helen McCarthy, thirty-two Crescent Lane, Llancastell.'

'What?' Ruth said, remembering that Helen McCarthy was the nurse they had questioned at the hospital.

Helen McCarthy? That doesn't make any sense!

'I don't get it, boss. Why would Helen McCarthy be following Mark Fisher?' Nick asked.

'No idea. I suppose we'd better go and ask her.'

'YOU NEED TO TELL US WHERE YOU WERE GOING WITH Craig at five-thirty in the morning last Sunday in such a hurry?' Sian asked, starting to feel frustrated.

She and French had been interviewing Derek Harrison at Llancastell nick for about ten minutes. They weren't getting very far. Even though it was a voluntary interview, Harrison had brought his solicitor whom he had consulted in hushed tones on several occasions already.

The solicitor peered over his glasses at Sian and pulled a supercilious expression.

Definitely a bit of a twat, she decided.

'As I understand it, my client has broken no laws. He is currently grieving for his son, who died tragically yesterday. If you do not have anything more substantial to ask Mr Harrison, then I ask that you allow him to leave here and be with his wife at this difficult time,' the solicitor said, holding his pen and waiting for Sian to answer.

'Mr Harrison. You lied to us about where you were last

Sunday morning. You must see why that would make us suspicious?' French asked in an appeasing tone.

'A lapse of memory doesn't constitute a lie, Constable,' Harrison replied.

'If you merely forgot, then you won't mind telling us where you were going?' French said.

'It was a personal matter and one I'm not willing to discuss,' Harrison said.

'This is a murder enquiry, Mr Harrison. You and Craig both have a very good motive to murder Mark Fisher. You were seen together, speeding away from the area where the murder took place, close to the time that Mark Fisher was killed. When questioned, you failed to remember what you had been doing on Sunday morning. And you are not willing to tell us what you were doing?' Sian asked.

'I can assure you that neither I nor Craig had anything to do with that man's death,' Harrison said.

'You used to work as a GP, didn't you, Mr Harrison?' French asked.

'Yes, that's right. Just over forty years,' Harrison replied.

'And that would have given you access to drugs and medical supplies, wouldn't it?' French asked.

'Yes, of course it did,' Harrison said, now sounding tetchy.

'I'm guessing you still have certain drugs from your time as a GP in your possession?' French asked.

Harrison leaned over and conferred with his solicitor and then looked at French. 'No comment.'

Jesus Christ! Are you really going to go 'No comment' now?

They really were getting nowhere.

.   .   .

Ruth and Nick marched down the corridor at University Hospital.

Nick nodded and pointed up to the Bunbridge Ward where Helen McCarthy worked.

'Here we go.'

Having used the hand sanitiser on the wall, Ruth and Nick arrived at the nurses' station that sat between two wards.

'DI Hunter and DS Evans from Llancastell CID. We're looking for Helen McCarthy?' Ruth said. The idea was to give Helen no warning before they interviewed her about why she had followed Mark Fisher out of a supermarket car park.

The nurses exchanged concerned looks.

What was that all about? Ruth thought.

'Is there a problem?' she asked, picking up on their apprehension.

'I'll just go and get the ward sister,' a young nurse said as she walked over to an open door and knocked.

The ward sister, tall and well into her sixties, appeared and approached.

'Can I help?' she asked.

Ruth showed her warrant card again.

'We just needed a chat with Helen McCarthy. This is the right ward, isn't it?' Ruth asked.

The ward sister gestured for them to follow her. 'If you could just come into my office for a moment.' She closed the door behind them. 'I'm afraid Helen McCarthy isn't at work today. Is it something I can help with?'

There is definitely something up here, Ruth thought.

'I'm afraid not. We need to speak to her directly,' Nick explained.

'Can you tell us why Helen isn't at work?' Ruth asked.

The ward sister looked awkward. 'She's been suspended.'

'Can you tell us why?' Ruth asked.

'I'm not sure I'm at liberty to divulge that information. You might need to talk to our HR department?' the ward sister said, looking worried.

'I understand that you're only doing your job. But this is a murder investigation. And as soon as we go to HR, they will have to tell us what is going on. So, it would be very helpful and save us a lot of time if you just tell us why Helen was suspended,' Ruth said with the utmost patience.

The ward sister considered what Ruth had said. 'Helen was allegedly caught stealing medical supplies and drugs from the hospital,' the ward sister said quietly.

Bloody hell.

Chapter 16

Gazing out at the garden in the darkness, Ruth sipped at her red wine and then lit a cigarette. She took the blanket from off her lap and draped it over her shoulders. Then she ran the evidence for the investigation over in her head. The multiple lines of enquiry were frustrating. Just when she thought they had a prime suspect and a focus for the case, more evidence was unearthed that shifted that focus to what was an entirely different story.

Ruth was now wondering how and why Helen McCarthy and Mark Fisher were linked? Why had she been following him? Her motive to kill Gerry Doyle was clear. In her eyes, he had 'murdered' her brother. But her interest in Mark Fisher was a mystery. Until they got a list of the drugs she had stolen from the hospital, there was little to go on. However, Ruth couldn't help but think about the toxicology reports for both Mark Fisher and Gerry Doyle that showed traces of anaesthetic drugs that would only be available to someone in a medical setting.

Ruth checked her phone again for emails. She couldn't

count the number of times she'd already looked since hitting send. It was bordering on compulsive. Now she had sent the email to Jamie Parsons, she had the anxious wait to see if and when he replied. Still nothing in her inbox. She turned it off and put it down on the side table.

Ruth watched outside as the wind whipped the brittle leaves around on the patio and grass. Someone was having a bonfire somewhere nearby and there was a faint hint of it in the air.

'Clown' by Emile Sandé was playing on the stereo. The taste of heavy red wine, the music, the autumnal light and skitter of leaves outside were powerfully redolent. Whether or not it had been deliberate, Ruth was transported back to the autumn of 2013. The Saturday before Sarah had gone missing, they had been to a friend's bonfire party in Peckham. Drinking warm cider, swirling sparklers in the darkness of night, spelling out swear words and howling with laughter.

Ruth allowed herself to visit those memories once in a while, even though it sometimes left her drained. That was the problem with grief. She could spend a day at work or with Sian and forget. And then, in a solitary, reflective moment, she would be caught off guard as she accepted the thundering realisation that Sarah had vanished and no one knew what had happened to her.

Just as Ruth moved to stand to go and get more wine, her phone buzzed. With her pulse quickening, Ruth opened her email app to see a message waiting for her from Jamie Parsons.

DEAR RUTH,

I have a completely free weekend this weekend. I know it's short notice, but we could meet during the day on Saturday. Otherwise, I'm away on business for a few months. If you are getting the train down to Euston, we could meet at the café in the British Library?

Best wishes,

Jamie

RUTH BLINKED AS HER HEAD RACED. SHE DIDN'T WANT TO wait months to meet. This weekend though? Maybe a phone call would do? But instinct told her to meet Parsons face to face. However, unless the murder cases were solved by then, she might find it hard to get a day off. It was rare for the SIO not to be available all day, every day.

DEAR JAMIE,

I'm in the middle of a big investigation but I am really keen to meet with you as soon as possible. The café at the British Library sounds like a sensible place to meet. Could you do Sunday instead? It gives me an extra day on the case.

Kind regards,

Ruth

THE PATIO DOORS FROM THE LIVING ROOM OPENED. SIAN came out, using her stick to aid her walking. She had been in the bath and was dressed in a huge baby-blue dressing gown with a pink towel wrapped around her head. She smiled at Ruth as she came out, which only served to make Ruth feel more guilty.

'Evening, gorgeous,' Sian said as she hobbled over, gave her a kiss and then sat next to her.

'Have you done your exercises?' Ruth asked in a slightly maternal voice, hoping to change the uncomfortable way she was feeling.

'I thought you might help me?' Sian said with a cheeky smile. It only served to make Ruth feel more shameful at keeping things from Sian.

'Yeah … Of course,' Ruth said, but her mind was drawn back to the email. She couldn't help herself.

'Everything okay?' Sian asked.

Ruth nodded, eager to hide her distraction. 'Yes, of course. Why?'

'Last few days, you seem to be away with the fairies,' Sian said.

Ruth shook her head. 'No. Not at all. It's just this investigation. Nothing seems to fit.'

Sian rested her head on Ruth's shoulder. She could smell the freshness of the shower gel and shampoo.

Ruth stroked her hair. 'That new shampoo smells amazing.'

'You can always talk to me, you know that, don't you?' Sian said.

Ruth smiled. 'Yeah, course. Thanks.'

Chapter 17

'Can you tell us what your connection is to Mark Fisher?' Ruth asked.

She and Nick had been interviewing Helen McCarthy at her home for a few minutes. Helen looked extremely nervous as she sat opposite them in the small lounge of her one-bedroom flat. Dotted around the room were various photographs of Helen that either featured her climbing mountains or at their summits with glorious views of the landscape behind.

Ruth watched as Helen furrowed her brow. 'Mark Fisher? I don't know who that is.'

Bullshit! You followed him out of the car park!

Nick frowned as he looked up from his notepad. 'Helen, are you sure you don't know who Mark Fisher is?' he said quietly.

Delving into her file, Ruth pulled out several stills from CCTV footage they had retrieved from the supermarket.

'This is you by the trolley station, isn't it?' Ruth said as she turned the photograph around for Helen to see. 'This person in the baseball cap is you, isn't it, Helen?'

Helen gave it a cursory glance. 'I don't know. It could be, I suppose.'

She's too nervous to even look at it, Ruth thought.

'Do you own a pink Adidas baseball cap?' Nick asked.

Helen thought about her answer. 'Yes, I think so.'

'You think you own a pink Adidas baseball cap, but you don't know?' Nick said, trying not to sound sarcastic.

'No … I do. Yes …' Helen stammered.

Ruth took out another photograph and showed her. 'And this man, who is Mark Fisher, comes out of the supermarket and you follow him across the car park while making a phone call.'

Helen shook her head. 'No. I was just going back to my car. I told you, I don't know anyone called Mark Fisher.'

Stop lying to us, Helen. What are you hiding?

Ruth then showed her another image. 'And this is your car?'

Helen leaned forwards and narrowed her eyes to take a closer look. 'Yes. That is my car.'

'And this vehicle here is Mark Fisher in his car. You're directly behind him,' Ruth said, pointing to the photograph.

'If I am, then that's a complete coincidence,' Helen said with an uneasy shrug.

'Mark Fisher was murdered last Sunday morning,' Nick said, looking up from his notebook.

Helen looked at them blankly and blinked.

'Where were you last weekend between midnight Saturday and six o'clock on Sunday morning?' Ruth asked.

'I don't know. I guess I was here asleep,' Helen said.

'Is there anyone that can verify that for us?' Nick asked.

'No, sorry, I was on my own,' Helen said with a slight tremor in her voice.

She's definitely lying, but what's the connection to Mark Fisher?

'Who did you phone from the car park?' Ruth asked.

'I can't remember,' Helen said, lacking conviction.

'Why don't you check your phone?' Ruth suggested.

'I'm not sure where it is,' Helen said.

'Really?' Nick said with a snort.

'No … I'm … sorry.' Helen looked down at the floor – it was getting too much for her.

Some people they interview, the pathological liars, show no sign of nerves. They are utterly convincing in the lies they tell – they don't believe they are lying most of the time. But others find it incredibly difficult. Their bodies react to the stress of not telling the truth – eyes that continuously move, sweat, red faces, short breaths. Helen McCarthy definitely fell into the latter category.

'You've been suspended from work, haven't you, Helen?' Ruth asked.

Helen nodded sheepishly, her eyes remaining fixed on the floor. The pressure was building.

'Why was that?' Nick asked.

'It was for … gross misconduct,' Helen replied.

That doesn't tell us anything.

'Helen, we know that you were suspended for stealing supplies and medication from the hospital,' Ruth said firmly.

Helen seemed to flinch at Ruth's statement.

'Yes. It was really … stupid.' It had now all got too much for her, and her eyes welled with tears. Then her shoulders juddered as she wept.

Ruth took a tissue from her pocket and handed it to her. 'Here you are.'

'Thank you,' Helen said, her hand shaking as she wiped her eyes and then her nose.

'What did you steal?' Ruth asked.

'Pain medication.'

'Why?' Ruth asked.

'I fell while rock climbing and injured my back a few years ago. I took painkillers for the pain. But when my back got better … I just carried on taking them,' Helen explained.

'How long have you been stealing pain medication?' Nick asked.

Helen looked at him. The game was up and she didn't have the wherewithal to lie anymore.

'Years …' She shook her head as if it was a relief to admit to it. 'Years and years. I can't get off them.'

Nick shot Ruth a look – he was all too aware of the pain of addiction.

'I'm going to need to see what you stole, Helen,' Ruth said.

Helen nodded, went off to the bathroom and placed an array of packets of painkillers and tranquillisers on the table.

Sian and French were making their way over to the police transport depot on the outskirts of Llancastell. Sian had checked the BMW specification for Craig Harrison's car, which had been in the possession of North Wales Police since his suicide. It was fitted with a GPS tracker so they hoped they could download the location information for its recent journeys; it could show them where Craig Harrison had driven on Sunday morning – and if he had been anywhere near where they had found Mark Fisher's body.

'Rather Be' by Clean Bandit came onto the radio and Sian turned it up. 'I love this song!'

'Clean Bandit,' French said.

Dan French has heard of Clean Bandit? Weird … Sian thought.

'How do you know that?' Sian asked.

'I went to university with them. Same college, actually …' French explained and then stopped.

'Erm, hang on. Rewind. Which college at which university?' Sian asked, knowing that the only universities that she knew of that had colleges were Oxford and Cambridge.

French looked at her awkwardly. 'Erm … Jesus College, Cambridge,' he said in a mumble.

'What?' Sian exclaimed. There weren't many DCs that even had a degree, let alone from Oxbridge.

'Yes. Sorry, is that a problem?' French said with a bemused, defensive smile.

'What did you study?' Sian asked. She couldn't remember if she had ever met anyone who had been to Cambridge University before.

'Law,' French answered.

Sian frowned. 'You've got a law degree from Cambridge. Next you'll tell me you got a first?'

Looking over at French, his face said it all.

'Bloody hell! You've got a first-class degree in law from Cambridge University. What are you doing as a constable in the North Wales Police?'

'I did two years in commercial law in London. It was horrendous and boring,' French explained.

'Bet the money was good?' Sian said.

'Yeah, it was amazing. But not worth it. Fifteen-hour days looking through the fine print of property contracts. I'm much, much happier doing this,' French said as he pulled into the police transport depot.

'Fair play to you, Dan,' Sian said, thinking of her own secondary education and sixth-form college in North

Wales.

Even though it shouldn't have made a difference, Sian saw French in a different light. Maybe it was the thought that he had turned down a six-figure salary to work as a police constable.

A FEW MINUTES LATER, SIAN AND FRENCH WERE SHOWN over to where Craig Harrison's white BMW X5 was being kept by the transport sergeant. The depot was noisy with the metallic sounds of a garage and the odd shout of police mechanics. The air smelt of oil and petrol. Sian knew this was also where the Forensic Collision Investigation team examined cars that had been used in crimes or had been in criminal road traffic accidents.

'That's it there,' the Sergeant said, pointing to the X5.

As the sun slid slowly from behind a cloud, the white paint of the X5 gleamed. It was a lovely looking car.

The sergeant opened the car with an electronic blip as the orange indicator lights flashed twice.

'Right. The Trackstar TM470 is the BMW-approved stolen car tracker. It has GPS, GSM and a movement sensor,' the sergeant said.

Sian groaned inwardly. *Oh God! He's a total car nerd!*

'As long as we can see where he was on Sunday morning and at the time of Gerry Doyle's death, we'll be happy, Sarge,' Sian said as she watched the sergeant open the door and get into the car.

As he started the engine, Sian and French went over and opened the passenger door to look at the screen on the dashboard.

Reaching over to click on the touchscreen, Sian saw the sergeant frown.

Not a good sign.

'The GPS has been turned off from here,' the sergeant explained.

Sian felt a little deflated and growled. 'So there's no way of us tracing where this vehicle was on Sunday morning?'

'Hold your horses, missy,' the Sergeant said, putting up his hand and turning off the engine.

Did he actually just call me 'missy'? Misogynistic twat ...

French gave her a look and stifled a laugh.

'The GPS antennae is housed just behind here,' the sergeant said, sounding like a teacher talking to his pupils.

Having pulled the dashboard away with a screwdriver, the sergeant began to rummage around pulling at various wires.

'Any luck?' French said with a bemused smile.

'I've got the antennae box, but the code has been changed by somebody. It's four numbers, but it's not the one installed with factory settings,' the sergeant explained. 'It might be written down somewhere in the car, or we're back to square one, I'm afraid.'

Sian reached up and pulled down the sun visor. Maybe someone had scrawled the new GPS code down somewhere in the car? She pulled down the driver's visor. Nothing.

As French went to the back of the car, Sian rummaged in the glove compartment and the compartments in the door.

Sian saw the sergeant slump in the driver's seat, grim-faced. 'Sorry, guys. Someone's completely dismantled the back of the antennae relay. I can't see that there's any way of you finding out where this car has been.'

Sian couldn't help but feel despondent. It could have provided a vital piece of evidence against Derek Harrison – or it could have eliminated him from the investigation.

French came to her side with a crumpled piece of paper in his hand. 'This was screwed up and in the back door.'

'Didn't you hear the sarge? In technical terms, the GPS is fucked, so we're fucked and we can't find out where the car has been.'

'Could you say "fucked" again?' French said with a grin as he unwrapped the piece of paper.

Sian could see that French's armour was coming down and he was starting to be himself.

French looked down at the paper and then at her. 'It's not a code. It's a banker's draft.'

'A banker's draft for who?' Sian asked, now interested.

'Derek Harrison withdrew ten thousand pounds in cash from his bank in Llancastell just over a week ago.'

RUTH AND NICK WERE HEADING ACROSS LLANCASTELL from Helen McCarthy's flat back to Llancastell Police Station.

'We had a little bit of a scare last night,' Nick confessed.

'That doesn't sound good. What happened?' Ruth asked.

'Amanda had these pains. Apparently, they're called Braxton Hicks? But I thought she was a soul singer,' Nick said with a grin.

'That's Tony Braxton, you twerp,' Ruth said rolling her eyes.

'Anyway, we rang the midwife and she said that false labour pains are normal,' Nick explained.

'Yeah. I had them all the time with Ella,' Ruth said.

'Bit of a wake-up call because I had about five miles of

petrol left in the car. Think I need to keep a full tank from now on,' Nick said.

As they stopped at a roundabout, Ruth checked her phone surreptitiously. She could see that there still hadn't been a reply from Jamie Parsons to her email. Maybe he had had second thoughts? Or he no longer wanted to meet her? Maybe he was busy? She could feel herself being drawn into swirling anxiety.

Wait. Be calm and try to put it to one side, Ruth said to herself.

'Did we get the results of the white powder that was found on Mark Fisher's body yet?' Ruth asked.

'Nothing yet, boss ... What do we think about our nurse junkie?' Nick said with a wry smile.

'She seemed to be genuinely ashamed of her addiction and being caught,' Ruth said. 'What did you think?'

'Yeah. She was all over the place. I don't know if there's a link to Mark Fisher. And maybe she was telling the truth. But she's not our killer. And she's got a rock-solid alibi for the time of Gerry Doyle's murder. She was three hundred miles away,' Nick said.

'Okay, but I don't want to eliminate her completely from the investigation yet,' Ruth said cautiously.

'I actually felt sorry for her. I've used pain medication before,' Nick admitted as they slowed at some traffic lights. 'Codeine, diazepam, all sorts of benzos. Anything that would make me feel soft around the edges.'

Ruth nodded. She had used codeine to 'smooth out the edges' too. 'Yeah, I used to have a sneaky gin and codeine once in a while.'

Her phone vibrated. Ruth's stomach flipped with the thought that it might be Jamie Parsons. However, when she checked, it was a series of images that the Tech lab had blown up and enhanced from 'Nicole Lace's' social media accounts. They were still a little blurred. Most of them seemed to be taken in pubs and clubs. One of them caught Ruth's eye. 'Nicole' seemed to be in a dark club wearing a black leotard and sitting with some men.

'You know, my mind keeps coming back to Zoe Tardelli …' Ruth said.

'Nicole Lace …' Nick said, correcting her.

'Whatever we call her. She's the only person that has a link to both our victims. She was raped by Mark Fisher, which gives her plenty of motive. Gerry Doyle had a well-known liking for underage girls. Maybe he sexually abused Zoe too?' Ruth said.

'That sounds plausible. And despite what the PM shows, we know it's highly likely that the same person or people killed both our victims. But Helen McCarthy was clearly following Mark Fisher,' Nick said.

'Can you get onto the hospital and get Helen McCarthy's mobile phone number? Let's see who she called from the car park.'

'Yes, boss,' Nick said as they pulled into the car park at Llancastell nick.

Ruth was looking at the images that Tech had sent her. As she peered at the photo of Zoe Tardelli, or Nicole Lace, sitting with the men, something struck her. She handed the phone for Nick to look at. 'This is a photo of Nicole Lace. What can you see?'

Nick looked at it. 'It's a pole-dancing club.'

Ruth nodded. 'That's what I thought. Any ideas where that is?'

Nick frowned in offence.

'Oh, come on, Nick. Don't be coy,' Ruth said, shaking her head.

'There is a place between here and Rhyl. Off the dual carriageway. The Rouge Lounge.' Nick said with a smile.

'The Rouge Lounge? Jesus!' Ruth said.

'Don't judge me!' Nick said in mock affront.

'I'm always judging you, Sergeant Evans,' Ruth quipped. 'When does it open?'

'I get the feeling that it doesn't ever close, if you know what I mean?' Nick said archly.

'You mean it's a front for a brothel?' Ruth asked.

'That's what I always thought. But I don't remember much about most of the times I went there,' Nick admitted.

'Come on then, let's go,' Ruth said as Nick turned the car around.

It was three o'clock by the time Derek Harrison arrived back at Llancastell Police Station with the same solicitor, now for an interview under caution. CID didn't have any solid evidence with which to arrest or charge Harrison, but it was clear he was hiding something.

Sian entered with French and they sat down. Harrison's solicitor put his pen down and looked at them.

'Just to make you aware, my client will not be answering any of your questions today. Although Mr Harrison is here under caution, he is also here voluntarily. It is our view that the constant harassment of my client when he is grieving the loss of his son is unacceptable and we will be putting in a formal complaint to the chief constable'

Sian shot French a look – even though they had new evidence, a formal complaint would have to be dealt with through the appropriate channels. That might well mean an interview with Independent Office for Police Conduct, IOPC, which was never a pleasant experience.

'Mr Harrison, we have new information that we would

like to ask you about in relation to our investigation into the murder of Mark Fisher,' Sian said, looking over the table.

Harrison didn't look at her but instead looked defiantly at the wall behind. His face was grey and drawn, and his eyes bloodshot.

'During an inspection of a car belonging to your son, Craig Harrison, yesterday, we retrieved this from the rear door,' Sian said.

Sian slid over a plastic evidence wallet that contained the banker's draft for ten thousand pounds that French had found.

'Can you tell me if you recognise this, please, Mr Harrison?' Sian asked.

Harrison rolled his eyes and then glanced down at the wallet. 'No comment.'

'It's a banker's draft for ten thousand pounds that you withdrew in cash last week from your bank. Is that right?' Sian.

'No comment,' Harrison grumbled.

'That's a lot of money to have in cash. Can you tell us what you were going to use the money for, Mr Harrison?' Sian asked.

'No comment.'

'Are you still in possession of the money?' French asked.

'No comment.'

French glanced over at Sian – he was going to start to apply pressure now as they had agreed on the way to the interview.

'Mr Harrison, is it right that you hated Mark Fisher?' French said.

'No comment,' Harrison said, trying not to react to the question.

'You blamed him for the death of your daughter, Donna, didn't you? After Donna's death, your son Craig went off the rails because he couldn't cope. So, you blamed Mark Fisher for that too? It was almost as if you had lost both your children, and Mark Fisher was to blame for that, wasn't he?' French said.

Harrison shifted awkwardly in his seat. Sian could see that French's hypothesis had clearly made him feel uncomfortable. 'No comment …'

'Mark Fisher showed no remorse for killing Donna, did he?' French asked, the volume of his voice growing a little.

Sian watched as, this time, Harrison just shook his head. He was no longer staring defiantly at the wall but at the floor.

'So you and Craig found someone who would kill him. To get revenge for taking your daughter away from you. No grandchildren, no cosy family gatherings at Christmas …' French said.

Sian could see that French's line of questioning was getting too close to the line, even though it was clearly rattling Harrison.

Harrison's solicitor put down his pen and rose slightly out of his seat, 'Detective, I really must protest at …'

'Sit down!' French thundered.

Harrison had now closed his eyes.

'You took ten thousand pounds in cash from your bank. Then you and Craig went early on Sunday morning to pay this person whom you had hired to kill Mark Fisher. And you paid him, either just before or just after he had carried out the murder. Isn't that right?' French growled.

Harrison shook his head slowly.

'That's what happened, isn't it, Mr Harrison?' French said loudly.

'No, it's not,' Harrison mumbled as he opened his eyes and shook his head slowly.

His solicitor went to whisper some advice to him, but Harrison wasn't interested. Whatever it was, he needed to get it off his chest.

'No? Then tell us what did happen?' French thundered.

'I … went with Craig to pay off his drug debts. He had been given drugs to sell, but … he spent the money. They said they were going to kill him. I took ten thousand pounds and drove with Craig to meet these men to pay them off and … save my son's life,' Harrison said quietly.

THE SKY HAD DARKENED AS RUTH AND NICK DROVE INTO A car park that seemed to serve around four or five shops. It was on the edge of Llancastell's industrial estate. Ruth knew that the council wouldn't hand out a licence for a lap-dancing or strip club anywhere near a residential area.

Looking out as they parked, Ruth could see a large builder's merchants, a shop selling car parts and a printing shop of some kind. In the far-left corner was a gaudy red neon sign – *The Rouge Lounge.* There were other neon signs that showed the silhouettes of women hanging suggestively from poles.

Jesus! What a classy place … Ruth thought.

As Ruth closed the passenger door, she could already hear the faint thud of the bass of the club's music. The wind died and became still as Ruth finished her ciggie, stubbed it out and followed Nick to the club.

'You take me to all the best places, Nick,' Ruth quipped.

'Looks a bit different in the daylight,' Nick confessed.

'I can't believe it's open now,' Ruth said, glancing at her watch.

They got to the ticket booth where a woman dressed in underwear and fishnets gave them a curious look. She looked decidedly fed up.

Ruth and Nick flashed their warrant cards and the girl confirmed that Nicole Lace did work there – although she couldn't remember if she was in there now.

Ruth walked down the red-carpeted stairs to a bar – it smelt of cheap perfume and beer. The bassline to some house music thudded.

As they entered, they could see about half a dozen punters and two women spinning and grinding around a pole on a raised platform. It was darker than Ruth thought it would be and she could just about make out the faces of the men that stared at the stage as if in a trance.

'Not your scene?' Nick said with a raised eyebrow.

'Not really …' Ruth said as she scoured the bar for any sign of 'Nicole Lace'.

'Not even, you know …?' Nick asked.

'Not even as a lesbian? No, Nicholas. There aren't many lesbians who get their rocks off in a lap-dancing club, I'm afraid. Despite your dirty little fantasies,' Ruth joked, shaking her head.

'I don't have dirty little fantasies,' Nick protested as he glanced at a waitress walking past in underwear and high heels.

'I think we both know that's bollocks. Come on, Romeo, let's find Miss Lace,' Ruth grinned as she gestured towards the bar.

The barman looked up and took a double-take. They didn't look like the usual clientele. And in a place like this, Ruth knew they looked like coppers.

'Afternoon. We're looking for a Nicole Lace? I understand she works here?' Ruth asked as she waved her warrant card.

The barman looked worried, but his glance right told them that Nicole Lace might be backstage somewhere.

'It's all right. Just a few routine questions. Nothing heavy,' Nick said to reassure him.

The barman nodded. 'Okay. I'll go and get her.'

The barman disappeared through a door as Ruth and Nick looked around.

'What's the attraction?' Ruth asked. Did the punters really enjoy just looking at women in their underwear swirling around a pole?

Bloody mystery to me, Ruth thought.

'Yeah, it's pretty grim sober,' Nick admitted.

Another two minutes went past and there was no sign of anyone.

Ruth looked back at the bar, then at the door, and then at Nick. They were both thinking the same thing.

'Shit! She's done a runner!' Nick muttered as he leapt over the bar, knocking a glass to the floor with a crash.

Pushing down with her arms, Ruth did the same, surprising herself at her agility.

Still got it, babe, she said to herself.

Crashing through the door the barman had vanished through, Ruth followed Nick down a dark corridor. There was a stock room, and then some dressing rooms for the dancers. A tall, blonde dancer, who was wearing nothing except a thong, looked at them startled.

'Close your mouth, Sergeant Evans,' Ruth joked.

Turning a dark corner, Ruth could see the light of a door up ahead. The green sign and long steel bar showed it was a fire exit. She assumed that was where Nicole Lace had made her escape.

Nick crashed through the door but Ruth was only a

second behind, even though sprinting was starting to burn her lungs. Squinting at the daylight, she and Nick had come out onto a huge, flat concrete yard somewhere in Llancastell Industrial Estate.

'Where now?' Ruth said as she sucked in air.

Smoking isn't really doing my lung capacity any good these days!

'There!' Nick yelled as he sprinted away towards a three-storey warehouse that had *Parcel and Courier Services North Wales* written in bright red on its side.

Peering up at the building as she ran to keep up with Nick, Ruth could see that a middle-aged woman with red hair was running up a metal fire-escape stairway. Nicole Lace. The woman stopped briefly to take off her heels before hitting the stairs again, full pelt.

'Stop! Police!' Nick thundered as they reached the bottom of the staircase.

'Jesus!' Ruth gasped as they stopped.

'Okay, boss?' Nick said as he began to clamber up the metal staircase.

'Never better,' Ruth panted. 'Where the hell is she going?'

'The roof ...' Nick replied as their shoes clattered noisily on the grey metallic stairs.

Even though they were only thirty feet up, Ruth looked down and felt a twinge of vertigo.

Keep looking up, Ruth! Keep looking up.

After the events with Craig Harrison, the last thing Ruth needed was another rooftop confrontation with someone who was feeling desperate.

Across to the left, Ruth could see the buildings of central Llancastell. The modern dome of the swimming pool, the spires of several churches and then beyond that, the dark ridges of Snowdonia on the horizon.

Dragging breath, Ruth could feel the muscles in her

thighs burning with lactic acid from going up step after step.

Reaching up with her hand, Ruth tried to steady herself – she was feeling dizzy. She looked down again and the ground seemed to roll and pitch below her with a stronger wave of vertigo.

Keep looking up, you pillock! she said to herself.

Turning onto the last ten or so stairs, she saw that Nick had already reached the roof and was out of sight. As she made it to the top, Ruth could see that the roof was flat concrete with a balustrade all the way around. There were cigarette butts a few yards away – clearly some of the warehouse workers came out here to smoke.

Nicole had stopped running and was now standing by the steel balustrade as Nick approached.

'Just stay there …' Nick said, breathing deeply to catch his breath. 'Don't do anything stupid.'

Bloody hell! I do not want to see two people jump to their deaths in as many days.

Nicole was trembling, holding one of her hands out, palm facing out. 'Stay there! Don't come any closer!'

'Okay. Nicole, we just want to ask you a couple of questions, that's all,' Ruth said in her well-rehearsed maternal voice as she approached where Nick was standing.

'I can't talk to you …' Nicole yelled at them as she put one foot over the balustrade.

Where the bloody hell is she going?

'Just stay there,' Nick said.

'Why can't you talk to us?' Ruth said. Nicole clearly frightened of something or someone.

'If I talk to you, they'll find me. And I've seen what they do to people and their families …' Nicole said as her eyes started to well with tears.

Ruth took a step forward. 'It's okay. Whatever it is, we can help you sort it out. We can protect you. You just need you to come away from the edge of the roof for us.'

Nicole looked at them and she nodded. She moved her body as if she was going to return back over the balustrade.

Thank God for that! Ruth thought.

Then suddenly, Nicole looked across at the next part of the flat roof. There was a gap of about six foot.

Do not try to jump across that. You won't make it, Ruth thought.

Nick had spotted what she was planning. 'Don't do anything stupid.'

Nicole turned around, took two steps and leapt at the adjacent roof. Her hand clasped the brickwork, then she lost her grip and dropped out of sight.

Oh my God! No!

'Jesus!' Nick said as they ran to the edge of the roof.

Expecting to see Nicole's body two hundred feet below, they instead saw that she had landed on another flat concrete section of roof about twenty feet below. She was unconscious.

Ruth looked at Nick. 'Call for the air ambulance.'

Chapter 18

Having overseen the transfer of Nicole Lace to Llancastell University Hospital, Ruth had returned to CID to regroup. Jamie Parsons still hadn't replied to her email. Maybe he was playing games. He seemed like that kind of man.

Ruth spun on her chair to look out of her office and into Incident Room One. Brushing a couple of loose strands of hair off her face, she took a hair clip and pinned them back. Looking into her 'The Real Boss' mug that Nick had given her, she drank the last inch of coffee. It was still warm.

She had asked Nick to arrange an impromptu briefing for those CID officers who were currently in Incident Room One and she could see that there were half a dozen officers assembled. Watching Sian hobble and sit down, Ruth felt a sharp twinge of shame. Sian was sitting there, safe in the knowledge that Ruth had drawn some kind of line under Sarah's disappearance. As far as she was aware, she and Ruth were moving forwards together in an honest relationship and building a life together. Except that wasn't true at all. Ruth felt the twist of guilt as she watched Sian sitting and laughing with French and Nick. It was too much to think about.

Grabbing her folders, Ruth came out into the incident room and headed for the scene boards. Getting stuck into a double murder case would keep her preoccupied.

'Right, everyone. There have been quite a few developments today, so I wanted those of us that are here to regroup and refocus.' Ruth pointed up to one of the photos of Nicole Lace. 'Nick and I tracked down Nicole Lace, formerly Zoe Tardelli, to a lap-dancing club on the industrial estate …'

'Ooh. How did you find that, Nick?' Sian asked, raising her eyebrows.

'Funny,' Nick said with a forced smile.

'Nicole did a runner, tried to jump across a warehouse roof, fell and is now unconscious in the hospital. She is stable and not critical. She told us that she was hiding from a person or people who are extremely dangerous. That's why she ran. We won't have any more intel on that until we question her when she regains consciousness.'

'If she had something to do with Mark Fisher or Gerry Doyle's murders, that would explain why she ran,' French suggested.

'Maybe … From what the boss and I saw, she was definitely scared that by talking to us, someone was going to find her,' Nick explained.

Ruth nodded. 'Nothing she said to us suggested that she thought we were there to talk to her about the murders. We'll see what she has to say when we question her.' Pointing to a photograph of Derek Harrison on the board, Ruth turned to Sian. 'You spoke to Derek Harrison earlier, didn't you?'

Sian nodded. 'We had evidence that he had taken out

ten thousand pounds in cash a few days before Mark Fisher's murder. He claims it was to pay off drug debts that Craig Harrison had racked up. The dealers had threatened to kill Craig, so Derek went with him last Sunday morning to pay them off.'

'What did you think?' Ruth asked French.

'I don't know, boss. Harrison has motive to kill Mark Fisher. But there isn't anything to tie him to Gerry Doyle.'

'Not yet,' Nick pointed out.

'I don't suppose he was willing to give you the names of the people he gave the money to?' Ruth asked, guessing the answer would be a resounding no.

French shook his head. 'No, boss. And the GPS in the car has been dismantled so there's no way of tracking where they went on Sunday morning.'

Ruth pointed to the photo of Helen McCarthy, 'Have we got the phone records back for Helen McCarthy yet? She was following Mark Fisher for a reason. And then she rang someone to tell them what she was doing. If she's not involved, I'd like to eliminate her sooner rather than later.'

'I spoke to Tech. We can have the phone log this afternoon,' French said.

'Anything else from today?' Ruth asked.

Sian picked up a printout. 'When we looked at the historical allegations against Mark Fisher, I assumed that Heather Morrison and Zoe Tardelli were never named. However, when I checked on the PNC, they are named in the police and CPS notes at the time.'

Ruth looked at her. 'What do the notes say?'

Sian gestured to the printout. 'Heather Morrison is her married name. The notes have her down as Heather Morrison, formerly Heather Kosminski.'

'Why do I know that name?' French asked.

'The investigating officer on Yewtree that Nick and I spoke to was a retired DI Graham Kosminski,' Ruth said.

'You think they're related?' French asked.

'I don't know. We've only just noticed,' Sian said with a shrug. 'I know there are lots of Polish people in North Wales, but it's not a common surname.'

Sian had a good point and Ruth nodded as she thought about the new information. 'Well, if they are related, why didn't he mention it to us when we talked to him? That would be very strange,' Ruth said.

'Not if he didn't want us to know,' Nick said. 'And Heather Morrison didn't mention it when we talked to her.'

'Okay, can we find out if there is any connection, please?' Ruth asked, looking at French and Sian.

At that moment, Drake came into the room. With his shirt sleeves rolled up and neat goatee, Ruth thought he looked back to his old self.

'Okay if I have a word with everyone, Ruth?' Drake said to one side. He didn't need to ask. There were many DCIs who would have come thundering in and just taken over. What Drake did was show respect in everything he did – and that's why he got it back.

'Course, guv. Fire away,' Ruth said, realising she had slipped into old habits from the Met and called him *guv*. That was strictly a London copper's thing.

Walking to the scene boards, Drake went over to the photograph of Nicole Lace. 'What I tell you stays within the confines of these four walls. I've had a call from the NCA and the UK Protected Persons Service. Nicole Lace, formerly known as Zoe Tardelli, has been part of the witness protection system for nearly twenty years.'

'Why?' Ruth asked.

'In 2003, she gave evidence against two drug dealers in

Cheetham, Manchester. They both got twenty years. However, there were two attempts on her life, so Zoe Tardelli was given a new identity as Nicole Lace and a new life in the south-west of England. Three months ago, she disappeared and failed to report to her protection officer,' Drake explained. 'She hasn't been seen since until she popped up on our radar.'

'What's she doing in Llancastell?' Nick asked.

'No idea. Have we done a check on her family?' Drake asked.

French looked over. 'Both parents are dead. Sister lives in Spain. Nothing else came up.'

'Maybe she felt it was time to come back and do something about the men who had abused her?' Ruth said, thinking out loud.

Chapter 19

I t was late by the time Ruth got home. Standing in the
kitchen, she took a cigarette, went out of the back
door and stood on the patio, looking up at the sky. It
was clear. On the radio, they had said there was going to
be a super moon. Apparently, it was when there was a new
full moon at exactly the same time as the moon was at its
closest to Earth.

'I'm going to go have an early night. I'm knackered,' a
voice said behind her.

Ruth turned to see Sian standing by the back door in
pyjamas and a dressing gown.

'Okay. I've got a few things to do,' Ruth said and then
turned back to look at the moon again. Ruth immediately
sensed that Sian wasn't going anywhere.

'What's going on, Ruth?' Sian asked, unable to hide
her frustration.

'What do you mean?' Ruth asked, but knew exactly
what she meant.

'The last couple of days. You're … you're somewhere

else.' Sian walked out onto the patio towards her. 'I've tried talking to you about it.'

'I'm sorry. My head's in this case. It's going nowhere and I'm the SIO,' Ruth said. The case had very little to do with why Ruth was continually lost in her own thoughts.

'I'm just scared that you're hiding something from me. And I'm not normally paranoid, am I?' Sian said.

Ruth walked over to her and put her arms around her. 'No, you're not. And I know that I've been a bit distant. But you don't need to worry. I'm not hiding anything from you. Trust me,' Ruth said, the guilt churning inside her at the outright lie.

Sian looked at her. 'I do love you. And before the last day or so, I don't think we've ever been happier.'

'I know. It's been so good. And I do love you too,' Ruth said. 'It's just work stuff. SIO on two murders means I'm under a lot of pressure.'

Sian nodded. 'Yeah, of course. Sorry. I forget sometimes because you normally take it in your stride … Don't be long, eh?'

'I won't be,' Ruth said as she watched Sian turn and go inside. *My ability for lying and deceit is repulsive,* Ruth thought. It was only a few months ago that Ruth had slept with her ex-husband. And now this.

Looking back at the moon, Ruth caught a glimpse of just how tiny and insignificant she really was. It seemed to be an overwhelming thought. A tiny speck on a dot of a small planet in a fathomless universe in a millisecond of time.

The buzz of her phone brought her crashing back to the actual reality of life and all perspective was lost. Unlocking the screen, Ruth could see that she had two emails waiting. She tapped out her cigarette, went into the kitchen, grabbed some wine and moved to sit in the living room.

Opening her email app with her forefinger, she saw the first email was from Jamie Parsons. Her pulse quickened.

HI RUTH,

Yes. Sunday is fine with me. How about midday at the British Library café then?

I hope the case is over by then.

Jamie

IT WAS HAPPENING THEN. RUTH'S MIND WHIRLED WITH THE thought of meeting Jamie Parsons. What was he going to tell her? There would be stuff that would be painful to hear.

Ruth's eyes zipped down to the second new email. It was from Steven Flaherty, who was Ruth's liaison officer from the Metropolitan Police's Missing Persons Unit. Steven had been an incredible support since they first met in 2013. He had gone above and beyond on many occasions, especially in the ongoing quest to find Jurgen Kessler. The previous day, Ruth had sent him an email asking if he could dig around and see if he could find anything about Jamie Parsons.

Ruth opened the email; had Steven managed to find something significant?

HI RUTH,

Hope you're okay?

I have done some digging around in Jamie Parsons' life. Asking around the Met, it would appear that Parsons is the man behind the company Secret Garden. It's a company that organises elite sex parties for the super-rich and beautiful people in London. As far as I can see, they're orgies for very rich men. I don't know if this helps? Otherwise, Jamie Parsons has no criminal record and is not a person of interest for anyone in the Met.

Speak soon and take care.

Steven

SIPPING FROM HIS LATTE, NICK LOOKED OVER AT HIS sponsor, Dundee Bill. They usually met at the Café Italia in the middle of Llancastell once a month to catch up and for Nick to chat about how his recovery was going. Bill had been sober for decades and had seen it all before. He also took no shit, which is just what Nick needed.

The air was cold, but Bill smoked so they had to sit outside whatever the weather.

'How are you feeling about becoming a father?' Bill asked, drinking his black coffee and tapping ash into an ashtray.

'Bit scared,' Nick admitted. If he remembered correctly, Bill had five children and a football team of grandchildren.

'You'll be fine,' Bill said with a paternal smile. 'How is Amanda doing?'

'I think she has had enough of being pregnant, but she's doing okay,' Nick said.

'Just be patient. She's in early sobriety, so she needs a lot of support at the moment,' Bill said and then looked directly at him. 'And remember to be kind to yourself, Nicholas. You've come a long way in a very short time. And that's lovely to see.'

Nick felt his pride swell. He was his own worst critic.

'Thanks. When I think about where I was a couple of years ago, it's a bloody miracle.'

'And how is our friend Peter?' Bill asked.

Nick shrugged. 'Early days. He says all the right things. But I think he tells me what I want to hear.'

'Peter is a lovely man, but he's been around for a long time. Then he disappears for years and then he's back for a while. Do what you can for him. And remember you can't get him sober,' Bill said.

'Yeah, I do get the feeling that he thinks I'm the answer,' Nick said.

'You're only just in yourself. It's good for you to be working with him, but you can only give him advice and your experience. If he doesn't truly want to stop drinking, there's nothing you can do. It has to come from him,' Bill explained.

Feeling his mobile vibrate, Nick took his phone out of his pocket. He recognised the number calling as University Hospital. His stomach clenched with nerves as he immediately thought of Amanda.

'It's the hospital,' Nick said to Bill. Bill nodded with understanding and continued to drink his coffee. Nick pressed the answer button. 'Hello?'

'Is that Detective Sergeant Nick Evans?' a female voice asked.

'Yes,' Nick said, his anxiety shooting through the roof.

'It's the A&E department at Llancastell University Hospital here …' the voice said.

Please God, do not let anything have happened to Amanda or the baby.

'Okay …' Nick mumbled.

'We have a Peter Wenger here,' the receptionist said.

Peter Wenger was Peter the Artist's' real name. Nick

was confused but relieved that the call wasn't concerning Amanda.

'Peter is very drunk but there's very little we can do for him here. He gave us your number and we wondered if you could come and get him?' the receptionist asked.

Nick's immediate reaction was anger. He didn't want to go and pick Peter up, and why had he given the receptionist his number? He was not impressed.

'Yes. That's fine. I'll be there in ten minutes,' Nick said and hung up.

'Everything all right?' Bill asked.

'That was the A&E department. Our friend Peter is down there drunk and they want someone to pick him up,' Nick explained.

Bill nodded and stubbed out his cigarette. 'I'll come with you.'

'Thanks. I'd better ring Amanda and tell her I'll be late,' Nick said, trying to remain calm.

'Remember, you're Peter's sponsor. You're not responsible for him twenty-four hours a day. You've got your own life. If you can help, then that's great. But he has to take some responsibility too. That's part of getting sober,' Bill said as they walked away towards the car.

Chapter 20

Ruth had received a call at 6.30 a.m. to say that Nicole Lace had regained consciousness at Llancastell University Hospital. She was being moved from the ICU but was going to remain under observation. Ruth had immediately sent a uniformed officer to 'babysit' her until their arrival.

Nick picked Ruth up on the way to the hospital – she needed to let other members of the team know that Nicole was conscious.

As they pulled into the Llancastell traffic, Ruth rang Drake. 'Boss, Nicole Lace regained consciousness about an hour ago.'

'She's out of danger?' Drake asked.

'Yes. Severe concussion and a fractured pelvis. I've arranged for a uniform patrol to go to the hospital straight away to make sure she doesn't go walkabout,' Ruth explained.

'Thank you, Ruth. I'll get onto Witness Protection. I'm sure they're keen to have a chat with her as well,' Drake said.

Ruth ended the call as they pulled into the hospital car park and stopped close to the main entrance.

What I really need is a coffee and ciggie, she thought. However, there wasn't time for that now.

'Christ, I'm just glad she's alive,' Nick said as he closed the car door.

Ruth nodded. 'Whatever she thought this gang were going to do to her, she certainly thought risking death was a better option,' Ruth said darkly.

They entered the hospital through two large glass sliding doors. Ruth looked over at the ground-floor café selling coffee and toast. Ruth's stomach growled. *I'll get some on the way out.*

They walked for a few seconds without talking. Ruth used it as an opportunity to offload what was on her mind.

'If we can clear this up, I'm meeting Jamie Parsons in London tomorrow. Otherwise it's going to have to wait.'

Nick's eyes widened for a second. 'Tomorrow? Bloody hell. How do you feel about that?'

The lift arrived and they got in. Ruth processed Nick's question. How *did* she feel about that?

'Apprehensive. I don't know what he's going to tell me,' Ruth confessed.

'Not my business, but do you really need to know?' Nick asked.

'Yeah. I'd prefer to know everything. That's what I'm like. But I'm guessing it will be hard to hear,' Ruth said as they came out of the lift and turned towards Bonney Ward. The smell of disinfectant and cooked food was much stronger now.

Nick nodded. 'Makes sense. I used to think that what you don't know can't harm you. But I know that's bollocks.'

'Thank you, Confucius,' Ruth said with a grin.

They reached the ward, showed their warrant cards and explained why they were there.

Nicole Lace was lying in bed in a private room with a uniformed officer outside. As they went in, she had her eyes closed. With her red hair pulled back off her face into a ponytail and the stark light of the room, she seemed to look ten years older than the woman Ruth had spoken to on the roof.

Nick shut the door behind them and the noise of it roused Nicole. She turned her head and looked up at them.

'Oh right. Wondered when you would turn up,' Nicole mumbled as she tried to sit up a little in bed. It was clearly painful and she winced as she shifted.

'How are you feeling?' Ruth asked.

'Like someone played football with my head. It's agony when I piss because of my pelvis. But apart from that, it's all tickety-fucking-boo …'

'You were lucky,' Nick said as they sat down beside the bed.

'Not really …' Nicole said in a withering tone. 'What do you want?'

'We know who you are. We know you were Zoe Tardelli,' Ruth said.

'Well done,' Nicole said. 'Is that it? When are you taking me back to Cornwall then? And where the fuck is Darren?'

'Who's Darren?' Ruth asked.

'He's my Witness Protection handler,' Nicole said.

'We're not with Witness Protection. We're from Llancastell CID,' Ruth explained.

'So, what were you doing at the club yesterday?' Nicole asked, clearly confused.

'We need to ask you a few questions. We're investigating the murder of Mark Fisher,' Nick said.

Nicole took a moment to process what Nick had said. She replied slowly, 'I haven't heard that name for a long time … And I didn't know he was dead.'

'I understand that Mark Fisher sexually assaulted you when you were a teenager? Is that right?' Ruth asked gently.

Nicole blinked and took a deep breath. Ruth could see that the question had thrown her. She nodded.

'When was the last time you saw Mark Fisher, Nicole?' Ruth asked.

Nicole frowned. 'I dunno. Twenty, twenty-five years ago. I was a kid.'

'You haven't seen him since you came back to Llancastell then?' Nick asked.

'No. Why would I? Why would I want to see him?' Nicole said with a sneer, shaking her head at the question.

'Can you remember where you were last Sunday morning between midnight and six?' Ruth asked.

Nicole shrugged. 'No. I don't know. At the club and then home.'

'But you don't know for sure?' Ruth asked.

'I've just fallen thirty feet onto my fucking head. I've had enough painkillers to stun a fucking horse. So no, I can't quite remember,' Nicole growled.

Ruth looked over to Nick. *No decent alibi …*

'Bloody hell! You think I had something to do with it?' Nicole sputtered.

'Did you?' Ruth asked.

'Don't be soft. I wouldn't piss on the man if he was on fire, but I didn't kill him,' Nicole said. After a couple of seconds, she added, 'Is that it?'

'No … We're also looking into the murder of Gerry

Doyle, who used to work at The Mill Recording Studios. Did you know him?' Ruth asked.

'Eh? Gerry Doyle's dead?' Nicole said with a scowl.

'You didn't know?' Nick asked.

'Yes, that's why I asked,' Nicole snapped. 'What happened to him?'

'We can't talk about the case. Can you tell us the last time you saw Gerry Doyle, Nicole?' Ruth asked.

'Same. Twenty, twenty-five years,' Nicole replied.

'And you haven't seen him since you came back to North Wales?'

'No. No, of course not … Gerry was all right. I don't know why anyone would want to kill him,' Nicole said.

'We've spoken to a couple of people that seemed to think that Gerry Doyle was inappropriate around teenage girls?' Nick asked.

'Yeah, a bit. He'd slap your arse. But nothing creepy like that other … one.' Nicole looked over at Ruth. 'Christ, you wanna speak to Gerry's wife.'

'Mary Doyle?' Ruth asked.

'Nasty piece of work. Everyone was scared of her,' Nicole explained.

'Sorry, Nicole. I'm lost. How did you know Mary Doyle?' Ruth asked.

'She did all the bookings at The Mill. She virtually ran the place,' Nicole explained.

'So why was everyone scared of her?' Nick asked.

'She was a bully. Gerry was terrified of her. I saw her beat the crap out of him once. Plus, she organised for all the girls to come to the studio,' Nicole explained.

'Do you mean Mary Doyle arranged for teenage girls to come to the studios to sleep with the bands?' Ruth asked, starting to feel that she was uncovering something far darker than they'd expected.

'Yeah, of course. That's why bands used to go there. Mary gave us booze and drugs. Told us to make the musicians happy. If you didn't, you'd get a smack, or you'd never come back. We used to call her Myra the Pimp. You know, after Myra Hindley. That woman was seriously evil.'

TAKING OFF HER JACKET, SIAN SAT DOWN AT HER DESK AND computer. The heating in the building had been cranked up, so now it was sweltering. That was the problem with being housed in a seventies tower block. It was either freezing or too hot. A pain shot up the left-hand side of her spine and seemed to travel up to her shoulder and neck. She had forgotten to do her stretches that morning. In fact, she hadn't forgotten. It was boring and a little painful, so she had sacked them off.

Sian had been onto records to check the intel they had got on Heather Morrison. There it was, confirmed: *Heather Kosminski, born 14 June 1983, University Hospital, Llancastell.*

Was Graham Kosminski related to Heather? Why didn't he mention it to Ruth and Nick when they interviewed him? That seemed highly suspicious. Heather hadn't mentioned any relationship to Graham Kosminski when she was interviewed either. That meant that either there was no relationship, or they had both deliberately decided not to mention it.

Sipping at her fruit tea, Sian glanced over to the DI's office where Ruth worked. She wasn't back from the hospital yet. Ruth had been distracted the last few days and it wasn't just work. It was more than that. If she had to guess, Sian would put her money on it being something to do with Sarah. Maybe that was paranoia. However, whenever Ruth became remote and preoccupied, it was usually to do with Sarah and her disappearance. She didn't know what she would do if Ruth was hiding anything from her again. She wasn't sure she could listen to the same apologies and promises that it would be different. Ruth would swear that she could move on, that she could put what had happened to Sarah to one side and this time they could build a meaningful life together.

The sense that someone had arrived beside her broke her train of thought. She glanced up to see French blinking at a piece of paper.

'Sian …' French said.

'Something up, Dan?' Sian asked.

'We got the phone call log from Helen McCarthy's mobile phone,' French explained.

'Any idea who she called from the supermarket car park?' Sian asked.

'The call was made to a burner …' French said.

'Shit …' Sian said.

'But I called the supermarket and they gave me the details of the credit card that was used to buy the burner. It belongs to Kathleen Taylor,' French said.

Sian needed a moment to register the name. Then she remembered. The woman who had been in the accident with Mark Fisher and whose child had suffered brain damage.

'How the hell does Helen McCarthy know Kathleen Taylor?' Sian asked.

RUTH AND NICK HEADED OUT TOWARDS THE SUBURBS OF Llancastell – they had arranged to meet Mary Doyle at her home. The revelation that she procured teenage girls for the bands and musicians using The Mill Recording Studios was a turn in the investigation that she hadn't seen coming.

Ruth's phone buzzed. It was Sian. 'Sian?'

'Boss,' Sian said, fully in work mode. 'Just to complicate things a little more, we've found out who Helen McCarthy was phoning from the supermarket.'

'Surprise me,' Ruth said in a droll tone.

'She rang Kathleen Taylor,' Sian said.

'What? Mrs Yoga-pants? How the hell do Helen McCarthy and Kathleen Taylor know each other?' Ruth said, getting exasperated.

'No idea, boss,' Sian said.

'Go and have a chat with Kathleen Taylor and see what she has to say,' Ruth said and then ended the call.

'Problems?' Nick asked.

'The case is driving me mad. I feel like we're going around in circles,' Ruth said. 'It seems that Helen McCarthy was ringing Kathleen Taylor the day she followed Mark Fisher.'

'What's the connection?' Nick asked.

'No idea. But it seems that just as we get a lead, something else turns up and we're back to square one,' Ruth explained.

'For what it's worth, I think both murders are linked to whatever was going on at The Mill,' Nick said.

Ruth nodded and took out a cigarette. 'Yeah. I'm with you on that one. That's my instinct.'

'Why did Mary Doyle hide the fact she had worked at The Mill from us?' Nick asked as they cruised around a roundabout.

'Maybe she wasn't keen for us to know about what she did up there?' Ruth suggested.

'But she's taking a risk because there were plenty of people who could have told us that,' Nick said.

'True. It's pretty unpleasant stuff, but I don't see anything that gives Mary Doyle a motive to kill her husband or Mark Fisher,' Ruth said, feeling uneasy the more she learnt about the goings-on at The Mill Recording Studios.

'What about the evidence of domestic violence we saw?' Nick said.

'That might explain Gerry Doyle's murder. But I don't see how that links to Mark Fisher,' Ruth said. 'Our killer knows both these men and has motive to kill them both.'

'You think Nicole Lace is our prime suspect then?' Nick asked.

'Mark Fisher raped her. Gerry Doyle had a reputation for liking teenage girls. We know all of them were at The Mill Recording Studios at the same time. It's the only theory that fits. Nicole Lace goes into hiding with witness protection. However, she still wants to get revenge on the two men that abused her when she was a teenager. Something happens to provoke her, she does a runner and ends up back in Llancastell. The two men who abused her end up dead. She has no decent alibi for the time of either murder.' Ruth looked over at him. Now she had said it out loud, it seemed to be an even more viable hypothesis.

'Motive, means and opportunity.' Nick said, nodding as they drew up outside the Doyles' home.

Sian spotted Kathleen Taylor as soon as she and French walked into the café at the fitness studio. She was sitting in the corner, drinking some kind of smoothie while thumbing through a magazine.

Sian nudged French and they approached the table and got out their warrant cards. 'DC Hockney and DC French, Llancastell CID.'

Kathleen's face fell and she rolled her eyes. 'I've spoken to two officers from CID already.'

Sian looked at Kathleen. She had an attitude and the kind of face she wanted to slap.

'We're aware of that, Mrs Taylor. However, there have been developments in our enquiry and we need to clarify a few things with you,' Sian said in a tone that made it clear that this was serious.

'Really?' Kathleen said with a huff as she put her lifestyle magazine down on the table.

'You could come down to the station if you would prefer?' French said.

Before Kathleen had time to say anything else, Sian and French pulled out chairs and sat down.

'That's great. Thank you for cooperating,' Sian said with more than a hint of sarcasm.

'I've explained already that I was out of the country at the time of that man's death,' Kathleen said.

'Yes, we've checked that. We know that you were out of the country,' French said.

'Well, I don't understand ...' Kathleen protested, her brow furrowed.

Sian leant forward. 'Could you tell us about your relationship with Helen McCarthy?'

Kathleen thought and shook her head. 'No, I'm afraid I don't know anyone by that name.'

'That's strange,' Sian said as she fished into the file and pulled out Helen McCarthy's phone records. 'Because these are the calls made by phone owned by Helen McCarthy. This here is a call to your number.'

Kathleen shrugged. 'That doesn't mean I know her. Maybe she dialled the wrong number?'

Okay. Let's see if she's stupid enough to hang herself going down this route, Sian thought to herself.

'Okay, that might explain it,' Sian said, nodding and

looking to French for confirmation that they were playing a game.

'Yes. Helen McCarthy could have dialled your number by mistake. But you would have remembered that because we can see that you answered the phone,' French said, pointing to the call log.

'Yes. That's right,' Kathleen said, unable to hide the fact that she was flustered.

You are walking straight into this, you snobby bitch.

'Oh okay. So, you did get a phone call from a wrong number? And you answered it?' Sian asked.

'Yes, I never said that I didn't get a call from a wrong number, did I? I remember it now,' Kathleen explained nodding with a growing sense of haughtiness.

Oh dear. Keep digging.

'What did you say?' French asked.

'It was a woman, so I suppose it could have been this Helen McCarthy woman. And I said that it was a wrong number and she apologised,' Kathleen explained, unable to stop her voice from wobbling a little.

'Well, that explains it then,' Sian said in a breezy voice. 'I guess you would have been on that call for a couple of seconds.'

French nodded at them both.

'Yes. Was there anything else?' Kathleen said as her shoulders dropped with an obvious sense of relief.

Sian shot French a look and then turned the printout for Kathleen to see.

'You know that's very strange because, according to these records, the phone call you admit to receiving lasted twelve minutes,' Sian said pointing to the column that detailed call duration. 'And you've just told us that the phone call lasted a couple of seconds.'

The blood visibly drained from Kathleen's face as her

eyes darted around. Sian couldn't help but feel a little pride in the flawless delivery of a well-rehearsed sucker punch.

I'd like to see you explain that away, Sian thought.

'I don't understand …' Kathleen stammered. 'I promise you, it was a wrong number. Maybe … the person making the call just forgot to hang up? I don't know.'

'Why are you lying to us, Kathleen?' Sian asked.

'I'm not …' She glanced down at her watch. 'It's just a mistake. Am I under arrest or anything?'

'No, but I'm pretty sure we'll be back to talk to you again,' Sian said.

'Well, I've got to go and teach a class now.'

Kathleen got up, gathered her things and left.

Sian turned to French. 'Well, she's lying her arse off.'

Chapter 21

Ruth and Nick were sitting opposite Mary Doyle at the kitchen table. They had shown their warrant cards and given her some of the developments in the case. Ruth was waiting for Mary to relax a little before knocking her off guard with some of the facts that she had hidden from them.

'We understand that you used to work at The Mill Studios, Mary?' Ruth asked in a very matter-of-fact way.

'Erm … well yes, but that was a very long time ago,' Mary said, taking a breath.

She wasn't expecting that.

'Strange you didn't mention it the last time we were here?' Ruth said.

Mary shrugged. 'My husband has been murdered. I wasn't thinking properly … I don't know.' She sounded a little flustered.

'It's almost as if you didn't want us to know?' Ruth suggested.

'I don't know what you're trying to get at. Gerry has

been killed … and you're asking me all this stuff,' Mary said, glancing over at Nick, her voice starting to shake.

Nick sat forwards in his chair. 'If we're going to find out who did this to Gerry, we need to know everything about his life, Mary.'

Mary nodded. 'I know … I'm sorry …'

'When we asked about Gerry's work, we asked whether he had ever mentioned a guitarist called Mark Fisher,' Ruth said, looking Mary directly in the eyes. She couldn't hide the fact that she was getting upset.

'It was a long time ago. I can hardly remember,' Mary said as she nervously moved her fingers around her coffee cup.

Nick looked down at his notebook. 'You were in charge of bookings, is that right?'

Mary nodded. 'Yes.'

'We know that Mark Fisher was at the studios. He was a session musician. How could you not have known who he was?' Ruth said in a slightly sterner voice.

'I did know who Mark Fisher was. But I didn't like him. He was trouble. There were all sorts of rumours about what he had done. And I saw in the paper that he went to prison. I just thought it was best not to bring it up …' Mary explained.

Ruth opened her phone and scrolled to an old photo of Nicole Lace, as she had appeared as Zoe Tardelli. 'When you worked at The Mill, you must have met this girl?'

Mary looked at the photo on her phone. Ruth could see that Mary instantly recognised her.

'Oh yeah … Zoe,' Mary said with a knowing expression.

'Why did you say it like that?' Ruth asked. What did her answer imply?

'No reason. But for a fourteen-year-old girl, Zoe was a

real piece of work,' Mary said with a meaningful shake of her head.

'Zoe told us that you organised for teenage girls to come up to the studios to hang out and sleep with musicians,' Ruth said.

Mary let out a sarcastic snort of laughter. 'Is that what she said? Jesus!'

What's that all about?

'Why is that funny?' Ruth asked.

'You must know,' Mary said, shaking her head.

'Know what?' Ruth was starting to lose her patience.

'Do you lot in North Wales Police not talk to each other or something? Bloody hell. Zoe Tardelli dealt all the drugs up at The Mill. She worked for some extremely dangerous people over in Manchester. You know what musicians are like? And she organised for her mates and anyone they knew to come to The Mill for the parties. Free drugs, booze and maybe shag a pop star. They had to be pretty, mind. No dogs allowed,' Mary explained.

'And you turned a blind eye?' Ruth asked.

'It was the eighties and nineties. Anything went. And we were booked solid all year. Everyone knew The Mill. Not because it had great acoustics or a beautiful setting or any of that. It's because we had decent drugs, booze and girls on tap.'

'You said someone in North Wales Police knew about this?' Nick asked.

'We had a few of your lot poking around. There was one detective that came a few times,' Mary said.

'Can you remember his name?' Ruth asked.

Mary shook her head and then a thought occurred to her. 'Yeah, actually. Kosminski.'

Bloody hell! DI Graham Kosminski?

'Kosminski? How do you remember that?' Nick asked in a dubious tone.

'Kosminski was the bloke that people thought was Jack the Ripper. So when this strait-laced copper comes in called Kosminski, I just thought it was funny,' Mary explained.

'Have you seen either Zoe or DI Kosminski recently?' Ruth asked.

Mary frowned – something had occurred to her.

'Whatever it is, you need to tell us,' Nick said.

'In town the other day. I got back to my car and someone had scratched it all the way down the side. I looked around. Across the road, there was this woman watching me. I wouldn't have recognised her, but she had this red hair,' Mary explained.

'Zoe Tardelli?' Ruth said.

'I thought I was just seeing things. I hadn't clapped eyes on her for over twenty years. But now you've said it, it must have been her,' Mary said.

It was an hour later. Ruth had called another CID briefing to regroup and share various bits of intel that had changed throughout the day. For some reason, the pieces of the case still didn't seem to fit together. Something felt wrong.

'Right, guys, listen up please,' Ruth said in an annoyed tone. The hubbub of Incident Room One continued. 'That means *now*.' The frustration about the case was getting to her. IR1 went quiet as she approached the scene boards, like naughty pupils who'd just received a telling off – they weren't used to seeing her angry. 'What we seem to be missing here is something that unlocks this case. We're chasing our tails and getting nowhere. And I'm starting to get questions from on high about what we're doing and why we're getting bloody nowhere. I'm not prepared to let this investigation make me or my team look stupid.' As she settled herself, Ruth went to the photo of Nicole Lace and pointed. 'Okay, this is what we've got. Zoe Tardelli. Aged fourteen, she was allegedly raped by Mark Fisher at a party in North Wales. We know that she used to hang around The Mill Recording Studios where our second victim, Gerry Doyle, worked as a sound engineer. Like Fisher, Gerry Doyle had a fondness for teenage girls and that's why he was eventually sacked from The Mill. Zoe and Gerry Doyle would have been at the studios on many occasions.

'Zoe Tardelli then worked for an organised criminal gang in Manchester in the early noughties, transporting and selling drugs. When she was nicked with a hundred grand's worth of coke in her boot, she did a deal with the CPS and went into witness protection with a new identity, Nicole Lace, and made a new life in Cornwall. Three months ago, Nicole Lace disappeared from Cornwall and popped up in Llancastell where she got a job as a stripper and lap dancer. And then last week, Mark Fisher and Gerry Doyle are murdered. Nick?'

Ruth watched as Nick got up to address CID. 'Nicole Lace doesn't have a decent alibi for the time of either of the murders. Mary Doyle claims that her car was vandalised in town and that she saw someone that could well have been Nicole Lace watching her from across the street. That would imply that Nicole had been watching and following Mary Doyle, and possibly Gerry.'

Ruth nodded. 'Eileen Fisher told us that in the week leading up to Mark Fisher's death, she had heard noises that sounded like someone was outside the house. Mark had gone to investigate but found nothing. However, we found a revolver in Mark Fisher's bedroom, which suggests that he was frightened of something or someone.'

'Maybe Nicole was following Mark Fisher as well?' Sian suggested.

'Yes, that sounds likely,' Ruth said.

'Boss, do we still think that Nicole Lace, or whatever we call her, is our prime suspect?' French asked.

Ruth nodded. 'She's our only suspect that has links to both victims. We know she has motive to kill Mark Fisher because he raped her. It's not hard to believe that Gerry Doyle's behaviour towards her was inappropriate. She has no decent alibi. She came out of witness protection to come back to Llancastell. Why?'

'What about the drugs that were used on both victims?' Sian asked.

'I don't know. But if you know the right people, you can get anything on the street. And Nicole Lace knows a lot of very dodgy people,' Ruth replied.

'We also think that DI Graham Kosminski was the officer investigating The Mill Studios back in the nineties for the supply of drugs. Mary Doyle remembers him being around. Why did he not tell us any of that when we interviewed him?' Nick asked.

'What about this link to Heather Morrison?' Ruth asked. 'Are they related?'

Sian shook her head. 'Still waiting on that, boss.'

'Anything else?' Ruth asked.

French looked up. 'Boss, we got a forensics report back on the white powder that was discovered on Mark Fisher's clothes. Turns out it's not chalk but magnesium carbonate.'

'What's that used for?' Ruth asked.

'It's a drying agent like chalk. It's used in the manufacture of magnesium oxide, which is found in the foam that comes out of a fire extinguisher or in fireproofing. Magnesium carbonate is also the stuff that gymnasts put on their hands when they're on parallel or uneven bars or the rings,' French explained.

'Thank you, Prof,' Sian said with a smile and then turned to Ruth. 'We spoke to Kathleen Taylor, boss. We know that she received a twelve-minute phone call from a phone owned by Helen McCarthy.'

'What did she say to that?' Ruth asked.

'Not a lot. But she looked guilty as hell,' French said. 'We think that Helen McCarthy was following Mark Fisher. She rang Kathleen Taylor as she was going to her car and continued to talk to her as she followed Mark Fisher out of the car park. What's that about?'

Ruth frowned. 'Can we check both their backgrounds against PNC and see if we can find a link?'

French glanced at his computer screen that he was sitting beside. He clicked a mouse.

'Boss, email from the superintendent registrar for Llancastell. Heather Morrison's paternal grandfather, Jakub Kosminski, is also DI Graham Kosminski's father.' French held up a photo of DI Graham Kosminski. 'So in answer to your question, yes, DI Graham Kosminski is Heather Morrison's uncle.'

As Ruth and Nick marched down the hospital corridor, two porters wheeled an elderly-looking woman, who was hooked up to oxygen and a drip, towards the lift.

As she held the doors open, Ruth looked at the woman's frail face that had lost its structure and colour. She looked scared and confused. Was that what she was destined for? If she didn't stop smoking, then it probably was. That's if she made it that far. What would she say to her fifty-year-old self looking back? She suspected that her advice to her younger self would be to get on with your life and enjoy it because it will be gone in a flash.

As they approached Bonney Ward, they went to the hand sanitiser on the wall, cleaned their hands and then made their way to the nurses' station.

Ruth flashed her warrant card. 'We're here to see Nicole Lace. She was down there?'

A young male doctor, who had heard them and seen the warrant card, stopped beside them.

'She's lucky to be alive,' the doctor said.

'How's she doing?' Ruth asked. She wanted to know when Nicole would be fit enough to leave the hospital.

'Physically, she's not too bad. But mentally, she's very fragile.' The doctor gave them a meaningful look and spoke quietly. 'She looks well for someone with her prognosis.'

Ruth shot a quick glance at Nick. 'Sorry. I'm not sure what you're talking about?'

The doctor frowned. 'Erm, sorry. I thought you would be aware of that. I'm not sure that I'm supposed to be discussing …'

'She's a suspect in two murder cases. You need to tell us what you know,' Nick snapped.

The doctor nodded. 'Nicole found out three months ago that she had stage-four pancreatic cancer … It's terminal.'

'Months or years?' Ruth asked.

'Months. She might not see Christmas,' the doctor said as he gestured to the ward. 'I'd better get on and do my rounds.'

Ruth and Nick looked at each other as they turned and headed for the single room where they had previously interviewed Nicole.

'That explains why she did a runner from Cornwall three months ago,' Nick said.

'Why come back here though?' Ruth said.

'Unfinished business,' Nick suggested.

As they arrived at the room, the door was closed. Ruth frowned and then saw a uniformed officer walking towards them with a coffee.

Ruth smiled. 'Thank God for that, Constable. I thought you'd deserted your post.'

Stepping forward, Ruth pushed the handle down and opened the door to the room.

The bed was empty.

Ruth looked back at Nick and then at the constable.

'Where the hell is she?' Ruth growled, looking around the empty room.

The constable's face drained of colour. 'She might be in the bathroom?' he said, gesturing to a door down the corridor.

'For your sake, she'd better be,' Ruth snapped.

Nick looked at a nurse who was dashing past holding a clipboard. 'We're looking for the patient that was in this room? Nicole Lace.'

The nurse smiled. 'She's gone for a walk down to the shop with her dad.'

'Her dad?' Ruth asked.

'I'm sure she won't be long,' the nurse said and turned to go.

The constable looked like he wanted the earth to open up right there and then. 'She's not coming back is she, ma'am?' he said in a quiet voice.

'No,' Ruth growled. 'I'm sure she's not. And according to her records, her dad died ten years ago.'

Chapter 22

I t was mid-afternoon by the time Sian and French arrived in the village of Tregeiriog. They soon identified Heather Morrison's home and French parked outside by the black metal gate. It had taken a while to get in contact with Heather Morrison's husband and arrange to come and talk to the couple.

Getting out of the car, Sian got the redolent smell of a bonfire somewhere nearby. It conjured images of carefree childhoods, kicking through thick blankets of autumnal leaves with her brother in the back garden of their home. Her father in his old purple gardening jumper, threadbare at the elbows, and his size-thirteen wellies, raking and carrying leaves in his wheelbarrow on a Sunday afternoon. Mum was in the kitchen cooking and singing to the radio. It felt like another life, but it had been perfect. And Sian, especially in this job, knew how lucky she was to have had a childhood like that.

Would she and Ruth ever have kids? Maybe they could adopt? She wasn't naïve enough to think that it would be easy, but there was a hankering inside her to have a child or two and give them that kind of start in life.

French opened the gate and they made their way to the front door. A short, wiry man in his thirties eventually answered their polite knock.

'Mr Morrison?' Sian asked as she showed her warrant card. 'We were hoping to have a word with your wife, Heather?'

Morrison, looking bleary-eyed, frowned. 'Erm, she's at work. Do you want to come in?'

Sian and French followed him into the hallway. He was still in his pyjamas and dressing gown, and his bed hair was a giveaway that they had woken him up.

Maybe he works shifts? Sian thought.

'Can you tell us where your wife works?' French asked.

'At the vet surgery in the village. She's a veterinary nurse,' Morrison explained.

Sian fished a police force contact card out of her pocket and handed it to him. 'Could you let her know that we do need to speak to her as soon as possible, please?'

'Of course. No problem,' Morrison said, reading the card.

Sian's eye was drawn to a wedding photograph on the hall window. It was a traditional shot of about twenty or so guests, with the happy couple in the middle.

Going over the photo, Sian had a thought. 'Oh, you got married at The Boat in Newnes? My sister got married there,' she said with a smile as she ran her eyes over the assembled guests.

On the right at the back was a man in his sixties with a cheesy grin. DI Graham Kosminski? It looked like the photograph French had held up earlier. The intel on the link between Heather Morrison and DI Kosminski was correct.

'Yeah. It was a spring wedding, but we were lucky with the weather,' Morrison said.

As they turned to go, French stopped. 'Your wife was a little uncertain about her whereabouts last Sunday morning. Early. Can you remember where she was?' French asked in an intentionally matter-of-fact way. Sian knew what he was really doing was seeing if Morrison would confirm Heather's actual alibi.

Morrison shrugged. 'At the stables up the road. That's where she is every Sunday morning. She gives riding lessons so she would have been there mucking out before that.'

Sian raised an eyebrow. *That's not what your wife told us.*

'WELL, NICOLE LACE DIDN'T VANISH INTO THIN AIR, DID she?' Ruth said, shaking her head.

Ruth and Nick had been in the security room of the hospital for nearly fifteen minutes. The burly security officer, who carried the faint odour of sweat and coffee, had been trawling through the hospital CCTV but was getting flustered. He was starting to annoy Ruth with his mixture of ineptitude and jobsworth conceit. He was one of those wannabe coppers who liked the uniform and the little bit of power the position afforded him. She had come across that type before and some of them wanted to show that they were cleverer than police officers. In Ruth's experience, they usually failed.

Ruth pointed to an image that was frozen on one of the monitors. It showed two figures waiting for the lift from the first floor. 'Right. We know that this has to be Nicole Lace and whoever came to pick her up. And they got into this lift at fourteen twenty-three.'

The security officer looked up at her and nodded. 'I

just don't understand why they don't come out on the ground floor here.'

Nick pointed to another monitor. 'And they don't come out of the main entrance within the next thirty minutes, which means that they left the hospital a different way.'

The security officer shrugged. 'There isn't a different way.'

Ruth thought for a moment. *That's ridiculous. There were other ways in and out of the hospital. He was talking bollocks!*

'You don't take dead bodies out of the front entrance, do you?' Ruth said, raising an eyebrow.

'God no. Of course not,' the security guard said, horrified by the suggestion.

Ruth gestured with her hands. 'Then where do they leave from?'

'There's a funeral director's bay at the rear, by the mortuary,' the security guard explained.

'So, there are other ways out of the hospital?' Ruth said in a withering tone.

'If you're dead, I suppose,' the security guard said under his breath.

Have the balls to say it out loud and to my face if you're going to be a sarcastic twat!

'What about medical deliveries, food, bed linen ...?' Ruth asked, desperately trying to keep calm.

'Yeah, there's a delivery and service entrance at the back of the hospital. But you can't get to it from the main stairs or from that lift,' the security guard said in a condescending tone.

Nick gave Ruth a forced smile and then looked at the security guard. 'So how do you get to the delivery and service entrance?'

'It's a different set of lifts that go from the fifth floor.'

Nick nodded and pointed back to the monitor. 'What if

these two people went up in that lift from floor one up to the fifth floor, got in the other lift down to the ground floor? Could they leave the hospital that way?'

The security guard rolled his eyes. 'I'm sure someone would stop them and ask where they were going or what they were doing.'

Nick forced another smile. 'Humour me for a second. It is possible to do that though, isn't it?'

'Yeah, I suppose so. Never heard of it, mind,' he said.

'And there's CCTV on the delivery and service entrance?' Ruth asked.

'Of course. Otherwise people would nick stuff, wouldn't they?'

'Can we have a look?' Ruth asked. 'Maybe from two twenty-three onwards.'

The security guard let out an audible sigh as he clicked through the various CCTV cameras and the files that held their digital recordings. After a few seconds, he brought the footage up and played it. He fast-forwarded it for seven minutes, but there was no sign of anyone.

The security guard shrugged. 'Nothing there.'

'Hang on. She's smashed her pelvis, so she's not going to be running,' Nick snapped.

A moment later, two figures appeared on the CCTV coming out of the doors of the delivery and service entrance. The man pushed open the door and they walked slowly down the concrete ramp and out into the loading yard.

'Who the hell is that?' Ruth asked, squinting at the CCTV footage.

The couple, who were looking around furtively, stopped and kissed. The man's face turned directly towards the camera.

'Stop it there, please!' Ruth said.

The frame froze on the man's face.

'DI Graham Kosminski,' Nick said.

SIAN AND FRENCH PULLED OFF THE MAIN ROAD TO Llancastell and followed signs to the North Wales Equine Centre. Spotting a series of one-storey buildings and stables, Sian pointed French over to the car park.

'You ride?' French asked, looking over at two teenagers in riding gear leading out a horse.

Sian gestured to the girls. 'Yeah, when I was a teenager. You?'

'No. Rugby and a bit of rowing,' French said.

'Rowing? Very posh. You went to public school, didn't you?' Sian said.

French ignored her as he opened the car door. 'Come on.'

Gazing up at the colourless sky, Sian inhaled the smell of straw and stables.

'I knew it,' Sian said, looking over at French.

'What?' French asked. Sian could see from his smirk that he knew exactly what she was talking about.

'I knew you were a public schoolboy,' Sian said with a slight tone of triumph.

'Does it matter?' French asked defensively.

'Not really. It does explain the slightly entitled attitude and childish sense of humour,' Sian said with a grin. She actually liked French's respectful attitude to women. She couldn't remember him ever making any comments about women's looks or crude sexual innuendos.

French forced a smile. 'I'll take all that as a compliment.'

A door to one of the buildings opened and a tall, ruddy-faced woman smiled at them as she walked over.

She's clocked us as coppers straight away, Sian thought.

'Can I help?' the woman asked.

Sian and French flashed their warrant cards.

'We're looking for Heather Morrison. We understand she works here?' Sian said.

The woman nodded. 'She used to. Not anymore, I'm afraid.'

Sian and French were confused. *What the hell is that about?*

'How long ago did she stop working here?' French asked, reaching for his notepad.

'Month or so. She said that her father's not well. Poor man has Alzheimer's. She needs to spend more time with him,' the woman said.

'Okay. Thank you,' Sian said and then stopped. 'Just to clarify, Heather Morrison wasn't here last Sunday. You didn't see her?'

The woman shook her head. 'No, I'm sorry. Like I said, the last time I saw her was when she said she couldn't work here anymore. I haven't seen her since.'

'Okay. Thanks for your help,' Sian said. As she turned to head back to the car, she saw that French had thought of something.

'Actually, quick question. This is an equine centre. Do you perform surgery on horses here?' French asked.

What the hell was French on about? Then she caught his train of thought.

The woman nodded. 'We have two fully equipped operating theatres here. We get horses from all over Wales and the north-west of England.'

'And excuse my ignorance, but I'm guessing that if you're doing a complicated operation on a horse that they are anaesthetised, just like we would be?' French asked.

'Yes, exactly the same,' the woman said, looking slightly bemused.

'Okay. Thanks,' French said as he shared a look with Sian.

'Heather Morrison could have had access to anaesthetics,' Sian said, confirming French's train of thought.

Chapter 23

Nick had been waiting for the manager of The Rouge Lounge for ten minutes. Having driven to the address that Nicole had given the hospital on her patient's form, they found that it didn't exist. Nick had dropped Ruth at Llancastell nick to look at the PNC and see if she could track her down. Nick also wondered if The Rouge Lounge had a different address for her as she had worked there for months.

As he sat by the bar, Nick got a waft of strong spirits. The barman that had tipped Nicole off on their previous visit wasn't anywhere to be seen. Nick had returned to make it clear to the club and the barman that they were lucky that they hadn't been charged with perverting the course of justice. Maybe they had given him the sack?

A barman came over and leaned forward. 'Do you want a drink while you're waiting? On the house.'

For the smallest second, Nick wished he could have said yes. Wished that he could have necked a double whisky and then another. The sharp edges of sober life would then melt away as the soft relief of alcohol did its trick. But

Nick knew that it wouldn't just stop there. He would get that overwhelming craving for booze that could never be satisfied. He had read an article on addiction recently. The neural pathways of his cortex in his brain had been rewired by the years of drinking and addiction, so now they reacted to the stimulus of alcohol with the destructive need to keep drinking. After the first drink, there was no defence against another.

'No thanks. I'm on duty,' Nick said.

The manager walked over. Dressed in a smart three-piece suit, he looked a little overdressed, as though he was going to a wedding.

'You're looking for Nicole, is that right?' the manager said.

'I'm looking for an address, actually. I don't think she'd be daft enough to come back here,' Nick said.

The manager raised an eyebrow. 'Actually, you just missed her.'

'What?' Nick asked.

Christ, she must be desperate to take that risk.

'She just came to get her wages for the last two weeks. Said she was leaving town,' the manager explained.

'Don't suppose she gave you any idea of where?' Nick asked, but he knew it was unlikely.

'No. Her dad was out in the car waiting for her, so I guessed she was going away with him somewhere,' the manager said.

Her dad? Graham Kosminski.

Nick then had a thought. 'This is going to sound weird, but what was she wearing?'

The manager frowned – it was quite weird. 'Puffer jacket. Leggings, white trainers.'

'You still want the address she gave us?' the manager asked.

Nick shook his head as he took his phone out of his pocket. 'No thanks. I don't need it anymore.'

Nick jogged outside, dialled Ruth's number and waited until she answered. 'Boss?'

'Nick?'

'Nicole Lace picked up her wages from The Rouge Lounge about half an hour ago. She was wearing different clothes to the ones that she had in the hospital. That means she's been back home. She was with Graham Kosminski. My guess is that they will be heading out of Llancastell and going to his house to hide out,' Nick said.

'Yeah, well they've no idea that we know they're together. That means they'll think that they're safe there,' Ruth said.

'Boss, I'll pick you up from the front of the station,' Nick said as he clambered into his car.

It was now four o'clock, and Sian and French were back at Llancastell CID following up on what they had learnt when trying to track down Heather Morrison. Sian was online looking through the PNC.

Clutching a printout, French came over from his work station.

'What have you got?' Sian asked.

'It might be nothing, but I've got the link between Kathleen Taylor and Helen McCarthy. According to the Inland Revenue, they both had time off work in April 2017. In that two-week period, they were both paid a salary and expenses directly by Mold Crown Court,' French explained.

Sian put two and two together. 'Jury service?'

'That was my thought. So I cross-referenced their names through the CPS and court records. They both did jury service at the same time at Mold Crown Court on the same trial in 2017,' French said.

That is *interesting,* Sian thought.

'Okay, so that's the connection. What was the trial?' Sian asked.

'I looked it up in the *Llancastell Leader*,' French explained, showing Sian a printout of a newspaper story. 'Lee Casey was on trial for the murder of a man in his forties in a street fight in Flint. But he was only convicted of manslaughter and sentenced to four years.'

'The same verdict as Gerry Doyle, who killed Helen McCarthy's brother Max,' Sian said, thinking aloud.

'I'm surprised that the CPS allowed her to sit on it,' French said.

'Unless she didn't flag it up. It wouldn't be on the PNC or even a DBS check,' Sian pointed out.

'Maybe Helen wanted to be at a trial for the exact crime that killed her brother and see justice done this time?' French suggested.

'Except it went exactly the same way again,' Sian said.

'Okay, so Helen McCarthy and Kathleen Taylor met on the jury of this case. Now we know how they know each other. Maybe they struck up a friendship?' French said.

'Kathleen Taylor has been through a very similar thing. Mark Fisher ruined her daughter's life by drink driving. But he only served a short sentence,' Sian said.

'But they have watertight alibis for the nights of the murders,' French said.

Sian nodded – French was right. Neither of them were in the country.

A CID officer came over and gave Sian a document.

French shrugged. 'Maybe. It's a waste of time taking this any further if we're barking up the wrong tree.' French then gestured to the document that Sian had just been handed. 'What's that?'

'Background checks on Heather Morrison. According to this, her father Bryn Kosminski died in 2015 aged sixty-seven.'

'Which means she was lying to the Equine Centre about caring for her sick father,' French said.

'YOU THINK NICOLE KILLED THEM BOTH, DON'T YOU?' Nick asked.

'Yeah, I do,' Ruth said.

Nick and Ruth were motoring along the A348 and getting close to Ceiriog, where Graham Kosminski's home was.

Ruth continued. 'We have to go on the evidence that we've got. She has probable motive to kill both men. When she finds out that she has terminal cancer, she comes out of witness protection and heads back to Llancastell. Why? She is having some kind of relationship with Graham Kosminski, who was the lead detective investigating the allegations at The Mill Studios back in 1997.'

'Do you think Kosminski is involved in the murders?' Nick asked.

'Maybe, he has motive too. His niece Heather was sexually assaulted by Mark Fisher and it was likely she came into contact with Gerry Doyle too,' Ruth said.

'Kosminski had been to suicides before as a police officer so he would know how to stage them,' Nick said.

'Except he fucked up. But I can't see Nicole doing both of the murders on her own. It makes a lot more sense to me that she had help. And the help of someone who felt a lot of anger towards both victims,' Ruth said.

'Who did we chase into the forest by the river then?' Nick asked.

'No idea. Could have been either of them, I guess.'

Nick nodded as they entered the village where Kosminski lived.

'But we don't have enough to arrest them?' Nick said, shrugging.

'Apply enough pressure and guilty people start to panic. They make stupid mistakes,' Ruth said.

Ruth and Nick pulled up outside Graham Kosminski's cottage. Getting out into the blustery wind, Ruth noticed the blue VW on the drive. She looked at the number plate and memorised it just in case.

'Somebody's home,' she said.

They walked up the neat pathway to the door. The sun was starting to drop in the sky and the shadow from the garden wall cut the path neatly in half. It was getting chilly.

Nick knocked on the door and stood back. A bird chattered noisily from a nearby tree. After a few seconds, Nick went to the door, knocked again and then peered through the frosted-glass pane.

Maybe they saw us coming up the path?

Nick shrugged as he went to one of the front windows, cupped his hands and peered inside.

'I can't see anything,' Nick said quietly.

Ruth gestured to the side of the house where it looked like there was a passage.

She followed Nick down the side of the house. The passage was neatly swept with two bins side by side. A road bike, partially covered with a protective rain tarpaulin, rested against the fence.

Nick got to the door. Ruth could see the glass was also frosted as Nick peered in again. He turned back to her. Nothing. No signs that anyone was home.

Taking a pen, Nick lifted the lid on the blue domestic wheelie bin and looked inside. He rummaged for a second.

'DS Evans, you do know that technically you need a search warrant for that?' Ruth said with a smile. It wasn't the first time she had seen Nick bend the rules.

'Sorry, boss. However, the wind must have blown the bin over and the rubbish was on the floor here,' Nick shrugged with a knowing grin.

Ruth looked at the green garden-waste bin.

'Anything?' Ruth asked.

Given the amount of time since the two murders, it was going to be a long shot to find anything of significance. If they found any hard evidence against Kosminski, Ruth would need to get SOCOs down to do a thorough examination anyway.

'Nothing that I can see,' Nick said.

Lifting the lid on the green bin, Ruth peered inside. In the shadows of the house, the bin seemed empty, but there was some kind of rubbish in the bottom. And it wasn't grass cuttings.

Ruth clicked on her torch and looked again.

'Nick, can I borrow your long arms?' Ruth said, thinking that she had seen something interesting.

'Great. I love scooping stuff out of bins,' Nick said as he came over.

'You'd better put your gloves on,' Ruth said.

Nick snapped on his purple latex gloves, pulled the bin onto its side and used his pen to hook something out of it.

As he pulled it free, they both saw what was an empty box of kitchen clingfilm.

'We need to get that into an evidence bag as soon as possible,' Ruth said.

Nick nodded.

A noise came from inside the house. It sounded like someone had dropped something.

They looked at each other. Ruth gestured to the side door.

Pushing the metal handle down, Nick pushed the door – it was locked.

Bollocks! If they're hiding inside, maybe I need to get back up? Ruth thought.

Nick leant down, peeled up the outside mat. Resting underneath was a silver key. He gave Ruth a knowing raise of his eyebrow.

'Christ, you couldn't write it!' Nick whispered.

Twisting the key in the lock, Nick unlocked the door and then opened it slowly.

Waiting for a moment before entering, Ruth strained her hearing. The house was silent.

Nick crept inside slowly. Ruth followed. She could feel her pulse quickening – the adrenaline was starting to kick in.

They went through a small room with a washing machine and then entered the kitchen. Ruth stopped and listened.

Should we make ourselves known? Ruth thought.

Nick went over to the kettle. He felt it with the palm of his hand.

'It's warm,' Nick whispered.

'All right, Columbo' Ruth said, rolling her eyes.

Beside a landline phone, there was a notepad and pen. Scribbled onto the pad in blue biro were a series of times – *13.48, 15.56. 16.12.*

Suddenly, there was the sound of a car engine.

'Shit! It's the car on the drive!' Ruth muttered as she shot a look towards Nick who was already running.

Crashing out through the side door, they ran up the path, only to see the blue VW speed away down the road.

Nick and Ruth sprinted down back towards their car.

Nick clicked his Tetra radio. 'Control, this is three-six. We are in pursuit of suspects, Nicole Lace and Graham Kosminski. In a blue VW Passat, registration alpha-tango-six-six, sierra-Oscar-sierra, heading east out of Ceiriog on the A-six-four-three. Over.'

'Control, received.'

Nick and Ruth got into the car. Nick turned the key in the ignition and hit the accelerator. The wheels spun as they set off in pursuit of Nicole and Kosminski.

'If I wasn't convinced that they're involved in the murders before, I am now,' Ruth thundered.

Nick nodded as he hit sixty miles per hour within seconds. Ruth could see that as the road straightened, they had nearly hit eighty.

Ruth's heart was pounding – the adrenaline had sharpened her senses. Gripping the door handle with one hand and the side of her seat with the other, she looked ahead as they hurtled past a small row of houses that blurred with the speed.

Nick sat forwards a little, peering through the windscreen. 'Where are you?'

Ruth watched as Nick overtook a car. She turned to him. 'Blues and twos.'

Snapping on the lights and sirens, Ruth saw Kosminski's VW come into view, speeding up a hill ahead.

Nick smiled. 'There he is.'

'You're like a kid.' Ruth couldn't help but laugh.

'It's the only rush I get these days,' Nick quipped.

They came hammering up the hill and over the crest. Kosminski's VW was now only about half a mile ahead and they were gaining. Nick pulled out to overtake a long, articulated lorry, which went past in a flash.

Ruth's mind went to the notes that Kosminski had made by the telephone.

'There were a series of times written on a pad by the phone. Thirteen forty-eight, fifteen fifty-six,' Ruth said as she glanced over at Nick.

'Train times? If they're trying to get away?' Nick suggested.

Ruth nodded. 'Kosminski was on the job so he'd know we'd track him through ANPR. The train is a safer bet if he paid with cash.'

'Could be plane times too?' Nick said. 'They could be at Liverpool airport in ninety minutes.'

Ruth nodded and then watched as the VW indicated right and pulled onto a road that was signed *A5, Llancastell, Chester*.

'They're heading for England,' Nick said as he slowed and turned to follow.

Ruth felt herself pulled hard left by the momentum of the car as she clicked the radio. 'Control from three-six. Suspect vehicle is now heading east on B-five-four-three-seven towards the A5, eastbound.'

They screamed through the tiny village. They were going so fast that Ruth felt that the stone walls were close enough for her to touch them. She closed her eyes for a second.

As she opened them, a green tractor pulled out of a field in front. Nick pulled the car into the opposite side of the road, missing the tractor by a few feet.

'For fuck's sake!' Nick bellowed.

I don't want to die today! Ruth thought, ramming her eyelids shut once more.

They careered around a bend. She dared to open her

eyes again. A red sign that read *Arafwch nawr – Reduce speed now!* went past in a flash.

You're taking the piss.

Nick was staring at the road with steely determination. He dropped the car into third when they reached a steep hill.

'So, do we think he's driving with somewhere in mind or just driving?' Nick asked.

'I'm not sure,' Ruth said, feeling the back tyres losing grip and slipping as they cornered another bend.

Nick looked over at her. 'You okay, boss?'

'Never better. This is my idea of fun,' Ruth said as her stomach lurched. She clicked the radio again. 'Three-six to Control. Suspect now heading north on the A-six-nine-four. Speed nine-zero. Please advise if a stinger operation is possible, over.'

'Three-six from Control, will advise.'

Kosminski's VW was only four hundred yards away. It pulled out to overtake two cars that hurtled past. However, as Nick pulled out to do the same, there was an enormous white motorhome coming the other way.

Ruth squinted and looked away.

Jesus! We're not going to make it!

Nick dropped the car down into third gear and the Astra roared. Ruth felt herself being pushed back into the passenger seat.

They made it past with inches to spare.

'Shit!' Nick said

'Shit indeed!' Ruth said, taking a breath.

Nick stared fiercely ahead at the VW, which was now only two hundred metres away.

'Just don't lose them,' Ruth replied.

If they lost Kosminski and Nicole now, they might disappear and go into hiding somewhere.

Out of nowhere, a recycling lorry pulled out in front of them. Kosminski's brake lights glared bright red as he slammed on the brakes.

'For fuck's sake!' Nick shouted as he hit the brakes hard.

'Nick!' Ruth yelled.

Nick turned the steering wheel, gripping it with both hands. With the car now skidding, Ruth glanced out and saw that Kosminski had swerved past the lorry and was now speeding away.

Ruth felt like everything in her body was contracting as the car skidded at speed. She instinctively pulled her knees up and screwed her eyes closed. A metallic thud threw her forwards.

Everything was silent.

'Okay, boss?' Nick's voice came from the eerie quiet.

Ruth nodded, opening her eyes slowly and checking she was still in one piece.

Clicking open the doors, Ruth and Nick got out to survey the damage. The rear window had cracked but was intact. There was a dent on the back bumper but otherwise the car and, more importantly, the tyres were undamaged.

'Can we drive it?' Ruth asked, her brain now whirring about what their next move should be.

Nick nodded. 'Looks okay. We'll give it a go.'

'At a guess, where do you think they're going?' Ruth asked.

'Llancastell train station,' Nick said.

Ruth dialled Sian on her phone as she worked through the various scenarios. 'Sian, it's me. Kosminski and Nicole have done a runner and we've lost them. They might try to leave the country so I need you to get to Liverpool John Lennon Airport. Phone ahead and give passport control their names and see if they can stop them at the security check-in. They're in a sixty-six plate blue VW Passat. Nick and I will head to Llancastell train station.'

'Will do. You okay?' Sian asked.

'We had a bit of a prang but we'll live. Let me know when you get there,' Ruth said and then ended the call. She looked at Nick. 'Come on, Wing Commander, let's get going, eh?'

Chapter 24

Having parked next to the departure gates at Liverpool John Lennon Airport, Sian and French came through to the large glass sliding doors that led inside. The clock was now ticking. If Kosminski and Nicole were here, they needed to stop them getting on a plane. Once they were out of their jurisdiction, getting them back was a logistical and bureaucratic nightmare.

French glanced up at the sign. *Liverpool John Lennon Airport.* 'Life is what happens to you while you're busy making other plans.'

Sian frowned at him as they looked frantically around for a police officer or security guard. 'What are you talking about?'

Sian weaved her way quickly through the hordes of passengers, but her lower back was killing her. French followed behind.

'Something John Lennon said. I like the sentiment,' French said.

'We haven't got time for your chocolate-box philosophy, Dan,' Sian said as they saw an Armed Response officer who had a Heckler & Koch MP5 submachine gun strapped across his Kevlar vest.

Sian flashed her warrant card. 'DC Hockney, North Wales Police. We have reason to believe that there are two murder suspects trying to get on a plane. I spoke to your head of security, Debbie something, about ten minutes ago?' Sian glanced at her watch. 'It's urgent …'

The ARO nodded, gestured for them to follow and broke into a fast walk. 'Debbie Joyce. Come this way.'

Sian and French followed the ARO to a small door that had a sign – *Authorised Personnel Only.*

Tapping in a code on the security keypad, the ARO swung the door open. Sian and French followed him into a corridor. Sian glanced at her watch. From her calculations, Kosminski and Nicole could have been at the airport for over half an hour now. If they were getting a short-hop flight, they could even be at the gate, waiting to board.

The ARO marched noisily up a steel staircase as they followed. They arrived at a large office with imposing windows that overlooked the runways.

A tall, well-dressed woman with auburn hair came out and walked over. 'DC Hockney? I'm Debbie Joyce. We spoke earlier?'

Sian nodded. 'This is my colleague, DC French.'

Joyce motioned them into her large office. 'I've only just got the passenger lists printed from all the carriers.'

'Great,' Sian said going to the desk where the paperwork was laid out. 'I need to sit down.' Sian's back was in agony as she lowered herself into a padded office chair.

On the wall to the right were two large screens showing the departures and arrivals.

'And you have no idea where they're going or what time?' Joyce asked.

'Sometime this afternoon. And if I was to guess, I think it would be short-haul,' Sian said.

French took a passenger list and began to scan down with his finger.

Joyce's phone rang. She answered it and walked away as she began to speak. Then she turned to them.

'That was passport control. Nicole Lace and Graham Kosminski have definitely been through security and must now be in departures.'

'What about a flight number?' Sian asked.

'Sorry. It won't have been logged on the system yet,' Joyce explained.

Sian felt frustrated. It was her job to find Lace and Kosminski and stop them leaving the country. She scanned down the passenger list in her hand – nothing.

French looked up. 'I've found them!'

Sian and Joyce went over.

'I need the flight number …' Joyce said urgently as she grabbed the walkie-talkie that communicated with police officers and security guards.

'M-A-two-nine-four, Liverpool to Sharm El Sheikh, Egypt,' French said loudly.

Sian froze as she watched Joyce click the walkie-talkie. Were they in time to stop Nicole and Kosminski from flying?

'Yeah, I need the gate number for flight M-A-two-nine-four,' Joyce said with a sense of urgency.

'Egypt?' French said, looking at Sian.

'It's hot?' Sian said with a shrug.

'Hi, it's Debbie. Have you boarded M-A-two-nine-four?' Joyce asked. 'Shit! Can you get me through to the cabin crew? … It's an emergency.'

They waited with bated breath.

French looked at Sian. 'What's M-A?'

276

'Med Airlines,' Sian said. She had flown to Spain with them before.

Joyce put the walkie-talkie down and pointed out of the window at an aeroplane that was rising slowly up off the end of the runway.

'I'm afraid they're on that plane,' Joyce said.

'I'll get onto the police in Egypt,' Sian said.

'Good luck,' Joyce said knowingly.

'Why?' Sian asked. Joyce's tone made her feel uneasy.

'The UK has no extradition treaty with Egypt and the police are notoriously reluctant to spend any time tracking down foreigners who have fled to its shores,' Joyce explained.

That wasn't what they wanted to hear.

AFTER THE EVENTS OF THE AFTERNOON, RUTH WAS utterly deflated. They had been so close to arresting their prime suspects and solving the case. Now the investigation was in limbo and Ruth felt exasperated on what had proved to be a challenging case. She had reluctantly called an evening briefing.

The news that Graham Kosminski and Nicole Lace had evaded capture had spread through CID and the murder team quickly. It wasn't good for morale to have your prime suspects sitting hundreds of miles away, drinking cocktails in the Egyptian sun.

Ruth had asked Drake to start the briefing off. The mood in Incident Room One was gloomy and low.

'I've spoken to Interpol and what you've heard is right. It's going to be very difficult to get Nicole Lace or Graham Kosminski out of Egypt at the moment. Diplomatic relations are at an all-time low and the noises I'm getting from above are that we shouldn't hold our breath. They are not going to be put on a plane for the foreseeable future,' Drake explained.

Ruth could see the look of frustration on her team's faces.

'I'm sorry, guys. I will do everything in my power to get them back to face trial,' Ruth said.

'What do we do now then?' Sian asked.

'We continue to build a strong case against them until we can get them back on British soil or they decide to come back,' Ruth said.

'How sure are we that we've got the right people?'' Drake asked.

'Nicole had motive to kill them both. It's likely that Mark Fisher raped her. Gerry Doyle was also around at that time. It's not a stretch to think that Doyle sexually assaulted her. She was traumatised by what had happened, goes off the rails and ends up in some Manchester drug gang before going into witness protection. When she was diagnosed with cancer three months ago, Nicole decides to run away from her new life in Cornwall and come back to North Wales? Why? Why take the risk? People know who she is. It's possible that being diagnosed with cancer sparked her into thinking that she wanted to get revenge on the two men that destroyed her life. She had nothing to lose. She remembers Graham Kosminski's name from the late nineties, looks him up. Something happens between them. Kosminski wants to get revenge on Mark Fisher for assaulting his niece, Heather Morrison. They plot and carry out the murders together.'

'Boss,' French said with some urgency.

'What is it, Dan?' Ruth asked.

'Heather Morrison lied about her whereabouts last Sunday morning. We checked with the husband and he says that she wasn't at home as she told us. Sian and I spoke to her boss at the North Wales Equine Centre. Not only was Heather not at work on the Sunday, she hasn't been to work for weeks,' Dan explained.

'Why is she lying to us?' Drake asked.

Sian looked up. 'There's more. Heather works as a veterinary nurse so she would have access to medical-grade drugs such as tranquillisers. She also told the stables that she was nursing her sick dad. Except her dad died four years ago.'

Drake looked up. 'You think that the three of them are working together?'

Ruth shrugged. 'It's possible. Heather Morrison has motive. And she is trained to administer anaesthetic drugs with a needle.'

'When we interviewed Kosminski, there was no reason for him to hide the fact that Heather Morrison was his niece. In fact, it would explain why he took particular interest in what was going on at The Mill Studios in the late nineties. He might have got himself involved in Operation Yewtree when he saw that Mark Fisher's name had been flagged,' Nick said.

'Right, well, we need to find Heather Morrison and find out why she's been lying to us,' Ruth said.

'Unless she's already flown out to Egypt to meet them there?' Nick said.

'Someone do a check on her, get her passport number and get it run through the border police. They should have exit data, but it's going to take a few days,' Ruth said.

'Before we scale this investigation down, do we have any other loose ends?' Drake asked as he got up to leave.

'Not that it matters now, but we found the link between Helen McCarthy and Kathleen Taylor. They both did jury service together in 2017,' French said.

Ruth nodded. 'That explains how they know each other.'

'If they formed a friendship while on the jury, that would explain why they spoke to each other on the phone,' Nick said.

Ruth knew that both women had watertight alibis. The evidence that they had built against Nicole and Kosminski felt compelling. Motive, means and opportunity.

'Thank you, Dan. We'll put that on the back burner,' Ruth said. She was exhausted.

As everyone was packing up, Drake gestured to Ruth that he wanted a word in her office. It was probably just a more open and honest discussion of how the case had gone. There was always an element of diplomacy when addressing her full CID team.

'Just wanted a word,' Drake said as he leant against Ruth's desk and crossed his legs.

Drake looked at her and Ruth was uneasy – it didn't feel like this was going to be a catch-up on the case.

'How can I help?' Ruth asked.

'You've probably heard the rumours that a detective-super job has come up in Cumbria?' Drake said as he smoothed his goatee and chin.

'Yeah, I heard something. But I assumed that you love it here and that line managing me has been a doddle,' Ruth said with a smile.

'Doddle? Jesus,' Drake said with a grin. 'Look, Ruth, you are a brilliant copper and more importantly, you're a brilliant leader.'

Oh, shit. He's going for the post.

'Which is a lead up to you saying that you're going to leave?' Ruth said.

'You know we've had a tricky eighteen months. Paula's

cancer really knocked me and the girls for six,' Drake explained.

Ruth nodded. She was aware of the toll that his wife's cancer had taken on Drake and his two daughters, even though he had remained the consummate professional.

'Yeah, and I'm so glad that she's okay now,' Ruth said and genuinely meant it.

'I think a new start somewhere else would be good for all of us. There's a great school up there for Jasmine and Ruby with a big focus on music. Paula can go back to nursing if she wants,' Drake explained.

'I can see that, boss. And I'm really happy for you. But for selfish reasons, I don't want you to leave. God knows who Jones will bring in as the new DCI,' Ruth said, feeling apprehensive at the thought.

'That's another reason why I wanted to talk to you. You need to apply for the position,' Drake said.

'Really?' Ruth said. She had already run that possibility through in her mind. Part of her was flattered and part of her was anxious.

'That CID team out there would do anything for you. They would walk through fire for you. You're their leader already. And you know you're working way above your pay grade. In fact, you're working as a DCI already but you're just not getting paid for it,' Drake said supportively.

Ruth swelled a little with pride, which was incredibly rare for her. But that pride was tinged with a little anxiety.

'You know, I came up from the Met for a quiet life and to wait for my pension,' Ruth confessed. There was part of her that could do with a quiet desk job for the next few years.

'Quiet life? Well, that hasn't happened. And with your experience, I will be recommending you for the position to those upstairs. And … I will be annoyed if you don't apply,' Drake said with a smile.

Ruth nodded, but before she could ask Drake more details about the job in Cumbria, Nick walked in with a memory stick.

'Boss, sorry to interrupt, but you need to see this,' Nick said and then turned to Drake. 'Actually, you both need to see this.'

Slotting the memory stick into her computer, Nick clicked the mouse and brought up a short clip of CCTV of an ANPR Traffic camera. 'We just got footage of the hits on Graham Kosminski's number plate.'

Ruth peered at the footage. It showed a small hotel on a country road. At the front, there were half a dozen or so cars parked up.

'This is the Buckley House Hotel. We see Graham Kosminski's car drive in at eight p.m. last Saturday evening. He gets out and this is Nicole Lace, as we know her. They go inside and check in,' Nick explained.

'Did you confirm that?' Drake asked.

'Yes, boss. I've just been speaking to the hotel reception.'

Nick played the next clip. 'Kosminski's car is still there at ten o'clock on the Sunday morning.'

What the bloody hell is going on? Ruth thought as she glanced between Nick and Drake.

'When did they check out?' Ruth asked.

'Midday.'

'They were there all night then?' Drake asked.

Nick shrugged. 'Reception said they checked in, had a meal in the restaurant and a drink at the bar. Went back to their room at about eleven. Came down for breakfast between nine and nine-thirty. Left at midday,' Nick explained.

Ruth knew this wasn't good. Buckley was a long way from Ceiriog.

'Technically they could have left their room, gone to a different car, driven and killed Mark Fisher and got back in that time frame,' Drake said, thinking out loud.

'And being in the hotel would have been their alibi,' Nick said.

'Except Nicole didn't say she was in the hotel with Kosminski,' Ruth said.

'Why didn't she just tell us that?' Nick asked.

'Because Kosminski is married and she didn't want his wife to find out about the affair. But that's the problem,' Ruth said as her mind raced, trying to put the pieces together.

'Sorry Ruth, you've lost me,' Drake said looking over at her.

'Let's say that Nicole and Kosminski preplanned going to a hotel so it would act as an alibi while they went out to murder Mark Fisher when challenged. If that were true, Nicole would have immediately told us where she was when Mark Fisher was killed. That's her alibi. She was in the Buckley House Hotel with Kosminski. But she didn't. She lied because she's having an affair with Kosminski, who is married,' Ruth said. 'And that was more important to her.'

Drake nodded. 'And if she lied to cover the affair because that was more important, she and Kosminski didn't sneak out to murder Mark Fisher.'

'Exactly. The fact that she lied and didn't use a pre-planned alibi shows she's innocent,' Ruth said.

'Back to square one,' Drake said, shaking his head.

Nick furrowed his brow. 'That means our prime suspects are probably in the clear.'

Ruth knew that was right. *So who the hell did kill Mark Fisher and Gerry Doyle?*

'Hang on,' Ruth said, getting up and wandering out towards the scene boards in the incident room. She cast her eyes around the various suspects and photographs. A very different hypothesis was starting to form.

Drake and Nick joined her.

'Helen McCarthy and Kathleen Taylor knew each other,' Ruth said, pointing to their respective photographs. 'They met on a jury in 2017. And we know that they spoke on the phone for twelve minutes only a day or so before Mark Fisher was killed.'

'Except these women have watertight alibis for the murders,' Drake pointed out.

Ruth looked at the photo of Helen McCarthy dressed in her hiking gear that had come from a social media page. A hypothesis was starting to fit together in Ruth's mind that no one had thought of yet.

'Yeah, they do have incredibly watertight alibis for the times of the murders of Mark Fisher and Gerry Doyle,' Ruth said, thinking out loud. She looked over to French. 'Dan, the forensic check on the magnesium carbonate that came back from the lab. Climbers use chalk, don't they? I've seen it on the telly. Can you check if they use magnesium carbonate instead of calcium carbonate?'

Nick furrowed his brow as he looked over at Ruth. 'We found magnesium carbonate on Mark Fisher's body, didn't we?'

Ruth nodded. 'Yeah, we did. And Kathleen Taylor was conveniently in Prague for the whole weekend … But where was Helen McCarthy that weekend?'

Before Nick could answer, Dan had looked up from this workstation. 'Yes, boss. Climbers use magnesium carbonate as a drying agent for their hands to get a secure hold on small spaces and gaps in the rock.'

'You think Helen McCarthy murdered Mark Fisher?' Drake asked with a quizzical look.

Ruth shrugged and then looked at Sian. 'Sian, the case that Helen McCarthy and Kathleen Taylor served on the jury for. What was it again?'

'A trial for the murder of someone in a street fight up in Flint. But he was only convicted of manslaughter and sentenced to four years,' Sian explained.

Bingo!

'That's it!' Ruth said as the pieces merged into a coherent picture.

'What's it, boss?' Nick asked.

'Grab your coat, you're driving,' Ruth said as she headed out of CID.

'Ruth?' Drake asked with a frown.

'I'll ring you en route, boss.'

As Ruth and Nick hurried down the staircase towards the car park, Ruth took out her phone and dialled.

'Hello?' said a voice. It was Helen McCarthy.

'Hi, Helen. It's DI Ruth Hunter from Llancastell CID. There have been a few developments in our ongoing murder cases and we'd like to clarify a couple of things with you,' Ruth said in a light, relaxed tone.

'Erm … okay. If you really need to,' Helen said, sounding completely baffled.

'I'll come by at around five o'clock this afternoon if that's okay?' Ruth said.

'Yes, I … I'll be at home,' Helen said.

'Oh, and just to clarify something for our records. I'm just making sure that you did serve on a jury at Mold Crown Court in 2017? Is that right?' Ruth asked as Nick gave her a confused frown.

There were a few seconds of utter silence and then, 'Erm, yes. I think … that was 2017.' Helen's voice was almost at a whisper.

I've got you on the ropes now.

'Great, I'll see you later then?' Ruth said and hung up.

'Are you going to tell me what all that was about, boss?' Nick asked.

'Not yet,' Ruth said as they turned and walked out into the car park.

Chapter 25

R uth and Nick had been sitting outside Helen McCarthy's flat for ten minutes.

'Are you going to tell me what the grand plan is, Sherlock?' Nick asked as he glanced at Ruth, who was deep in thought.

I knew there was a reason that this case never felt right, Ruth thought to herself.

Suddenly, there was movement at the door to the flats where Helen McCarthy lived. A woman came out in a coat, scarf, sunglasses and a baseball cap.

Helen McCarthy, right on cue.

'Where is she off to?' Nick asked.

A white 4x4 pulled up on the road; Helen got in, and the car drove away.

'Follow that car,' Ruth said as Nick started the engine and they pulled off.

Nick gestured to the 4x4. 'Is that who I think it is?'

'Yes. I did a PNC check earlier.'

'Before this turns into a bad episode of *Columbo,* can

you tell me what we're doing?' Nick said, starting to lose his sense of humour.

'Okay. So Helen McCarthy and Kathleen Taylor meet on a jury in 2017. The case is a man who has killed someone in a street brawl. He gets away with a four-year sentence for manslaughter, of which he will serve two. Helen is reminded of her brother's trial, which ended in the same way,' Ruth said as they followed the 4x4 to a roundabout and then onto the main road out of Llancastell.

'Okay. That makes sense,' Nick said.

'Helen tells her new friend Kathleen how angry she is that the justice system has let the victim down again. Kathleen shares her story of how Mark Fisher killed his wife and severely injured her son and got away with a light sentence too. They both agree that their lives have been ruined by these two men who have not been punished by the British justice system,' Ruth explained.

Nick glanced at her with a furrowed brow. 'So they agree to carry out each other's murder?'

'Yes. Exactly,' Ruth said.

'What? That's crazy!' Nick spluttered. 'People don't do that.'

'They do in *Strangers on a Train*,' Ruth said.

'That's a film! ... You phoned Helen McCarthy to rattle her, knowing that in her panic, she would meet with Kathleen Taylor?' Nick said.

'I thought it was likely. They're not going to talk on the phone. And they don't want to be seen at each other's property,' Ruth explained.

'You seriously think that they swapped murders?' Nick said, shaking his head.

'After the trial in Mold, they agree to wait and plan their revenge on these men. Mark Fisher came out of prison three months ago. So the plan starts and they arrange watertight alibis for the time of the respective murders. They travel to Prague and Glasgow on the planned dates. Helen has access to medical-grade anaesthetics. She tells Kathleen where to inject Gerry Doyle on the neck, except Kathleen misses,' Ruth said, still thinking out loud. Was this plausible or ridiculous?

'Yeah, okay, we could never work out how Nicole Lace had moved the bodies before Kosminski was on the scene. But neither Mark Fisher nor Gerry Doyle are particularly big,' Nick said.

'Helen McCarthy is a nurse who is skilled at moving people and bodies. She's also a climber, so she is seriously strong,' Ruth said.

'And Kathleen Taylor can hold her own bodyweight on her arms upside down for hours on end,' Nick said.

As they turned onto a quiet country road, the 4x4 pulled into the car park of a country pub. A moment later, Nick pulled in and parked on the other side.

'Here we go. Give them a minute to sit down,' Ruth said as she took off her seat belt.

Turning off the ignition, Nick sat back. 'Ever seen this kind of thing before?'

'Nope, never,' Ruth said.

There have been a lot of things I've never seen before until I moved to North Wales, Ruth thought to herself.

'Come on,' Ruth said as she opened the door.

As the smell of damp leaves and autumn dew filled the air, Ruth reached the pub and went inside.

Walking across the carpeted floor, Nick turned to Ruth. 'You think they're going to cough for this now?' he asked.

Ruth shrugged. 'I bloody hope so.'

In the far corner, beside a window, Helen McCarthy

and Kathleen Taylor were just taking their coats off and settling.

'I hope we're not interrupting anything, ladies?' Ruth said.

Looking up from their chairs, Ruth could see that they were tired and worried.

'What are you doing here?' Kathleen snapped.

'I'm afraid you're both going to have to come with us,' Ruth said.

'We're not going anywhere. And if you insist, then I will be calling my solicitor,' Kathleen said.

'I'm afraid you are going to need an exceptionally good solicitor … We know about your jury service and the trial at Mold. The stolen meds, the planned alibis,' Ruth said. She could see that Helen was beginning to shake as the colour drained out of her face. She had no fight left in her.

Kathleen shook her head. 'I have no idea what you're talking about.'

'Don't piss us about. We haven't crosschecked Mark Fisher and Gerry Doyle for both your DNA. And you thought we never would. But there is no way that your DNA isn't somewhere on the evidence, clothes or bodies,' Ruth said.

Helen had tears in her eyes. 'That man killed my brother. He wasn't sorry and neither am I.'

'Shut up, Helen!' Kathleen growled.

Helen looked at her across the table. 'I can't do this anymore. I can't sleep, I can't eat. I can't do anything … I'm sorry.'

Helen got up and began to put on her coat. She was still shaking.

Kathleen put her head in her hands and muttered something inaudible.

The game was up.

Ruth looked at them. 'Helen McCarthy and Kathleen Taylor, I'm arresting you both on suspicion of the murder and conspiracy to murder Mark Fisher and Gerry Doyle. You do not have to say anything, but it may harm your defence if you do not mention when questioned something you later rely on in court. Anything you do say can be used in a court of law against you.'

IT WAS NEARLY MIDNIGHT AND RUTH WAS EXHAUSTED. Helen McCarthy and Kathleen Taylor were both down-stairs in holding cells but wouldn't be interviewed until the morning. It was clear that Helen McCarthy was going to confess straight away. Ruth wasn't so sure about Kathleen Taylor.

Coming out of her office, she saw that Nick was still finishing paperwork.

'Will you go home, Nick?' Ruth said.

Nick nodded and looked at her. 'Do you think some-thing happened between Kosminski and Nicole back in the nineties?'

'Maybe. It would explain why they weren't keen on talking to us.' Ruth thought for a second and said. 'She came back to Llancastell to be with him.'

Nick looked up. 'They must have been in touch the whole time she was in witness protection.'

'And when she gets her diagnosis, Nicole heads back to Llancastell to be with him. Except they have to keep it quiet until Kosminski sorts out everything before leaving his wife,' Ruth said.

'Why did they run when we got to Kosminski's?' Nick asked.

'They've got two flights booked to Egypt. If we pull them in for questioning, they miss the flights. And if we start digging around in their past, they're stuck here in the middle of an investigation. Nicole doesn't have time for that, does she?' Ruth said.

'It's kind of sweet, in a strange kind of way. True love,' Nick said.

'Go home, Nicholas. Or you'll be sleeping on the sofa,' Ruth said.

'I'm afraid that ship sailed a few weeks ago, boss,' Nick said, getting up and putting on his coat.

'You're going to make a great dad,' Ruth said.

'Thanks, boss. Good night,' Nick said as he went.

Chapter 26

Euston Road was busy. Ruth could already smell the fumes from the waiting traffic and queues of red double-decker buses. The hiss of the air brakes made her jump. She hadn't been in her home city for over two and a half years. The smells, noise and chaos took a few minutes to get used to, even for a native. Everything seemed louder and faster than she remembered it.

London used to be a quiet, restful city on a Sunday. Ruth remembered travelling to relatives across South London on empty roads. Then they relaxed the Sunday trading laws and then the licensing laws in the nineties; the city's day of rest became the busiest day of the week.

Glancing right, Ruth could see the top of Eversholt Street and then Tavistock Square a little further up, which she had wandered through at times looking at its sculptures of Mahatma Gandhi and Virginia Woolf. Now all she could think of was the terrorist bomb on 7 July 2005 that blew up a red London bus and killed thirteen people. She hadn't been back since that day.

As Ruth continued striding east, she could feel the

tension building in her stomach. She was making the short walk from Euston train station up Euston Road to the café housed inside the British Library. She checked her watch. Fifteen minutes before she was due to meet Jamie Parsons. She had spent the journey down on the train from Chester preparing the questions that she wanted to put to him.

Ruth arrived at the vast red-brown brick piazza that stretched out from Euston Road to the main glass doors of the British Library. Even though it was chilly, there were a dozen or so people sitting outside at the café in scarves and coats. Looming above them was an enormous dark bronze statue of Isaac Newton by Eduardo Paolozzi.

Ruth sat down and pulled a ciggie from her coat pocket. As she looked around, she felt glad she had made the move to North Wales. London didn't feel like her city anymore. She was too old to try to keep up with it and the way it changed incessantly. The pace of life in Snowdonia suited her now.

She took a deep drag, held it for a second and then let it out, watching the smoke scuttle and dance away on the wind that whipped around the modern piazza.

How did you first meet Sarah? How long were you seeing her for? The questions rattled around chaotically in Ruth's head. And then the more difficult ones. Do you know Jurgen Kessler? Was she going to ask him that, or would that alert Kessler that she was on to him?

The cigarette had done little to calm her anxiety. If anything, it had made her feel a bit sick. She stubbed it out on the shiny metallic ashtray on top of a nearby bin. Maybe she should go in now. Get a coffee and get settled.

Suddenly Ruth's phone began to vibrate in her pocket. For a brief second, she thought it might be Parsons, but he didn't have her number.

She looked at the screen – Sian. Her immediate reaction was guilt. She had told Sian that she was following up some witness statements out on the North Wales coast and would be out for the whole day. Sian wasn't suspicious. Working seven days a week, fourteen hours a day on a murder case was the norm.

'Hiya? You okay? I left you snoring …' Ruth said in a bright, sing-song voice but feeling horrible inside.

'Where are you?' Sian asked. Something about her tone made Ruth feel uneasy.

'I'm sitting looking out at the sea near Caernarfon,' Ruth said, hoping the strong wind that rattled and zipped around the piazza would sound vaguely coastal.

'Where are you, Ruth?' Sian said very quietly but with a clear sense of anger.

'What do you mean?' Ruth asked.

'You phone is linked to mine via iCloud. I told you I was doing it after Ella was kidnapped. All our phones are linked. And you've enabled your location,' Sian said.

Oh shit! This is not good. Ruth's stomach lurched.

'For fuck's sake, Ruth! What are you doing in London?' Sian barked down the phone.

'It's such a long story. Let me tell you when I get home,' Ruth said, trying to sound as conciliatory as she could.

'Either you tell me now, or I pack my bags and walk out of here now!' Sian growled.

'A woman came to see me at work …'

'What woman?' Sian asked.

'Her name was Lucy Parsons. She had evidence that her ex-husband, Jamie Parsons, had an affair with Sarah in the summer of 2013,' Ruth said.

'So what?' Sian yelled down the phone. 'So fucking what?'

'I just needed to …'

'I knew it. I'm so bloody stupid because I fucking knew it!'

Sian hung up on her and the phone went dead.

Ruth dialled her straight back. Her phone went straight to voicemail – Sian had turned her phone off.

THE TELEVISION WAS BLARING WITH A FOOTBALL GAME AS Nick came in with a tray of tea, biscuits and cakes. Amanda's father, Tony, and Nick's father, Rhys, were sitting on armchairs chatting and laughing about the football. It was the first time that they had met and they were getting on like a house on fire.

'John Charles. Best Welsh footballer there has even been,' Rhys said as he took a mug of tea.

'Cliff Jones. Now he was a fantastic player,' Tony said. 'I saw him play for Spurs at Anfield once. Up and down the wing, they couldn't catch him.'

'Aye, that's right. He won the double with Spurs in sixty or sixty-one,' Rhys said, smiling.

'I saw him on that YouTube the other day doing a fitness workout. No word of a lie,' Tony said with his eyes widening.

'Eh? Cliff Jones? I didn't know he was still alive!' Rhys said.

'He's in his eighties and as fit as a fiddle. He does these bloody videos in his back garden. Christ, he's like a twenty-year-old,' Tony said, laughing.

Nick swigged his coffee. After the frenzied pace of a double murder investigation, he was happy to sit quietly and listen to the two men reminisce.

Feeling a buzz on the arm of the sofa, Nick picked up his phone. Peter the Artist had left him a text message: *Hi Nick. Would you be able to give me a call? Thank you. Peter.*

Peter would have to bloody wait.

I'm not his bloody mother, Nick thought as he reached for a piece of chocolate cake.

THE CAFÉ AT THE BRITISH LIBRARY WAS RELATIVELY EMPTY. Ruth was still reeling from the conversation with Sian. She had tried to call her back four times, but Sian's phone was still turned off.

Ruth chose one of the booths with padded dark-chestnut seats that lined one side. Having got herself a flat white, she settled in, but her stomach was doing cartwheels. Was Sian in the process of moving her stuff out? Ruth couldn't bear the thought of it. Maybe she should have come clean about the whole Jamie Parsons affair …

Oh God, Ruth. You're such an idiot. You're going to lose the best thing that's happened to you in years!

Nick had texted her to say that they hoped she got what she wanted out of the meeting. Ruth wasn't sure what that was. After the phone call with Sian, she was finding it hard to think straight.

There was the sound of low chatter and the clink of china or cutlery. As the smell of fresh coffee and pastries wafted over, Ruth looked up at the high ceilings of the library.

She became aware of a presence beside the table. It was Jamie Parsons. He was smartly dressed and his Omega watch glistened in the light.

'Ruth …' Parsons said, holding a mug of coffee. 'I saw you already had a drink. Unless you want something else?'

'No, I'm fine, thank you,' Ruth said, but as he sat down everything around her felt surreal, as though she were detached from reality. She needed to stay focussed.

'Good trip?' Parsons asked as he adjusted a cufflink.

Everything about him was just so, as if he had walked out of GQ magazine.

'Yes.' Then Ruth looked at him directly. She needed to muster the kind of focus and strength that she possessed as a detective inspector. Getting emotional wasn't going to be helpful. 'Listen, there is little point in us making small talk. I'm not remotely interested in your life and you're not interested in mine. But I am grateful that you agreed to meet me today,' Ruth said, feeling calmer and back in control.

'Okay, to the point,' Parsons said, arching a bemused eyebrow.

'I'm a police officer. Force of habit,' Ruth said.

'How can I help?' Parsons asked, leaning forwards as he took his coffee cup. She noticed he wasn't wearing a wedding ring.

Ruth took a moment to think. 'How long did your affair with Sarah last?'

'Three or four months, thereabouts,' Parsons said with no hint of shame or embarrassment.

'Why did you stop?' Ruth asked.

'Sarah stopped it. She said she was confused and it was upsetting her,' Parsons said.

'Having an affair?' Ruth asked to clarify.

'Yes,' Parsons said. 'She felt terribly guilty.'

Ruth couldn't help but be relieved that Sarah had felt guilty enough to end the affair. It was something positive — albeit a very small one — to take away.

'So, you knew that Sarah had a partner?' Ruth asked.

'Yes. We were both clear about that,' Parsons said.

'And did you know I was a woman?' Ruth asked.

'Yes, I knew that too,' Parsons said. Ruth thought she saw a glint in Parsons's eye as he thought about the question.

Don't you fucking dare smirk, you arrogant bastard.

'Didn't you think that was weird? That she was living with a woman?' Ruth asked.

Parsons shrugged. 'I'm very broad-minded.'

'Was that the attraction then?' Ruth asked, trying not to sound scathing.

'No. Sarah was a very beautiful, charming and intelligent woman. I would have been attracted to her if she had been straight,' Parsons explained.

'You had a three-month affair and then what?' Ruth said.

'Nothing. Sarah said she needed some time. I called and sent her a couple of texts, but she didn't reply. I knew it was over. That was that,' Parsons said nonchalantly.

'And when she went missing?' Ruth asked.

'I was shocked, of course,' Parsons said, but Ruth thought the comment sounded hollow.

'You didn't come forward or talk to the police?' Ruth asked.

'What could I tell them? I hadn't seen her for three or four months. I didn't know anything worth telling anyone,' Parsons said.

Ruth looked at him. Everything he said was slick and sounded rehearsed. 'And you never saw her again?'

Parsons frowned. 'No, I just said that. Do you think I'm lying?'

'I'm not sure yet,' Ruth said. Her comment seemed to make Parsons uncomfortable.

'Listen, I felt that meeting you today was the right thing to do. That's all. Especially after what happened to Sarah,' Parsons said, leaning away from the table.

'How did you two meet?' Ruth asked sharply.

'We met at a party. A friend introduced us,' Parsons said.

'What kind of party?' Ruth asked.

'I don't know. It was a party …' Parsons said with a frown.

'Not a Secret Garden party then?' Ruth asked.

Parsons shifted in his seat – for the first time he actually looked uncomfortable. 'Oh right … If you must know, then yes, it was at a Secret Garden party. Does it matter?' Parsons said.

'Who was the friend who introduced you?' Ruth asked.

'Just a friend. Someone I worked with,' Parsons said.

Jurgen Kessler?

'You worked at a German bank at the time, didn't you?' Ruth asked.

'How do you know that?' Parsons said slowly.

Something about this is rattling him, Ruth thought. *All the slickness and polished charm has gone.*

'Was that the only time you were at a Secret Garden party with Sarah?' Ruth asked.

'No,' Parsons said.

Ruth was confused. The Sarah she had known had been private when it came to sex. Ruth never saw anything to indicate that Sarah would have enjoyed a sex party.

'Secret Garden parties are sex parties, aren't they?' Ruth asked.

'Are they?' Parsons asked.

'Come on. You don't think I came here without doing my homework thoroughly, do you?' Ruth said.

'I don't know what you're getting at?' Parsons said.

'Were you and Sarah exclusive at these parties? From what I understand, there are no rules in the Secret Garden,' Ruth said.

'It's a discreet club for discreet people,' Parsons said as he finished up his coffee. Ruth could see he was getting ready to go.

'You didn't answer the question,' Ruth said.

Parsons looked angry. 'What do you want me to say? I fucked other people. Sarah fucked other people. That's what happens.'

Ruth was a little winded by his brutally honest response – it was painful to hear. But she needed to keep pushing Parsons.

'This friend from work that introduced you. I'm assuming he was German, is that right?' Ruth said.

'Why? Not everyone that works there is German. It's a merchant bank,' Parsons said impatiently.

'Right. I'm sorry. I just had in my mind this tall German man, blonde hair, blue eyes, glasses. Racial stereotype, I'm afraid,' Ruth said with a shrug.

Of course, she was describing Jurgen Kessler and wanted to see what Parsons did with that.

Parsons blinked, sat back, pursed his lips and nodded. 'It's been nice to meet you, Ruth. But I think I've told you everything that I want to tell you. So if you'll excuse me, I'm going to go now.'

Getting his coat, Parsons edged out of the booth, walked swiftly away and disappeared down the escalator that led to the ground floor.

As the final whistle went for the football game on the television, Amanda stuck her head through the door.

Nick smiled up at her. She yawned and rubbed her eyes.

'Dad, you're gonna stay for tea, aren't you?' Amanda asked.

'Yeah, lovely. If that's okay?' Tony said.

Nick looked down at his phone and noticed that he had a missed call and text.

'And Rhys. We won't take no for an answer, so you're staying too,' Amanda said with a cheeky grin. She looked at Nick. 'Give me a hand?'

'Course,' Nick got up, grabbed his phone and headed for the kitchen.

'Chicken and roasties are in. Carrots are peeled. Can you make the gravy, sweetie?' Amanda said, pinching Nick's behind.

'Do I have a choice?' Nick asked.

'No, get on with it,' Amanda said in a mock angry tone.

Leaning back on the counter, Nick opened up his phone and listened to the message that Peter had left. It was twenty seconds of silence – just noises and some banging about.

Nick opened the text:

THANKS FOR YOUR FRIENDSHIP, OLD MATE. AND THANKS FOR agreeing to be my sponsor. I've let everyone down. So this is not a cry for help. I've gone past that point. Love and fellowship, Peter.

NICK FROZE FOR A SECOND AND THEN HE LOOKED AT Amanda.

'I've got to go!' Nick said grabbing the car keys.

'Go? Where the bloody hell are you going?' Amanda asked.

'Sorry. Won't be long,' Nick said as he dashed out of the front door.

THE SKY WAS A DARKENING SHEET OF BLUE AS RUTH manoeuvred her way down Euston Road, trying to avoid being detected. She had been following Jamie Parsons for five minutes and keeping a decent distance. She had had plenty of surveillance training over the years.

Ruth had no real idea of why she was following Parsons. He was probably just going home. However, she also reasoned that she had somehow got to him. The questions about the Secret Garden and his 'German friend' had certainly flustered his calm, controlled manner. Would Parsons now act on the fragments of information that she had deliberately fed him?

Parsons turned left and headed south, past Slade School of Art. Ruth followed. He was now about a hundred yards ahead of her and talking on his mobile phone. Gesturing with his left hand, Parsons seemed to be getting more worked up as he spoke.

Was that a clue? It could be nothing. But if there was any link between Parsons and Kessler, he might have thought to ring Kessler immediately. Was she just clutching at straws? Yes. But that was all she had.

Parsons looked back as if to check who was behind him. A cyclist courier coming the other way managed to block Ruth from his view as she skipped to one side. *Bloody hell, that was close!*

Cutting left down Grafton Way, they were now heading for the Hampstead Road. This wasn't Ruth's manor at all. She thought that they were close to the BT Tower. Grafton Way was dangerously quiet. Ruth had to give Parsons another fifty yards or more and now she was in danger of losing him if he made any sharp turns.

She watched as Parsons put his phone away and looked at his watch. He sped up into a virtual trot. It looked like he was meeting someone and was late.

Ruth sped up behind him. Parsons crossed the road

onto the main high street and then disappeared out of sight.

Shit!

Breaking into a run, Ruth followed and got to the main road about thirty seconds later – but Parsons was nowhere to be seen.

How the bloody hell did I miss him?

Glancing impatiently from left to right, she saw that Parsons had vanished into thin air. How was that possible? Her heart sank.

Then out of the corner of her eye, she spotted a black London taxi in the traffic heading south, but stationary in the traffic. She caught the profile of the man as he looked out of the taxi window – it was Parsons. He didn't see her.

Ruth waved down another black London taxi. It pulled over, and she opened the door, clambered in and closed the door behind her.

'Where to, love?' the cabbie asked.

'Follow that cab?' Ruth said loudly.

'Eh? You're joking, aren't you?' the cabbie asked.

Fumbling inside her coat, Ruth got out her warrant card and held it up so he could see it in the rear-view mirror. 'No …'

'Oh right. I've been waiting thirty years for someone to get in my cab and say that,' the cabbie said with a smile. 'This cab here, is it?'

'Yes. Please,' Ruth said as they pulled away into the traffic.

They followed the taxi down through Fitzrovia and then swung north onto Great Portland Street. As they reached the one-way system, Parsons's taxi slowed down outside Great Portland Street underground station. It was instantly recognisable with its cream, thirties, stone-clad exterior.

'You want me to pull over too?' the cabbie asked, gesturing to the taxi they had been following. 'Not too close though, eh?'

'Yes, please,' Ruth said, undoing her seatbelt and getting ready to jump out. 'How much do I owe you?'

'It's on the house. I'm gonna be telling this story for months,' the cabbie cackled. 'Who's the geezer you're following then?'

'Can't tell you that,' Ruth said as she opened the door.

'Right. Say no more. Wrong 'un, is he?' the cabbie said.

'You could say that. Thanks,' Ruth said as she watched Parsons hand over money to his cabbie and make his way into the entrance of the station.

Ruth slowed and peered carefully into the ticket lobby of the station. Parsons was standing to one side, talking to a man in a dark overcoat.

As he turned, she saw the man had blonde hair, blue eyes and glasses.

Jurgen Kessler! Oh my God …

Ruth felt sick as she moved backwards in shock.

Her instincts had been right.

The two men were in an animated conversation. Parsons clapped Kessler on the back in a friendly gesture. They went to the top of the escalator and disappeared down and out of sight.

Breaking into a jog, Ruth followed across the ticket office and took the middle escalator instead, trying to keep out of their sight.

As they reached the bottom, Parsons and Kessler went left towards the Circle line and disappeared again. Ruth broke into a run down the metal stairs, coming off the bottom of the escalator and nearly falling.

Don't lose them now!

Her head was whirring. Heading down a small flight of stone steps, Ruth could feel the rush of air as a tube train approached. She started to run flat out and came out onto a busy platform.

The front of the approaching Circle line train whooshed towards her ominously. The noise was thunderous.

Where the hell are they? They couldn't have gone any other way!

Anxiously, she glanced around again. Nothing. The platform was too long and too busy.

With her frustration building, Ruth moved left and right, trying to get a clear view.

Oh my God. I cannot lose them! Bloody hell!

Then suddenly, she saw the back of Kessler's coat and blonde hair as he stepped into a carriage at the other end of the platform.

Got him!

The electronic beeps of the train sounded and the doors began to close.

The train was going to go without her.

And with that, Kessler would be gone.

No! No way!

Leaping forward, Ruth put her shoulder and arm into the gap where the doors were closing. The black rubber squashed her for a moment. Ruth knew they would have to open again – much to the other passengers' annoyance.

As the doors opened again, Ruth stepped into the carriage and caught her breath.

Two passengers scowled at her, but she didn't care. She was on. Now what?

The beeps sounded again, the doors closed and the train pulled out of the station.

Enjoy this book?
Get the next one on pre-order
on Amazon NOW.
Publication date August 2020

www.amazon.co.uk/dp/B08CF3WSFD
www.amazon.com/dp/B08CF3WSFD
The White Forest Killings
A Ruth Hunter Crime Thriller
Book 6

Your FREE book is waiting for you now

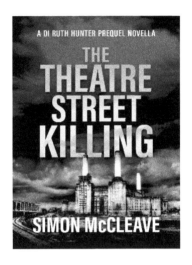

Get your FREE copy of the prequel to
the DI Ruth Hunter Series NOW
at www.simonmccleave.com
and join my VIP Email Club

AUTHOR'S NOTE

Although this book is very much a work of fiction, it is located in Snowdonia, a spectacular area of North Wales. It is steeped in history and folklore that spans over two thousand years. It is worth mentioning that Llancastell is a fictional town on the eastern edges of Snowdonia. I have made liberal use of artistic licence, names and places have been changed to enhance the pace and substance of the story.

Acknowledgments

I will always be indebted to the people who have made this novel possible.

My mum, Pam, and my stronger half, Nicola, whose initial reaction, ideas and notes on my work I trust implicitly. And Dad, for his overwhelming enthusiasm. Without their support and encouragement, these novels simply wouldn't exist.

Thanks also goes to my amazing Advanced Reading Team for their invaluable feedback on earlier drafts. Detective Sergeant Ben Wild of the North Wales Police Force for checking my work and explaining the complicated world of police procedure and investigation. My incredibly talented editor Rebecca Millar who has held my hand through the rewriting and editing process again and is a joy to work with. My proof-reader Eden Flaherty. My excellent designer Stuart Bache for the incredible cover design and Bryan Cohen for the blurb and advertising copy.

Milton Keynes UK
Ingram Content Group UK Ltd.
UKHW020908100724
445379UK00013BB/354